bloodline

What did Tristan Sr see? Not a future president of a company but the President of the United States. He saw a world-class athlete, a great musician or writer, a doctor, a church leader. He saw unlimited potential. Tristan Jr would learn a lot, forget a lot. He would be a force for good or for bad. He would shun the limelight or he would be up there, basking in it. He would earn a lot, or he would reject materialism. He would make lots of friends, some enemies. Whatever, Tristan Jr would always have Tristan Sr's love and support.

The boy was perfect. At least, he was perfect on the outside. Inside, he had one twisted gene that Tristan had hoped his company would be able to correct. This tiny, vulnerable creature of infinite possibilities wasn't even ill, but he carried an invisible flaw that would sleep inside him for ever. One day soon, though, it could be used to kill him.

D0733699

Malcolm Rose

■SCHOLASTIC

Scholastic Children's Books,
Commonwealth House, 1–19 New Oxford Street,
London WC1A 1NU, UK
A division of Scholastic Ltd
London ~ New York ~ Toronto ~ Sydney ~ Auckland
Mexico City ~ New Delhi ~ Hong Kong

First published in the UK by Scholastic Ltd, 2002
Copyright © Malcolm Rose, 2002

ISBN 0 439 99402 0

Printed and bound in Great Britain by
Cox & Wyman Ltd, Reading, Berks.

1 3 5 7 9 10 8 6 4 2

The right of Malcolm Rose to be identified as the author
of this work has been asserted by him in accordance
with the Copyright, Designs and Patents Act, 1988.

For The Malcolm Rose Fan Club
based at Denbigh School, Milton Keynes

With special thanks to
Carol Barac
Wendy Barnaby (*The Plague Makers*)
Peter Krugg (*Fire in the City*)
MC 900ft Jesus (*The City Sleeps*)
Siouxsie & the Banshees (*Shadowtime*)

It is predicted that the human genome will be sequenced by the year 2005. The information is expected to lead to radical new treatments for a broad range of human disease. It cannot be ruled out that information from such genetic research could be considered for the design of weapons targeted against specific ethnic or racial groups.

UK contribution to United Nations Background Paper on New Scientific and Technological Developments Relevant to the Convention on the Prohibition of the Development, Production and Stockpiling of Biological and Toxin Weapons, 1996.

There is another horrifying possibility of genetic engineering: a weapon made to attack a specific ethnic group. Thus, it has been suggested, a mixture of influenza or diphtheria could be designed to affect mainly blacks; a designer toxin could be aimed exclusively at Serbs; or people with blue eyes might be given Alzheimer's disease.

Wendy Barnaby in The Plague Makers, *Vision Paperbacks, London, 1999.*

Recipes for developing biological agents are freely available on the Internet. As genetic manipulation becomes a standard laboratory technique this information is also likely to be widely available. Developing effective control systems within the next five to ten years will be crucial to future world security.

British Medical Association report on Biotechnology, Weapons and Humanity, 1999.

prologue

The wide avenue with its big whitewashed houses set well back in their own lush gardens was an insult. The plush white Lexus was an insult. Shadow knelt by the car's fuel tank, the perspiration glistening on his brow and arms. Like rain on dark glass, a drop of sweat ran down his left cheek, over his short muscular neck and into the cotton of his worn T-shirt. For a fifteen-year-old boy, Shadow was built big and solid. At his side were the tools of his trade: a rag, a can of gasoline. In his pocket was the means to a magical end: a box of matches.

The night was not just hot. It was stifling, stale and empty like nights in only the southern states can be. A night when tempers on the street were short. A night when everyone kept a handkerchief in their moist hands. It was a night for the whites to stay inside their air-conditioned homes. No sweat. The breathless avenue was deserted.

Shadow drank the smell from the gas tank. Sheer bliss. The smell alone could transport him to paradise. Quickly, he stuffed the rag into the wound in the side of the car, letting a few centimetres hang out like a wick. To make sure there was enough food for the fire, Shadow splashed gasoline over the cloth and down the side of the car. Slowly, working his way backwards, away from the Lexus, he laid a trail of gasoline. In the warmth of the night, the fuel evaporated and filled the air with its sweet hungry smell. Twenty metres from the car, behind the shiny liquid fuse leading to the Lexus, Shadow stopped.

He was eager to see the greedy flames and yet he wanted to linger, to savour the moment that was about to make him important once more. He called it Shadowtime. His fingers gripped that little box, slowly extracted a match. Such a tiny thing, like an exclamation mark. One simple strike, a quick twist of the wrist, and the cleansing began with a graceful yellow plume like a candle in a church. Shadow's spine tingled, his heartbeat raced. He was about to see the most beautiful show on Earth. He dropped the lighted match and the eager fuel reached up and embraced Shadow's gift of life.

The seductive flame danced silently, slickly down the road towards the white car. The itchy yellow fingers clawed up the side of the Lexus, blistering the paint, and loitered for a few seconds on the wick before worming their way into the interior.

Time stood still. It was the moment that Shadow craved. He knew that he should have run by now, making his escape before the white world woke to his handiwork, but he could not. He couldn't turn his back on the coming display any more than he could look away from a lit firework. Of course, that's exactly what he had made of the car.

2

Fluttering yellow birds flew out into the darkness and sucked the oxygen from the night air. Some of the flames flashed beneath the Lexus and baked the car as if it were on a gas cooker. After a delicious delay, the windows blew out and the vehicle leapt a metre off the road in an exquisite explosion, engulfed by a fiery yellow sheath, as if it were being carried to heaven by a host of shining angels. The flame shot upwards into the night, pushing aside the darkness, illuminating the sky. The shock wave rushed past Shadow, pushing him backwards and roaring in his ears. A split-second later, Shadow felt an extra ripple of unnatural heat wafting over him, sensing it most on his bare skin. He did not even blink. This was what he lived for. Forget school. This was what life was all about.

Only when he detected movement in the street was it time to retreat. At first, Shadow jogged backwards so that he could keep an eye on the still burning wreck, so he could keep the image on his retina for as long as possible. In the coming days he would replay it many times – until he ached for a different image. But the next one would also be that magnificent combination of yellow and black. Street-lamps at night, gold on skin, flame scavenging among charred remains. For now, he could see it wherever he looked. The flickering flower was reflected in every window of every house and every parked car. It was like a dream that the whole world was on fire. Paradise.

When the gathering crowd looked up and, yelling, began to point at him, it was really time to fly. Time to leave the sprawling cosy suburbs of Memphis and return to his own people's territory – downtown inner city. Shadow turned and dissolved into the blackness, sprinting joyously as if he too were assisted by angels' wings.

1

Kyle looked around carefully again. He was nowhere near a sink or a tap and no one was using water anywhere near him. He'd already moved the water-filled test-tubes to the far end of his bench. He dabbed the oil from the grey cube of soft metal. He was always surprised how easy it was to slice through the metal with a blunt spatula. And he was always surprised by the beauty of the glinting colour that it revealed, like opening a cracked rock and finding a spectacular fossil. The fresh surface of potassium was purest shiny silver. Yet, almost immediately, contact with the atmosphere dulled the gloss. The metal was sucking oxygen from the air, tarnishing its lustre. Wasn't life always like that? As soon as something began to breathe, pollution inevitably followed.

Kyle was sweating a little. He could feel it seeping into the back of his shirt. Wearing the protective lab coat didn't help, but really it wasn't the heat. Lab 47 was a state-of-the-art, air-conditioned, safe working environment. No. It was the procedure. He didn't like working with potassium. It was a temperamental and unreliable metal. He'd filled in a COSHH form, of course, but a bit of paper didn't make it safe. Besides, potassium could not read. The Control of Substances Hazardous to Health document was lying on the lab bench and Kyle could see the sentence he'd written in capitals. POTASSIUM REACTS VIOLENTLY ON CONTACT WITH WATER; WATER WILL BE EXCLUDED FROM THE AREA OF THE EXPERIMENT. He checked the lab once again. There weren't many researchers left. It was getting late. None of the nearby ones needed water for their work. The only tap that was turned on was at the other end of the biotechnology laboratory. Jill was using a rotary evaporator. No problem. To relax himself, in his mind he played the new tune that he was creating.

Kyle worked for the drugs company Yttria Pharmaceuticals International, in the science park at Cambridge, UK. He was the new kid in Lab 47, straight from university, a first-class degree in chemistry, twenty-one years old, bags of potential. A great future with YPI beckoned but the present offered mostly the dirty jobs that the more established members of staff didn't want to touch. Kyle felt like a young footballer, restricted to cleaning the boots of the star players. Ah, well. It wouldn't always be like that. Things would soon change when they saw yields increase in his hands, when they heard his bright ideas. Right now, he was appreciated most in the lab for his skill of filling test-tubes to different levels and tapping out tunes on them. Earlier in the day, he'd produced his own jazzy rendition of "Happy Birthday to You" for Jill.

Jill let out a groan that ripened into a cry. "Damn! Damn!" The evaporator had lost its vacuum and the rotating flask fell from the glass spindle into the water-bath. It bobbed on the surface for a moment, but then drank the water and sank. The remains of the solvent flooded from the flask, formed a layer on top of the hot water and bubbled away. Rapidly, the flammable vapour wafted towards the electrical contacts. Unable to stop what was about to happen, Jill stepped back. She didn't lose her cool, though. She couldn't reach over the contraption and switch it off at the mains because, if it went up in flames, her arm would be burned. She went to the end of the bench and grabbed the fire blanket but she was too late to stop the fire before it started. On her way back, the blaze began. The yellow flame danced on the pan of water. It looked like a meal set on fire by an overzealous chef. Across the other side of the bench, one of her fellow researchers laughed and another stood gawping. It wasn't serious. Just a nuisance. Yet before Jill flung the grey cloak over the flames and extinguished them, the fire alarm sounded.

They all sighed and looked up at the alarms set in the ceiling. There was no smoke but the detectors were also tuned to the flicker of a flame. It was the glimmer that had set them off.

"Sensitive, aren't they?"

"Too sensitive."

Without warning, the full force of modern automatic safety features came unthinkingly into play. The sprinklers started to spray a fire that had already been doused by the blanket.

"Damn!" Jill repeated.

Someone began to sing, "Raindrops keep falling on my. . ."

Across Lab 47, through the instant mist, water gushed down on to the potassium in Kyle's hand and the metal ignited spontaneously. Kyle froze, aghast, unable to react. For a split second he watched in horror as the bright purple flame licked his fingers. Strangely, he felt nothing at all. He was numb to pain. Then the explosion in his hand ripped away the tips of his thumb, forefinger and middle finger.

2

Walking towards Kyle's bed in Addenbrooke's Hospital, the nurse told Stuart Urling-Clark, "He's upset – understandably – but he's recovering nicely. If it wasn't for the shock he'd be back home by now."

The young researcher was sitting up in bed, reading the latest *New Scientist*, a copy of *New Musical Express* across his legs, his right hand covered in bandages.

"How are you?" asked Stuart.

Kyle put down the magazine and shrugged. "OK, I suppose." His tone suggested otherwise.

"Sure?"

"I don't like hospitals."

Kyle's boss at Yttria nodded sympathetically. "Do any of us?"

"No. I mean I *really* don't. . . Never mind."

Immediately, Stuart realized that Kyle was locking him out of whatever was bothering him. Stuart sat down in the chair beside the bed. "Have your family – your mum and dad – been in to see you?"

Kyle shook his head. "No."

In his expression, Stuart saw disappointment and resentment – a grudge, even. He also detected that the young chemist didn't anticipate a visit from his mum or dad. That was really sad. Having failed to connect with

Kyle through small talk, Stuart decided to get to the point. "The hand?" he enquired.

"I've had a lot of microsurgery. When the fingers have healed, they're going to rebuild what they couldn't fix," Kyle replied. "That's the power of modern silicones for you."

"We'll pay for the best plastic surgeon, you know. YPI won't argue about it."

Kyle didn't need to be told. He wasn't stupid. He knew that the managers at Yttria would be sweating in case an injured employee decided to sue the designer suits off them. Right now, they would bend over backwards to placate him.

"Yeah, I can have the best patch-up, but I won't feel anything with them ever again."

Stuart nodded compassionately. "I know it'll affect your career."

A raw nerve exposed, Kyle turned away. When he looked back at his visitor, it was obvious that he wanted to keep their meeting businesslike. That was easier than talking about his emotions. "You want me to run through the accident."

"If you're up to it."

"Apart from. . ." He lifted his bandaged hand and glanced at it before continuing. "Apart from this, it was trivial really. Comical, even."

It didn't take long to relate Kyle's side of the story. As laboratory accidents went, his was straightforward, unforeseeable and unlucky. "An unfortunate no-fault incident," Stuart said, emphasizing *no fault*.

"But it brought the management team out in force. Why's that?"

Stuart looked puzzled. "Because we care. Don't forget, the workforce is our most important asset."

"So why did you rush to the... Nothing." Kyle turned his eyes away again.

Urling-Clark guessed what Kyle was going to say but did not pursue it.

When the Lab 47 alarm had sounded, an impressive array of top brass had swarmed in, checked out the safe, and then attended to Kyle. If he was such a valued asset to YPI, why wasn't he at the top of the list of priorities? With the floor by the bench running pink, the sprinklers having washed away the rest of his blood, why did a metal box come first?

Kyle didn't even know what was in the safe. The powers-that-be made sure that individual workers knew only what they had to know. They were excluded from the big picture. After all, in an industry where one big-selling cure could earn hundreds of millions of pounds, the management was going to do all it could to keep the successful formulas secret. Kyle had all the information he needed on the two reactions that he performed in Lab 47 but little else. He was aware only that the chemicals he made were used in the development of a new drug for combating a type of anaemia.

Maybe the safe held a brilliant remedy or the instructions for making it. But the unseemly and undiplomatic rush made Kyle believe that something sinister was going on. Now that he had forfeited his fingertips to it, Kyle felt he had the right to know what it was.

"By the way," Stuart Urling-Clark asked, "why have you got unlabelled test-tubes on your bench? There's two racks of them with different volumes of some liquid."

Kyle smiled at last. "They're my version of a xylophone. I can get a pretty good tune by hitting them with a bit of plastic or wood. The other people in the lab enjoy it."

Urling-Clark frowned. Makeshift music had nothing to do with company business. "Well, when you come back to us. . ."

Kyle's fleeting good humour had gone again. With another glance at his useless right hand, he muttered, "What use am I now?"

"Yttria doesn't have a scrap-heap policy, Kyle. We think positive. It's no problem to find a new role for you. That's assuming you play ball with us as well and don't involve the press. We don't need journalists and lawyers. Rest assured, we look after our own."

Kyle didn't want a new role. He wanted what he couldn't have: a perfect hand.

Stuart stood up. "Is there anything else you want to say to me?"

Taking the *New Musical Express* in his left hand, Kyle said, "Thanks for coming."

Outside the hospital, Stuart could not wait until he got back to work. He called YPI's Press Office on his mobile phone as he crawled along Cambridge's cluttered streets in his company car. "Just make sure the media doesn't get hold of it," he demanded. "I don't want to see YPI *playing fast and loose with employees' limbs* splashed over the front page."

"We'll have that Victoria Scates sniffing around again, no doubt."

"Well, get rid of her or, if she finds out about Proctor, get on to your contacts and block her story. Full stop." He put his phone away and turned on his wipers. As September rolled over into October, the fine drizzle threatened to turn into a downpour.

3

Once, for a brief while, Dwight Grant had it all. He had credit cards and even a car. Now, he had almost nothing – not even his freedom. He was left only with his healthy fifteen-year-old body and his prized place in Westland Youth under-18 football team. He did not realize that, on a rainy Sunday in December, he was about to lose those last two assets.

Compared to some of the teams in Cambridge's local league, Westland Youth were well off. They had new home and away kits, a superb all-weather pitch, a real pavilion, and floodlights, all courtesy of their wealthy sponsor. Their home kit had *YPI* emblazoned across the front. The away kit had *Yttria* written on the back from shoulder to shoulder. That way, the pharmaceutical giant ploughed something back into the community. Westland Young Offender Institution also benefited in other ways from its association with YPI. The well stocked library, medical centre and indoor sports hall had also been funded by YPI. With its enviable facilities, it was surprising that Westland had a higher than average suicide rate among its young offenders. Noticing that most of the suicides occurred among Westland's black inmates, a group called the Black and Asian Defenders had latched on to the embarrassing statistics and begun to voice its concern.

It was cold, but not yet cold enough to feel like winter. Besides, Dwight never felt the chill while he bewildered the opposition's defenders with his tireless runs on goal. At 1–0, his marker pulled back from a crunching tackle in the penalty area but Dwight hit the deck acrobatically, as if he'd been poleaxed.

The defender threw up his hands. "I didn't touch him, ref! That was a dive." He mimicked the action of a swimmer about to plunge into a pool.

The referee reached into his pocket.

Dwight's marker cried, "You can't be serious!"

Abruptly, the ref said, "Shut it. I'm booking *him* – for diving." Yellow card in hand, the ref loomed over Dwight but he hesitated and frowned. The black striker was uncannily still. It wasn't that bad a fall. Suddenly concerned, the referee turned to Westland's manager and waved him urgently on to the pitch.

Frankly, Dr Crear hadn't got a clue. Sure, she'd seen the blood tests, brain scan and toxicity tests. Sure, Dwight Grant had inherited the sickle-cell trait from one parent, like one in twelve blacks worldwide. It was in his bloodline but that didn't mean he had the full-blown disease. It was no reason for him to collapse. As far as she could tell, his brain showed normal activity and there was no sign of the common recreational drugs in his blood. Dr Crear did not know why Dwight was now reliant on life support in Addenbrooke's Hospital.

Actually, she did have one clue. She'd been told that Dwight had volunteered for a drug trial with Yttria. Young offenders at Westland seemed to get special favours, especially when their cases were reviewed, if they signed up to act as guinea pigs for YPI's new medicines. So, having been found guilty in one trial, they took their risks with another. Helen Crear had no idea if Dwight's condition had anything to do with the experimental drug he'd been given but she owed it to her patient to find out. After three abortive attempts, she had YPI's Head of Clinical Trials on the phone. His name was Cameron Ingoe and he was ducking and weaving like an expert boxer.

Ingoe made a show of sympathy but Helen guessed that his concern was exactly that: a show. "Grant's in a coma? Poor lad. That's nothing to do with us, though."

"First, can you confirm what I've been told by his parents? He was participating in one of your drug trials."

"Yes, that's true. But. . . How did he come to get into this state?"

"At one minute he was running through some local football team's defence, the next he was flat out on the penalty spot," Dr Crear explained.

"Bad, is it?"

"Suffice it to say, if we turn off life support, we lose him. Now," the doctor said forcibly, "I need to know what he's been taking."

"I want to help of course, but I don't see what it's got to do with — "

"Neither do I," Dr Crear said, butting in impatiently. "So you have to give me the opportunity to find out if there's a connection between Dwight's present condition and his drug regime."

"I'm afraid I can't do that."

"What? Why not?"

"Let's be frank, Dr Crear. In my trade, secrecy is the key to success. I have a drug development programme to protect from competitors."

"And I have a patient to revive."

"I sympathize, but— "

"Has this happened before?" Dr Crear asked.

"We're not in the habit of poisoning our human subjects," Ingoe said in his smooth voice. "It doesn't make commercial sense, does it? Look, the best I can do is assure you that the drug's quite harmless. Then you can look elsewhere for a reason for this boy's ... illness. I don't want to waste your time barking up the wrong tree. That wouldn't be fair to you or him."

Dr Crear hesitated, swallowed, and tried to keep calm. She decided to try a legal line of reasoning because it might be the sort of language this Ingoe could understand. He was immune to the humanitarian angle but perhaps he'd respond to a threat. "If Dwight dies, I guess his family will sue you for every penny they can get and splash the YPI drug trial

17

across every newspaper. Bad publicity whether there's a link or not." Through gritted teeth she added, "Both his family and I would appreciate your co-operation."

Infuriatingly unruffled, the Head of Clinical Trials replied, "No, that won't happen. You see, before Dwight Grant – or anyone else – embarks on a drug trial they sign a consent form. It covers most eventualities, including a no-publicity clause. And in the unlikely event of ill health, volunteers waive their right to bring proceedings against us."

"How very convenient. What type of drug was it? You must be able to tell me that."

With barely a pause, Cameron continued, "As I said, I have every sympathy, Dr Crear, but there are limits. For obvious commercial reasons, our drug trials must remain confidential. I'm sure you know the law: drug companies are not obliged to reveal their results to doctors, volunteers, patients or the public. Now, I'm sorry but I'm a busy man."

Helen snapped, "And I've got nothing to do all day but put my feet up while my patients drop like flies." Exasperated, she said, "For someone in the health care business, your attitude stinks. I haven't signed one of your contracts so I'll make sure everyone around here knows how helpful you've been."

"That would be unwise," he warned. "Your management knows we're very generous to the hospital. You get advanced treatments from us under extremely favourable terms."

"You mean we give you access to our terminal cases as guinea pigs?"

"Dr Crear." His tone suggested reproach, like a teacher cautioning a pupil.

"Go to hell." She slammed down the phone and dashed back to Intensive Care.

4

Yttria's premises in Cambridge were only a few years old. The building was a large futuristic dome. Outside, it was all glass and steel framework. Inside, it was spacious and airy with potted plants and trickling fountains. It was so suave that it was almost sickly. It was tainted only by the homeless man who slept outside the gates most nights, even in a dank and gloomy December. When Kyle arrived at work, he often gave the beggar his change before the security officers moved him on. Behind Yttria's sophisticated architecture, there lurked a security system that MI5 would have been proud of. Getting beyond reception required both a pass and a retina scan. The labs and animal house were located within a fortress, a picturesque fortress but a fortress all the same.

Kyle Proctor stood by the door and allowed the discreet camera in the wall to scan his left eye. There was a quiet click and his pass was ejected from the security post like a credit card from a cash machine. The door could be opened for a few seconds but, just in case a crazed intruder was holding a knife to his throat, the closed-circuit TV camera set into the ceiling monitored his entrance. If he'd had someone with him, a vigilant guard in the security office would have overridden the door mechanism, forbidding access until his visitor had been identified, checked in and authorized. Or arrested and taken away.

Kyle's new workplace was not a laboratory at all. It was a computer room. On the benches, where he wanted to see bottles of chemicals, flasks and rotary evaporators, there were computers. Along the walls, where he wanted to see fume cupboards, incubators and chromatographs, there were shelves of books, CD-ROMs, and more terminals. There was no possibility of making musical test-tubes. Stuart Urling-Clark was trying to make a virtue out of necessity. He was trying to convince Kyle that his injuries were a blessing in disguise because they obliged him to change the direction of his career. Stuart was saying, "All the best chemistry's done on computers these days. That's where the real innovations are, Kyle. Not in the lab."

"Really?"

"Really."

It was a game they were playing. Stuart had found a way of retaining Kyle whilst removing him from the lab where his disability would be dangerous. He had found a job for Kyle in the computing section and he wanted to paint a glossy picture of it. His words were rubbish, of course. Stuart knew it and Kyle knew it. The real innovations were being made exactly where they had always been made: in a real lab, with real chemical reactions and real genetics. Even so, Stuart talked up Kyle's new and exciting assignment.

21

By the normal rules of the game, Kyle should have played along with Stuart despite knowing that Stuart was spinning a yarn. Kyle should have welcomed the deceit because he should have been grateful and optimistic. He couldn't quite manage a brave face, though. He didn't refuse to play the game altogether but his indifference made the meeting uncomfortable for both of them.

"With a bit of retraining you'll have two roles really," Stuart told him. "The design of potential molecules for fixing known sites of disease – that's where all the excitement is – and scouring the literature for new chemicals and reactions that'll assist our laboratory chemists. Just think. No more COSHH forms, no tiresome practical considerations, no restrictions on your imagination, no getting your own hands dirty. OK?"

What choice did Kyle have? He nodded unenthusiastically. "OK, I guess."

"Once you get stuck into it, you'll wonder how you ever thought experimental chemistry was fun."

"Yeah."

"How goes it, then?" Jill nodded towards Kyle's hand with its reconstructed thumb and two fingers.

Kyle thought that she was referring to the computer keyboard. "Great," he muttered. "No more COSHH forms, no tiresome practical considerations, no restrictions on my imagination, no getting my hands dirty. That sort of thing."

22

Jill realized that it was premature to expect him to show any zeal for his new role in YPI. "I meant your hand," she said.

"Oh. Sorry. Well, it's . . . strange. My fingers are longer than they feel. I keep bashing them. It takes a bit of getting used to. My brain's not accepted them as part of me yet."

Trying to inject a little humour, Jill replied with a smile, "No more playing guitar, then."

Her comment had the opposite effect. Kyle grimaced and turned back to his monitor.

"What's that?" asked Jill, pointing to an icon on the screen.

"A virus protection package. A very powerful one. According to the technicians we get five attempts to hack into the system every day. A lot of those are carrying a virus."

"And the zapper works?"

"Mostly. If not, I don't have to worry about it. The computer technicians come in and sort things out." Kyle wished that he was still able to combat real, biological viruses and not virtual ones.

"Well, I'd better get back to work. I just came to see how . . . you know . . . how you're doing."

"Thanks."

Kyle knew that he should stop work and consult the technical staff straight away, but the file that appeared

23

mysteriously in his computer mailbox was too enticing. When he doubled clicked on *BAD Vibes*, he got a file from the Black and Asian Defenders that claimed to list YPI drug trials that had gone wrong in Cambridge, complete with casualties. He was glad that he'd dared to open the document because the most recent entry caught his eye. Apparently, a volunteer called Dwight Grant was lying unconscious in the Intensive Care unit at Addenbrooke's Hospital, just along the corridor from the ward that Kyle had left a couple of months ago. Kyle shuddered unpleasantly. It wasn't his own stay in Addenbrooke's that made him react. He was thinking of his brother. Apparently, Dwight Grant was wasting in the room where, four years ago, Kyle's older brother had lost his own fingertip grip on life.

Kyle did not have the nerve nor the time to print out a copy of the e-mail message before a team of technicians flooded the computer laboratory, ordering all workers to vacate their terminals. Between the scientists trooping out and back in as if on fire drill, the *BAD Vibes* were eradicated.

Most of the time, Kyle searched the biochemical literature on behalf of his lab-based colleagues like Jill. They would ask him to find new ways of making speciality chemicals. To Kyle it was utterly boring. He'd been promised a course on molecular graphics but the opportunity hadn't arrived yet. He couldn't even relieve his boredom on the Internet. His computer was moni-

24

tored by someone or other. If he downloaded some MP3 files or logged on to the *NME* site to read reviews of CDs, he'd cop it from a supervisor. For light relief from work, he had to make do with the occasional incursions by hackers from animal liberation groups, computer freaks who relished a challenge, and environmentalists. But such files were spotted very quickly by those vigilant supervisors and deleted almost immediately.

It was an open-plan room. Kyle guessed that the design discouraged staff from misusing the state-of-the-art computers. It was dangerous to log on to a favourite website when a colleague or a supervisor could walk past and see it at a glance. The screens were full of three-dimensional molecular models, biochemical articles, synthetic schemes or internal documents.

To e-mail the results of a literature search to one of the chemists in Lab 47, Kyle logged on to the staff list. He copied the e-mail address that he wanted and he spotted two other things. The file had not been updated because he was still listed as a worker in Lab 47. More interesting, at the bottom of the staff list there was a reference to a Professor Brandon Fleetwood (Head of Laboratory, resigned). Kyle had never come across a senior biochemist called Fleetwood, although he remembered samples in the lab with code numbers beginning with BF. Now he understood why those initials had been used. More importantly, he had found out that the scientist in charge of the Lab 47 project had quit. Kyle was amazed. In YPI, resignations were almost unheard of, especially from high-ranking staff.

Yttria did not want to lose workers simply through another drug company offering more money. High salaries and super pension schemes discouraged members of staff from resigning, moving to competitors and taking YPI secrets with them. Of course, the bosses weren't really being generous to personnel, they were simply protecting company inventions. But Brandon Fleetwood had moved on.

The missing Head of Laboratory and the boy in a coma further heightened Kyle's sense of intrigue.

5

Mr and Mrs Grant were distraught. Their Dwight wasn't a bad boy. Sure, he'd been in a young offender institution but that didn't make him bad. In England, a white boy who'd done what Dwight did would have got off with a caution. In parts of England, skin colour was a substitute for evidence and Dwight had got the wrong sort. In Cambridge, blacks were more likely to be stopped, searched or arrested by police, and much more likely to be locked up. OK, Dwight had someone else's credit cards and his fingerprints were on a stolen car, but he was led into all that by friends. His mam and dad would have stopped him mixing with those sorts of boys. The police could have handed him back to his family. His dad's belt and a lengthy grounding would've sorted it out. But no, the police decided to follow procedure. Strange it wasn't followed with white suspects.

Sure, Dwight had done wrong. Mr and Mrs Grant knew that. They even reckoned they knew why. Dwight looked up to his Uncle Akoda. Akoda had got himself a flashy Internet business and a flashy lifestyle and a flashy motor to go with it. Dwight was always talking about being a footballer so he could have tonnes of money, a flashy lifestyle and a flashy car as well. But maybe his friends told him there was a short cut to flashy lifestyles and flashy cars. Dwight didn't want to hear the problems that go with those things. The police thought only one thing when they saw a black man in a flashy motor. A black man isn't supposed to be able to afford that. A black man in a flashy car means he's just nicked it. Akoda's record was getting stopped by police in his flashy car twenty-seven times in three months. Akoda got political. He got himself a flashy lawyer, took the police to court for harassment and won the case. So that was it. End of problem. Except that, when he drove home from court, the police stopped him again, arrested him for suspected car theft. Dwight closed his ears to all that hassle. He still wanted a flashy lifestyle and, to try and get it, he got sucked into bad things by bad people.

Dwight was sent to Westland's juvenile wing. And then he was sent to YPI. After that, he got himself a place in Westland Youth. In the team, he was as happy as anyone in a young offender institution was going to be. Then he fell over during a match and didn't get up again.

He was a normal healthy boy, not a weak old man, so why was he hurt so bad? His mam and dad were convinced it was to do with that drug trial. They didn't want to get dragged into politics like Akoda but when they had been contacted by BAD, they were so angry they'd talked to a man called Linton about Dwight. Then they got worried that the pressure group was taking over Dwight's case. They were determined not to get elbowed out so they took it in turns with Akoda to camp at Dwight's bedside to make sure BAD didn't exploit their unconscious son.

They didn't want to score political points. They just wanted Dwight back.

There was something of a commotion around Dwight's bed – too many visitors. Along with Dwight's emotional parents, a loud uncle in sunglasses, and a sister, there were two men in their early twenties. They were all speaking excitedly in a dialect that Helen Crear could not follow when it came so thick and fast.

She put up a hand. "Hold on! All this isn't going to help Dwight, is it?" She glanced down at the unconscious fifteen year old, connected to this world only by tubes, wires and machines. "What's going on?"

The Grant family looked towards one of the other visitors. He introduced himself briefly, as if there were more important things to say. "Linton Okri, of the Black and Asian Defenders."

Helen had heard of the pressure group called BAD. She groaned. "Look, you're not going to turn Dwight into a political football, are you? I'm not interested. I'm a doctor, trying to make him better. That's all I care about. Now I suggest you—"

Interrupting her, Linton said, "I agree. That's all we want as well. But we've brought some information that'll help you – and him."

More interested but still sceptical, Dr Crear replied, "And what's that?"

"Other cases in Westland," Linton said.

The second BAD representative waved a file in the air.

Helen looked from one man to the other. "You mean cases like Dwight?"

"Not exactly," Linton answered. "But there's a pattern. All documented."

"Let's find an empty office to talk," Helen suggested.

"You have to understand," Linton Okri said to Dr Crear in the small staff room, "I'm not a medic or any sort of scientist but I'm perfectly capable of smelling something rotten. And Westland reeks." He pushed the BAD file towards her and allowed her a few minutes to scan through it in silence. Then he commented, "What you've got is a whole catalogue of disasters, from nausea to suicide, among young offenders who volunteered to take YPI drugs."

Helen nodded. Still scanning the report, she said, "Interesting, worrying, but these cases haven't got anything to do with Dwight. He's several steps beyond dizziness and fainting and, as far as I know, he's not contemplating suicide."

"There's got to be a connection, though. Take depression. Ninety per cent of inmates classified as clinically depressed are blacks when the population inside is only sixty-five per cent black. Of those depressed blacks, all but one are on Yttria drug trials. Don't tell me that's coincidence."

Helen wasn't going to tell him anything. She wanted information *from* him. Besides, Dwight wasn't depressed. In fact, his parents told her that he was really cheerful now he was in Westland Youth football team. "Do you know what they volunteered to take? What sort of drug?"

"They're told a lot of guff. But these lads don't exactly ask for facts and figures. That's not what they're after."

"Why *do* they keep volunteering?"

"They're desperate, Dr Crear. The only facts and figures they're interested in are measured in months off and privileges inside. They'll sign any bit of paper if they're promised some money and suddenly they get the best cells, no sharing, the best food, the prize jobs. On top of that, they get outings to YPI for the tests. There's even rumours that early release might be on the cards. They'd swallow anything for that." Sensing in Dr Crear a sympathetic audience, he added eagerly, "Our counterparts in America have put together a document with the same sort of results on black prisoners volunteering for Yttria trials in Atlanta, Georgia."

Helen asked, "Does YPI recruit whites into its drug trials, do you know?"

Linton smiled because he believed he had converted the doctor to his way of thinking. "Some, but not many. They're keener on black lads."

"That's useful to know, but. . ." She shrugged, no wiser.

She asked if she could keep the BAD file, thanked the activists, and then went back to her patients.

Uncle Akoda stripped off his shades for a moment. "I think they blame me, your mam and dad," he said, more subdued than usual. Although Dwight wasn't listening, he continued, "They likely reckon I set you a bad example, but it ain't true. No way." He looked around and then slipped his sunglasses back on before anyone saw his tortured eyes. "I wish you'd wake up, though. Come on, Dwight. Play the game." He shook his head and slumped into a bedside chair. "How'd you get like this anyway? What happened to you, man?"

Dwight wouldn't have been a real man if he hadn't gone out that night with his mates. Before he went, he'd told himself he wouldn't have anything to do with any bad stuff. But they told him what they did last time. It sounded easy and exciting. They got themselves nice clothes, shoes, mobile phones and CDs, things Dwight couldn't afford. In Dwight's family, only Uncle Akoda had that sort of heavyweight stuff. And it didn't really count as stealing because they were taking from rich whites who could afford to stay at a big hotel. They were like black Robin Hoods, taking from the rich and giving to the poor. Robin Hood was a good guy.

With Dwight as lookout in the darkened car park, they broke into a BMW in fifty-two seconds. Another one minute and fifteen seconds and she was purring, ready to fly away from the hotel. Under three minutes and the tyres were squealing as she rocketed on to the main road. For the next couple of hours, Dwight owned that beautiful car as she revved, accelerated, swerved and sped. He had the fantastic adrenalin rush that came with getting something for nothing.

It was the boys' lucky night. When they stopped in a lay-by on the A14, screened from the main road by trees, and opened the boot, they found a briefcase. And when they broke open the briefcase, they found a load of credit cards, a mobile phone and quite a bit of money. One of Dwight's friends kept the mobile phone and shared out the cash. He let Dwight have the credit cards. Someone else grabbed the radio and CD player from the car. The boys were going to torch the BMW, they were going to make a firework display, but it was too good for flames. Besides, it might have alerted the police. They abandoned the car instead.

Alone again in Cambridge later that night, Dwight wanted to feel that adrenalin buzz again. He wanted money and goods like other people had, like Uncle Akoda had. He wanted something for nothing again. He tried out the Visa card in a cash machine but didn't know how to bypass the PIN number so he didn't get any joy. Instead, he went late-night shopping with the Switch card. That felt really good. He could grab anything he wanted – anything at all – and someone else, someone with money, would pay the bill. He didn't realize at the time that his spree had been captured by the bank's security camera and two shop videos.

It wasn't Dwight's lucky night after all. How was he to know that the BMW belonged to a high-ranking police officer who was not going to let the theft of his car and its contents stack up with all the other unsolved crimes? How was Dwight to know that the vindictive policeman had enough power to assign a whole team to the case? And Dwight didn't reckon on closed-circuit television making the team's job easy. The case was closed in a matter of days and Dwight was in a cell with no chance that he'd get off with a warning or a suspended sentence. It was clear that the police were going to lay it on thick.

Dwight was the only one who got caught because he wouldn't shop the others. He took the entire blame.

That was the beginning of how Dwight got into a coma. If he hadn't been seduced by that flashy lifestyle and the wrong sort of mates, he wouldn't have gone on the jaunt. He wouldn't have got himself arrested, charged and convicted. He wouldn't have been caged in a young offender institution. And he wouldn't have gone on a drug trial. He would still be living – not just festering – in the real world along with everyone else.

He was guilty only of having an ambition that was bigger than society's expectation of him.

Uncle Akoda sighed heavily in distress, then he pulled a bundle of crisp notes from his trouser pocket. Furtively, he slipped a tenner under Dwight's pillow. "Something for you when you wake up," he whispered. He got up and left his unresponsive nephew.

6

Paul Turrell opened the padded envelope that he was expecting and then held the vial for a moment in his hand as if it were precious to him. There was a sad smile on his handsome face. He was in his early thirties, white, tall and fit, dressed casually but tidily. He turned to his research assistant and said, "Here it is, that blood sample from Addenbrooke's I told you was on its way."

"And the idea is to look for anything? Anything at all."

Paul nodded. "Let's call it a challenge rather than a problem. As Helen explained it to me, the sample's from a lad in a coma. It's possible he's taken a trial drug and he's reacted badly to it. If so, the question is, are there still traces of it in his sample?"

"Surely the question is why she hasn't asked whoever supplied the drug what it is," the research student replied.

"Good point, but think about it."

"Ah. It's a drug giant's next best-seller, all hush-hush?"

"Precisely," Paul replied. "She's not getting anywhere that way."

"All right. I'll work it up and take a look but it won't be easy when we haven't got a clue what we're looking for."

"True. But if you do find something and identify it, Helen's promised us a joint publication. That way she releases the details to everybody and gets her own back on an uncooperative drug company. And, of course, there's the little matter of you helping to save a boy's life."

Paul's assistant held up the sealed vial. "Is it . . . you know . . . safe?"

"Helen's checked. The lad's not HIV-positive, but treat the blood carefully because there might be a toxic agent in there if her patient's anything to go by."

Once the research assistant had gone, Paul put his work aside and walked to the window. It wasn't a good view. His office overlooked the university's ring road and the grey concrete buildings opposite. Lost in thought, he watched three cars cruise past without really seeing them at all. He hoped that he had not come to Helen Crear's mind just because he ran one of the country's best analytical units at the University of Warwick in Coventry. Years ago, they had been trained together at Cambridge and they had shared much more than academic life. But something had torn them apart. Lots of things had torn them apart. A great opening for a chemist in Coventry, Helen's love of Cambridge and a great opening for a junior doctor at Addenbrooke's, two busy schedules, two important careers, 140 kilometres. Why had they let these obstacles – none of them insurmountable – end their relationship? Really, they had surrendered in the face of trivial opposition. It was just that, with one thing and another, they never got around to meeting any more. Helen would be on duty when Paul saw a free weekend. Paul would be away at a conference when Helen got a bit of free time. Somehow, Coventry and Cambridge seemed to be on opposite sides of the globe.

7

Five disaffected, pot-bellied, middle-aged men lounged on the shaded wooden balcony of the huge opulent house and surveyed the unending crop of maize, parted only by the narrow dirt road across the plain. The nearest neighbour was forty-three kilometres away. Four of the men were wearing handguns and three rifles were propped against the wall of the house. It was stifling, the beginning of summer in South Africa. The mercury had just crept over the 30°C mark. The wind and the sky told them that there would be a rainstorm soon. It would last between thirty minutes and an hour and it would leave great pools of water that the sun would evaporate in the heat soon afterwards.

It was the sixteenth of December – the Day of the Covenant – and the Afrikaners had gathered to celebrate the Battle of Blood River in 1838. Actually, the battle between Afrikaners and native Zulus took place on Buffalo River, but it became known as Blood River once its water was reddened with the blood of 3,000 slaughtered Zulus. Swords and spears were no match for cannon and guns. Four Afrikaners were also wounded in the fighting. The battle confirmed that God Almighty had put blacks on this earth to serve Afrikaners.

Esron took another gulp of chilled beer. He was the

smallest of the men yet he carried the biggest gun. He never used to arm himself, but an attack on his farm by disgruntled blacks had persuaded him otherwise. "The place is full of crime now," he complained, his eyes hidden behind sunglasses. "In town, no one stops at red lights any more – not if you're white and especially not women." A stationary car was an automatic invitation to poke a gun through the window and rob or abduct the driver. It could be worse if the driver was female. In South Africa there were forty times more rapes than in the average European city, and murder was common. "It's even worse out here," he added, exaggerating. "No one can hear an attack on our farms. They take everything, you know, even the floorboards and make them into furniture to sell. Remember, the blacks stole a farm school – desks, chairs, roof, walls, the lot – apart from the concrete foundations."

Pieter Fourie spat over the balcony on to the cracked earth, still waiting for the rain. "That raid on your place was your own fault, Esron. I told you."

A week before the attack, Esron had caught a black couple taking a short cut across his land. To punish them, he made them both strip. He sprayed the man's entire body with silver paint and he forced the naked woman to lie in a coffin for five hours. Eventually, when the police arrived, the petrified couple were fined three months' wages for trespass.

Esron was not prosecuted. In Hartswater, where

Free State, Northern Cape and the North-West Province met, the law was friendly with the farmers. There was an understanding between white farmers, the old police and judges. It was a gentleman's agreement, a white gentleman's agreement, and even the new democratic regime could not shift such entrenched alliances. The new police – blacks recruited straight out of the ANC army – were overrun with city crime and demoralized. On any night shift, a police officer stood only an eighty per cent chance of getting home in one piece. In a location where an eleven-year-old boy could be murdered for his bag of footballs and his body parts used in magic potions, the police couldn't be expected to appear every time a farmer had to beat his labourers – or punish black trespassers. The police did not have infinite resources. They had to prioritize. When, occasionally, the unreconstructed white force turned up to deal with countryside crime, they prioritized trespass by blacks, theft by blacks from white land, and attacks by blacks on white properties.

The problems were easy to see. It was Mandela's fault. Under the apartheid system, blacks could not roam across the province without a pass. They didn't see the whites' affluence, much less experience it, so they could not be envious. Once Nelson Mandela banished passes, blacks were free to wander anywhere. They could see the luxuries that they had been denied. They could not read or write – the old state had not provided them with schooling – so they could not hope to better themselves. The only way to get a piece of the action was through crime. Guns and knives were cheap, sold on every street. Gun licences were scattered around like confetti at a wedding and licence holders were allowed to loan their firearms to someone else. Almost everyone was armed. And the plush white farms were isolated – perfect for raids, perfect for self-improvement. Even if the police set out to investigate, it took them so long to reach the scene on bush roads that they usually arrived far too late to catch anyone.

Pieter continued, "You created a grievance, Esron. After you'd finished spraying the kaffir he was real photogenic, so the story got in the press. You asked for trouble. They were bound to come back – with reinforcements – looking for revenge. Why didn't you kill the trespassers in the first place? No pretty pictures then. Paint's for decorating. It's bullets that are for blacks. Before the election we shot them when they trespassed without passes."

The other murmured approval.

Pieter Fourie was an immense man in his fifties with a long straggling beard, bushy black hair erupting from his large ears, shaggy arms like a gorilla's and, behind his shirt, a chest to match. He had a particularly simple view of life. He was a rich landowner, an energetic member of the Afrikaner Freedom Front, and he was under a suspended sentence for putting a bullet in the head of a worthless black teenager who had stolen some fruit from his land. Pieter's brother, Wouter, wasn't at the gathering. He was serving a token prison sentence for beating, strangling and decapitating one of his black labourers who had called him by his first name rather than "baas".

Nicholas complained, "Now the damn kaffirs can claim back the land we saved from them and, if they live on your farm for long enough, they have the right to stay on it. Do you believe that?" He shook his head in exasperation.

Hendrick said, "When they peg out, I won't bury workers on my land no more. The relatives'll use the grave as the basis for a land claim under this crazy government."

The police had refused to charge Hendrick after he'd killed the labourer who had accidentally driven a tractor over his dog. Hendrick argued successfully that the value of his dog's life was greater than that of his worker.

"Time we got back to the old ways."

Their guest, Eugene Knobel, sat silently and smiled at the thought.

Nicholas threw an empty beer can into the air and Hendrick pulled out his gun, took aim, and missed it. Once it landed on the ground, though, he salvaged his wounded pride. He hit it twice in rapid succession, sending the can tumbling over the dried mud.

A tractor rumbled past, driven by one of Pieter's workers on his way to the labourers' quarters. At the wheel was a mere boy, not yet in his teens, but Pieter didn't know his name. Pieter looked beyond the tractor and pointed to the distant wall of mist. "Ah. Here it comes. About time."

His eyes on the coming rain storm, Hendrick murmured, "If there was a way back in time, I'd take it, no matter what the price." He had been infected by the spirit of the Day of the Covenant – and several beers.

Of course, the old ways were gone for ever. Everyone knew that. But the members of this group – the last white bastion of apartheid – were constantly looking over their shoulders.

Quietly, Eugene said, "What's the most important commodity around here?"

Immediately, the others were attentive and respectful. Through their minds ran several ideas: weapons, crops, property, money, gold, diamonds, a white skin. But Pieter came up with the right answer. The foundation of their wealth and livelihoods. He cleared his throat and muttered, "Water."

Lying back on his chair and toying with the spectacles in his hands, Eugene nodded with satisfaction.

They were obsessed with the management of water. Paranoid even. Without the Vaalharts irrigation scheme, their farms and food were finished. Without the irrigation system, they would be at the mercy of the weather and deep, unreliable boreholes. Each of them would defend their water supply with their lives because their farms and their food were the source of their power.

"Water," Eugene repeated softly. He didn't have to raise his voice. He knew his listeners would strain to hear his every word. "Your irrigation system provides white water. The blacks take what they can from the storms in summer and scrounge from boreholes to get them through winter."

Pieter replied, "The kaffirs have got their eyes on our water."

Mysteriously, Eugene said, "Good."

Huge drops of rain began to thunder on the wood above them. Pieter and Nicholas moved back from the edge of the veranda, suddenly smattered by the storm.

Still not speaking up against the din, Eugene said, "You could show your goodwill and lay on a water supply for them."

Puzzled, they were all leaning towards him, waiting for an explanation.

Even in the gloom of a storm, Eugene's vivid eyes shone. His enthusiasm, excitement and fanaticism dispelled the dark. "Are you really serious about . . . how shall I say . . . resisting recent changes?" he asked. When they all nodded, he said, "There *is* a way."

No one – not even on an isolated farm kilometres from prying ears – would use Eugene's real name. Although they all knew who he was, he remained anonymous. They were so in awe of him that they would never whisper his name or threaten his cover in any way. He was far too precious to put at risk.

"You see, if you gave them a good supply of water, you also provide yourselves with a medium for . . . controlling them." He looked into the faces of his rapt audience, checking that they had understood him.

"Controlling?" Nicholas queried.

Behind his bushy beard, Pieter beamed. "Poisoning," he said, spelling it out for his colleagues.

Eugene nodded. "A medium for whatever you want to do."

"You've got something in mind," Pieter guessed.

Eugene shrugged and smiled playfully. "Water's a gift from heaven. There are so many possibilities. . ."

Eugene Knobel was not Dr Adriaan W Bresson's only pseudonym. To the press, he was known as Dr Death. Courtesy of modern cosmetic surgery, Adriaan's bald head had acquired thick locks of hair, his nose was smaller and he had lost a lot of weight. He had shaved off his beard and he wore glasses but, as he held them in his hand most of the time when he was talking with friends, they were probably fake. As with Superman, the spectacles did more for his disguise than for his eyesight. Only one thing hadn't changed since the comfortable days of being former President P W Botha's prized and spoiled doctor. Adriaan's mischievous eyes still shone. Nothing could hide that. He had the bright eyes of an adorable cheeky child.

The catalogue of Adriaan Bresson's crimes was almost endless. He was wanted by the police for murder, conspiracy to murder, theft, fraud, and drug trafficking. According to the Truth and Reconciliation Committee, he had headed a project to sterilize blacks by chemical and biological warfare, assassinated a Russian adviser to the African National Council by dosing his food with anthrax, murdered two hundred activists from the Namibian liberation movement, supplied apartheid security police with muscle-relaxing drugs which were used to suffocate Swapo activists, and ordered the dumping of black prisoners' bodies at sea from state helicopters. He was responsible for poisoning the black consciousness leader, Steve Biko, with thallium and unsuccessful plots to poison Nelson Mandela and a former Head of the South African Council of Churches.

Dr Bresson had used fraud, drug trafficking, and theft of government research money to set up a company to fund the purchase of chemical and biological warfare agents. He had forged many useful contacts in pharmaceutical companies based in the USA, UK, Serbia, Croatia, Israel and Iraq. Only the downfall of the apartheid government had prevented him from achieving his aim of developing or buying germs and chemical weapons that affected only blacks.

As individuals, the four farmers sitting with Adriaan would take the necessary steps to ensure dominance over their own black workers but, as an organization, they were ineffective, bigoted, irrelevant, laughable. Now that Adriaan Bresson was hiding amongst them, though, the white Afrikaners had become sinister, as dangerous as a wounded animal.

"So you see," Eugene was saying in his relaxed voice, "it depends what you want to do: spread disease, incapacitate, or more. All these things are technically feasible and a few are achievable right now. Drinking water is a fine means of delivery."

"What if it got into our own water supplies?" Esron asked.

"Ah. Then it's high-tech you'll want. Genetics." Eugene pronounced the word like a young person whispering in awe the name of a favourite pop group. "It's the secret of life, literally the mother of all discoveries. Genetics will change everything. It's the key to curing cancer, putting off old age, and adjusting personality. Already it's giving us drugs – and maybe poisons – for specific groups of people. It's possible that someone's made chemical or biological weapons that'll only attack blacks."

"Only attack blacks?" Pieter sat up in his eagerness. "Who is this someone?"

Eugene took another drink of clear iced water. He never touched alcohol because it was a poison to the human body. "I've got good contacts with drug companies," he replied. "It'll cost you a bit but I'm sure I can find one that'll be able to help."

Abruptly, the five men were illuminated momentarily by lightning as it sought a path to earth. The image was burnt for a few seconds on their retinas, like a map of a river and its tributaries. Then thunder crashed loudly all around them. The hollow reverberation seemed to press them together in their isolated refuge from the storm.

Duma had four sisters. Four sisters! That's not just bad luck, it's total misery. Four of the disastrous things! Real torture. Two big sisters, two little sisters. Duma was in the middle. Twelve years of age. Of course, he would've had a little brother as well, a friend in the face of the common enemy, if the baby hadn't gone and died before he saw out his first month. What was the problem with so many sisters? They were bossy and bitchy. They all thought they knew better than he did. They stuck together and whispered a lot. And if there was trouble, they always blamed him. Well, all right. Fair enough. He was always the one creating mischief. But it was still annoying that his sisters always pointed their fingers at him. "It was Duma," they'd cry in unison like a girl choir when they could have taken a share of the blame. That's what he imagined a brother would have done. But, no, it was always Duma's fault. They ganged up on him, all girls together. That was the problem with four sisters. To get his own back, he teased them, even though he was in a minority. But what did Duma and his folk know of democracy? Besides, being a boy, he was the important one.

He jumped down from the cab of the tractor on to the dusty track and, holding his arms out, waited for a few seconds. Almost immediately, shadow displaced daylight. As the lightning flashed and the thunder rumbled through his body, Duma looked like a scarecrow. He didn't think of the danger. He thought only of water, precious water. Within seconds, the large drops had drenched him, washing the dirt from his scraggy clothes, arms, legs and face. He blinked the rainwater from his eyes and felt the drops running off his hair, nose and ears. It was a wonderful, refreshing feeling, helping to clear his headache. The baths and drums at the edge of the village would be filling. No doubt, at the end of the day, he'd be sent with the other children to fetch bucketfuls back to the shacks. While Duma could joke around with almost anything, he'd learned that water was a much more serious business. It was life and death to the sheep, pigs, goats and donkeys, and it made the workers' existence bearable. When Duma

50

was messing about, he could put donkey dung in the teacher's desk; he could chase the ostriches if he felt brave; he could lace his sisters' drinks with his dad's alcohol, but he wouldn't dare spill a drop of water.

No opportunity to hoard clean water could be missed. Right now, pots, pans and buckets were appearing outside each cottage in the village. The exception was Duma's neighbour where something even more important than a supply of water was happening. No one appeared at the door of the shack, no one was celebrating the rain. Instead, the man of the household was fighting for his life.

8

A boisterous party was under way in the hired community hall that was more accustomed to gentle over-60s waltzing and bingo. The drums cracked, the bass thudded relentlessly, the keyboard droned, the guitar screeched, and the singer's voice boomed. Around the sides of the hall there were tables, chairs and a queue for the bar. At the far end, the Short Cuts were playing live on the raised stage. Most of the partygoers were dancing wildly in the centre of the room, oblivious to the lead guitarist's occasional wrong note.

It wasn't a big thing. The Short Cuts were never likely to break into the big time, never likely to stumble into the big money, but it wasn't about fame and fortune. It was about passion, the odd gig here and there, five mates having a great time and letting other people have a great time. It was about a little fee and a lot of free drinks. And occasionally it was about impressing the opposite sex. So, if the new guitarist sometimes bummed a note, it wasn't the end of the world. Once he was more familiar with the songs, he'd get better anyway.

At the entrance a morose solitary figure, sidelined by the party, was watching the band and counting every clashing chord as if he were nursing a grudge. After a few minutes, Kyle shuffled sadly away, his eyes fixed firmly on the ground. Jill's unintentionally hurtful words rang louder in his head than the muffled music behind him. "No more playing guitar, then." She was absolutely, devastatingly right. His injury had forced him to leave the Short Cuts.

The on-line Phone Directory listed five Fleetwoods in and around Cambridge but none of them was B Fleetwood. Kyle decided to try a different tack. A search of the biochemical literature in the last ten years brought up fourteen papers written by Professor B N Fleetwood, FRSC. His address was given as the University of East Anglia but he had not published anything for the previous six years. Kyle deduced that he had moved from academic life in Norwich to Yttria six years ago. Staff at YPI were not allowed to publish their results in the open press.

Kyle presumed that, after resigning from Yttria, Brandon Fleetwood had not returned to a university because he had not published any research papers recently. But he might have moved back to the Norwich area. Maybe he had retired and was spending more time with his family or with his garden. Maybe he was pursuing some other hobby. Quickly, Kyle searched the directory again and took down the numbers of two B Fleetwoods in North Norfolk. Tonight at home, he would try both of them.

Kyle kept his repaired right hand in his pocket when he

wasn't using it. It was unnecessary because no one would have noticed that he had nails on only two fingers of that hand, and that the other three didn't look quite normal. Even so, he felt self-conscious about it. He lingered uncomfortably outside Intensive Care, shuffling anxiously from foot to foot, not knowing if he was allowed to go in, not really wanting to go in. He was remembering an intolerable queasiness in his stomach as he waited outside that same ward four years ago with his mum and dad and a pregnant Oonagh. He couldn't recall the corridor, the room and the bed, but his parents' expressions, Oonagh's bloodless, vacant stare, and his own feelings of dread were fixed in his brain for ever.

The fifth nurse to walk past busily was the first to hesitate and ask, "Can I help you?" The others were too flustered and rushed to deal with muddled visitors.

"I've come to see Dwight Grant."

"Dwight Grant." She paused. "He's Dr Crear's patient and I doubt if she'll allow you to see him. Are you family or a friend?"

"I'm a friend, I guess." Then he added, "Actually I work at YPI and I wondered. . ." He stopped, questioning why he was being honest. To find out about Dwight, he should be telling the nurse that he was a close personal friend. With his skin colour, he could hardly claim to be a brother.

"You work for Yttria Pharmaceuticals?" the nurse

54

asked, as if she needed confirmation before she could believe him.

"Yes."

"Why don't you wait in the day room?" The nurse pointed to it. "I'll get Dr Crear as soon as I can. I think she might want to speak to you."

In the quiet room, colourful Christmas decorations hung limply, almost apologetically, around the walls. Kyle might have been in there before but he would have been too stunned to remember. In the corner, three old folk were gathered lamely in front of the television which was showing some Australian soap. One of them kept exploding into dry horrible coughs as if his lungs were rusty. The other two were asleep or dozing. Another patient with bandaged legs sat in the corner, surrounded by her family. A walking frame stood to attention beside the group. A teenage girl, almost completely bald, was clearly recovering from cancer treatment. Keeping himself to himself, Kyle sat on his own near the door and tried unsuccessfully not to think about his brother.

Kyle had been at school when that awful phone call had come in. He'd known that it was serious when one of the teachers volunteered to drive him to the hospital. Outside Intensive Care, he'd joined Oonagh and his parents with their horrified, haunted faces. His brother had been taken inside to a high-tech bed that would be his last home, the victim of a simple and ordinary car accident, like thousands of others. "I'm sorry," a detached voice said. "The damage was just too. . ."

And that was it. Kyle's brother had been killed by half-a-tonne of rapidly moving weapon called a car. Oonagh lost her partner and her unborn daughter would never know her dad. Kyle's family was destroyed by it. Kyle's father did his best to hold everything together; Kyle's mother fell apart and resigned from her teaching job; Kyle tried to be normal again. His early guitar work became dark and menacing. He used it to extract the rage from himself.

What hurt Kyle the most? What still shocked him? What still made him wake in the night covered in sweat, feeling sick? His mother. Ever since the death of her first son, she'd had nothing left for Kyle. She was empty. Kyle knew how to interpret her attitude. If he could not be a consolation to her, if she could think only about the son she had lost, then he must be worthless.

Startling Kyle, Dr Helen Crear arrived after half an hour and apologized for keeping him waiting. She looked at him with a mixture of suspicion and hope. "I hear you're from YPI and you've come to see Dwight Grant."

Kyle nodded.

"Is it an official YPI visit?"

Surprised that she could think such a thing, Kyle said, "No, not at all. I just. . . It's just me."

56

"Are you all right, by the way?" she asked. "You look very pale."

"I'm fine," Kyle lied, still trying to free himself of the nightmare of his brother's death.

"So, what's your relationship with Dwight?"

"He's my mate," Kyle replied unconvincingly.

"If you're his friend," Dr Crear said, "you'll know how many sisters he's got."

Reddening, Kyle said, "Not that big a friend. I don't know his family."

"How about which football team he played for?"

Kyle sighed in defeat and took his right hand out of his coat pocket and extended it towards the doctor.

She examined the damage and the repair. "Nice job. But. . .?" Her puzzled expression told him that she didn't understand the connection between his hand and his hospital visit.

In a quiet voice, Kyle explained his accident, his new position at YPI, his disappointment, his brief sighting of the BAD file, and his hope that Dwight Grant was now conscious. If so, maybe Dwight could tell him something about the drug he had been taking, and maybe that was related to Kyle's accident. It was a long shot but Kyle was increasingly desperate to discover the cause for which he had sacrificed his career and his ability to play guitar. He hoped that Dwight was a signpost along the way.

Dr Crear shook her head. "I'm sorry, Dwight can't

help you. He's still unconscious. But you could help him – and me. You must have some sort of clue about the drugs Yttria's testing at the moment."

"Not really. In my lab we were working on some sort of anaemia. . ."

"Anaemia?" To Helen, that made sense. Dwight Grant did not have full-blown sickle-cell anaemia but he was a carrier. That might have made him useful for testing a treatment of the condition. The disease was caused by abnormal haemoglobin in the blood and it affected only blacks, so Yttria would need plenty of black volunteers. The company would need just a few whites as control subjects – to check that the drug did not harm people who couldn't possibly have sickle-cell anaemia. Suddenly, Helen suspected that she was nearer to the substance that Dwight had taken, but she had no idea if it had anything to do with his coma and, even if it had, she still didn't know how to treat him. She also realized that she might be barking up the wrong tree altogether. She told Kyle her suspicions and then said, "I really need this guesswork confirmed or denied, you know. You work at YPI so you could—"

"Can't you just analyse his blood?"

"I tried. I gave a sample to the best analyst in the country, Paul Turrell, up at Warwick University. No joy. Not in the early tests anyway."

Kyle sighed. "OK. I'll see what I can do." He walked away, shaking his head. He had come to help himself and he'd left with an obligation to help someone else. It was an obligation that could get him into a great deal of trouble.

At home that night, Kyle poured himself a long cold drink and wrapped his fingers around it. Not all of his right hand felt the chill. He tried to forget the past and concentrate on the future. With the phone perched on his lap, he soon found out that neither of the North Norfolk Fleetwoods had got a clue about Professor Brandon Fleetwood. He had drawn another blank. He sat back and drank. It was the sort of restless, long night on which he would have loved to call his mates in the Short Cuts and set up a practice session. It wasn't the practice that he needed, it was the companionship and the sound.

Idly, he took an elastic band from the telephone table, stretched it over the arm of his chair and twanged it with the unscathed little finger of his right hand. It was years ago, as a curious and playful child, that he'd first plucked a crude tune on elastic bands. His early fascination with vibration, stretching and noise had turned him on to physics, chemistry and music.

His mind turned instead to that search of the scientific literature. The man who had become the chief of Lab 47 was listed as Professor B N Fleetwood, FRSC. Fellow of the Royal Society of Chemistry. Using his home computer, Kyle logged on to the Royal Society of

Chemistry's website and searched it for information on Professor Brandon Fleetwood. It didn't take long. An archive of the Society's magazine mentioned him many times. The most recent extract came from the magazine's obituary page.

The article went through Professor Fleetwood's illustrious career. First degree and PhD at Oxford, England; post-doctoral research at Harvard, USA; Lectureship at Bath, England; Reader and Head of Department at East Anglia; Head of Laboratory at YPI, Cambridge; resignation; death. The cause of death wasn't given but the article referred to a tragic accident. The end of the obituary caught Kyle's eye. *Brandon leaves a wife, Ellie, and three daughters. He will be sorely missed by both the chemical community and his family.*

At least Kyle now understood why he had failed to trace Brandon Fleetwood. Earlier, when he had checked local telephone numbers, he'd been looking for B N Fleetwood. But maybe Mrs Ellie Fleetwood had changed the entry since her husband's death. Kyle put down his drink and grabbed the phone book. There was only one candidate: an E J Fleetwood lived in Cambridge. Before he tried the number, he thought carefully about what to say if E J Fleetwood was Brandon's widow. It would be very easy to make a slip and upset her. He didn't relish the call but, to steel himself, he thought of Dwight Grant in a coma and the moment when he saw the tips of his fingers shredded by that explosion in his hand. He thought of the gushing blood. And he thought of the Short Cuts performing at New Year celebrations without him in the line-up.

9

Memphis was built above the Mississippi River where the borders of Arkansas, Tennessee and Mississippi meet. Home of the blues, Elvis Presley, cotton carnivals, and the Lorraine Motel where the black civil-rights leader, Martin Luther King, was assassinated by a sniper's bullet in 1968. Segregation as an official policy had ended many years ago but it continued unofficially. Black and white communities were still divided by mutual suspicion and money: the white minority in comfortable suburbs, the black majority crammed into the inner city. Always barriers. Invisible ones, but barriers none the less.

Nathan McQueen had become a political celebrity. "Today in America, skin colour substitutes for evidence as grounds for suspicion, you know. If you're black, you're more likely to be stopped, searched, arrested, jailed or shot by the police." Nathan wasn't the only black man to have been beaten by white police officers, but he was the only one to get lifted from an inner city street in Memphis and beaten so spectacularly that he got himself on international TV. It had helped that a bystander with a camcorder got the whole thing on tape, of course. Ever since Nathan's televised beating last summer, the racial temperature in Tennessee and the Deep South had soared. And Shadow had begun his fiery vengeance.

The radio interviewer could hardly get a word in edgeways as Nathan continued his practised protest at pace, like a rap artist. "Check this out, man. Number of whites shot dead by the police this year as they fled the scene of a crime? One. Number of blacks shot dead by the police as they fled the scene of a crime? Thirteen. Now, ain't that funny? And most of the shootings were at night so the whites would've showed up better," he said with a wry grin that was wasted on the radio audience. "The police seem to be much more accurate when the suspect's black. What else? For starters, there's failure to respond to race-hate crimes, a conspiracy of silence around racist police officers, retaliation against good officers who report racist colleagues, unnecessary physical force on young black men with gang problems, overenthusiastic raids on suspected black drug dealers—"

The radio presenter butted in. "That's all well documented. We know it, for sure. But does it excuse the antics of the man who calls himself Shadow?"

"Shadow's messed up some properties and vehicles real good but he hasn't messed up any lives."

"It's only a matter of time before he does," the interviewer responded sharply. Insisting on an answer to his question, he repeated, "Does corrupt policing excuse him?"

Nathan replied, "Maybe not, man, but it explains him. Don't forget, for us, it's corrupt police officers and then some. Schooling's designed for the white middle classes, employers discriminate every day, white extremists promote race hatred on the Internet like they'd got their own TV show. . ."

Storm Force operated throughout Tennessee, Alabama, Mississippi and Georgia. Its members were anonymous individuals. They didn't wear ridiculous Ku Klux Klan outfits in public or in private, they didn't have a badge or regulation tattoo, they couldn't even be identified through a funny handshake. They looked like normal human beings: old, young, handsome, ugly, tall, short, wealthy, poor. They were born-again Christians, farmers, secretaries, managers, police officers, louts, self-styled "reverends", anything. They wouldn't even recognize each other in the streets because they were joined mostly by the World Wide Web. So what did these rednecks have in common? White skin and hatred.

Their neo-Nazi website exploited the First Amendment's protection of free speech to the extreme. *You got your drive-by shootings, your drug dealing, your car theft, your arson, your gangs. And who are the perpetrators? Your niggers.* The site contained hit lists of black activists, Jews, gays and lesbians. It contained an Aryan Dating Page with suitable mates for breeding. It sold white supremacist books and race-hate rock CDs and it provided tips on making explosives and using firearms. The last two pupils who'd walked into a high school with automatic weapons and massacred their fellow students and teachers had made many visits to the Storm Force website where they'd learned how to amass an arsenal of weapons and how to use it. The next cold-blooded kid to do the same thing will probably have also visited the same site – or one of many similar sites.

Storm Force posted Nathan McQueen's name, picture and address on its bulletin board, offering $500 for a better beating than the police gave him or $10,000 to any white brother willing to assassinate him before he could spread any more lies. It was plain why the Storm Force bulletin board was actually called *The Bullet Board*. There was also a reward of $1,000 for outing the arsonist dubbed Shadow and a tempting $25,000 for his elimination. The offer brought a swift response by e-mail from Atlanta.

How do you counteract Shadow? With Light, of course. I despise these niggers who say they commit crimes because America is racist. By targeting whites, Shadow is the biggest racist of them all. None of us are safe while he prowls the streets. I don't know who he is but I'll be able to eliminate him and his kind soon. Watch out for a whole bunch of news. Feeling angry, Light.

The reply was short and sweet. *Go get him, Light. Best wishes, Storm Force.*

10

The interchange at the porch was awkward. Kyle would not offer his right hand to anyone any more so he did not initiate a handshake with Ellie Fleetwood. "Hello," he said, his breath forming small clouds of condensation. "I'm Kyle Proctor. I called you last night. It was good of you to agree to see me."

Ellie was in her fifties, still attractive in a worn sort of way, and wary of her visitor. She stood to one side. "You'd better come in out of the cold, Mr Proctor." Guiding him into the L-shaped living room, she took his coat and asked, "Can I get you a coffee, tea, anything else?"

"Coffee would be great."

She disappeared for a few minutes.

It was a big, expensive house. In the hall, Kyle had noticed that stairs led up to two more floors and down to a basement. A substantial conservatory had been built on to the side of the living-room and, beyond it, there was a large, well kept garden on several different levels. The living room was decorated with large antique vases and the hi-fi, television and DVD player were state-of-the-art. Other than the unlit Christmas tree, it was sparse and tidy. Its unusual stone floor made it feel a little cold, but a colourful, authentic Turkish rug provided warmth. As Kyle expected, YPI had paid Brandon well until his untimely death.

Ellie returned, carrying a tray. She had a natural elegance but she was not aloof. "I'll leave you to organize your own milk and sugar."

"Thanks." Kyle guessed that Ellie Fleetwood was a teacher, maybe even a headteacher. He thought that she might have the right combination of authority, energy and grittiness.

Ellie sat back and watched him pouring the milk with his left hand. "Well, Mr Proctor. . ."

"Kyle."

"OK, Kyle. What can I do for you? On the phone, you said you work at YPI and you're concerned about research my husband started."

"Yes. I . . . er. . ."

"You can speak freely," Ellie told him. "I agreed to see you because it's fair to say Brandon had his concerns as well. That's why he resigned. I wonder if you share something with Brandon."

Kyle took a drink. "Mmm. That's good. What exactly did he do at YPI?"

"At first, he was really proud of his work. The company recruited him to develop a cure for sickle-cell anaemia. He was excited at the prospect of cracking a serious, more-or-less worldwide problem. He specialized in genetic engineering and he thought. . ." She put her mug down on the coffee table for a moment.

"What's your interest in this, Kyle? If you work at YPI, don't you know it all?"

Kyle knew that, like most pharmaceutical companies, YPI had put a lot of effort into the human genome project to generate a detailed set of instructions on how people were constructed. Increasingly, the company was using that chemical map of human beings to make the next generation of drugs. Scientists like Brandon Fleetwood called it gene therapy and pressure groups called it messing with the stuff of life. Kyle played down his knowledge so he could get a complete picture from Ellie. "No," he answered. "I don't get told a lot."

Ellie picked up her mug again and wrapped both hands around it. She still wore a plain gold wedding ring. "Brandon was fond of telling people that, in terms of genetic make-up, they're almost identical to chimps. That was one of his party pieces. 'Ninety-nine per cent of chimp DNA is the same as yours.' Even now, I can almost hear him saying it. He'd follow it up with, 'There are even fewer differences between different people.' He used the argument to show that us humans should all be one big happy family. He was very ... humane. 'It's only a tiny fraction of genes – point one per cent – that gives us our different skin colour, height, nose shape and so on. It's that drop in the ocean that distinguishes one ethnic group from another.' He had a few examples of differences that I can't remember. There was something about Caucasians being able to digest a chemical in milk but most Africans, Asians and Hispanics can't. Is that right? Anyway, the most obvious difference, he thought, was sickle-cell anaemia. It's inherited and it affects blacks. Obviously, some black people have got a faulty gene that whites don't have. Brandon thought he could design a smart drug, as he called it, to target that gene. Is this making sense to you?"

Seeing Kyle nod, she continued. "He said he had a cunning way to repair the fault that causes the anaemia. Now, this is where it gets really technical and loses me. I'm trained as a mathematician, not a scientist but, as I understand it, he made a bit of DNA that attaches to the sickle-cell gene. I remember he said he could get the DNA into the body using a virus. That always struck me as strange. We hate most viruses and avoid them like mad but here's a harmless one that's carrying a cure. Anyway, when the DNA finds the target gene, it latches on and that's supposed to trigger the body's own repair mechanism to come and fix the damage. And there you have it: a cure that hunts out only one target and repairs it. He didn't really like a military comparison but he called it a smart drug because of those missiles you hear about on the news. They're aimed at one target and they're called smart because they're supposed to miss civilians. Brandon's drug would sort of do the same: attack the source of the disease without side effects and without affecting people who don't have the sickle-cell problem."

"Yes, that all figures," Kyle said. "You said it was *supposed* to fix the disease. Did it?"

"He got a real shock one day. The drug worked in a test-tube and it was fine in experimental animals. But human trials were a different story. There was no problem with whites because they don't have the sickle-cell gene that the drug was aimed at but, instead of curing black volunteers with the gene, it seemed to make them more poorly. After that, he didn't talk so much about what was going on, but I knew something was bothering him. It must have been to make him clam up. I remember, just before he resigned, he said, 'It's a wallet-widening job all right but I don't like having to leave my principles at the gate every morning.'"

"What did he mean?" asked Kyle. "Trying to cure a disease and having a failure first time is nothing to be ashamed about. In fact, it's par for the course."

Mrs Fleetwood shrugged. "He didn't say exactly, but he certainly got disenchanted."

Kyle put down his empty mug. He took a deep breath and said, "Do you think he was worried someone might turn his smart cure into a smart poison? Do you see what I'm getting at? Genetic engineering to make new medicines is exactly the same as genetic engineering to make new biological weapons. It means people and companies who are keenest to promote human health – like your husband and YPI – can get drawn into making weapons, whether they mean to or not. He had a bit of bad luck and gave YPI a virus that's got no effect on whites but targets a lot of blacks. That's a smart poison."

Ellie sighed. "It's crossed my mind. Brandon hated weapons of any sort. If he thought he might've developed a new type. . ." She shook her head eloquently. Then, cheering up, she added, "If YPI *was* contemplating a weapon rather than a medicine, at least Brandon's resignation forced a rethink. By the time he left, they'd promised they'd drop that particular drug."

Kyle believed that Ellie Fleetwood was naïve about the pharmaceutical business. Yttria had sunk vast sums of money into developing gene therapy. Now it needed a best-seller to get back those millions of pounds and dollars. Then, on top of that, it needed a profit. Could the company afford to scrap Fleetwood's pet drug and try again when they could do very nicely by selling it as a smart weapon instead? The knowledge of how to develop smart biological weapons would itself be a very exportable expertise. After all, there was no shortage of ethnic clashes in the world. There was more than enough hatred to exploit.

Kyle realized that Ellie was looking for the silver lining and he didn't really want to disillusion her but he felt the need to talk about his own worries. "I don't think the promise means much," he replied.

"What?" she exclaimed.

"Volunteers are still having problems. There's a particularly bad case going on right now: a boy called Dwight Grant. I can't swear he's had the sickle-cell treatment but even so. . ."

Ellie stared at the ceiling and then out of the window before turning back to Kyle. "Couldn't they just be tinkering with Brandon's design to try to make a better medicine?"

Kyle shrugged. "They could be, yes. Equally, they could be modifying it to make it a better weapon."

Ellie looked utterly disgusted. The possibility that YPI had broken its promise and betrayed her husband's work made her angry. It was no way to start a new year.

Deciding that it was best to deal with all of the disturbing questions at the same time, Kyle said tentatively, "Can I ask you about your husband's accident?"

Aghast, Mrs Fleetwood sat bolt upright and stared at her visitor. "Are you saying it's connected with YPI?"

He shrugged. "I don't know."

After clearing her throat and swallowing to regain her composure, Ellie said, "Brandon lived for three things: chemistry, family and flying. He was a pilot, you see. He flew a Cessna 150. It's a small training plane – and one of the safest aircraft ever made. But. . . Anyway, apparently it all happened very quickly. Air investigators were amazed. He was only up a few minutes, four or so

72

kilometres out from the runway and banking round. A witness said he saw the plane spin out of control." She gulped down some of her drink. "It nose-dived and burst into flames when it hit the ground. He, er . . . he didn't stand a chance."

"I see. I'm sorry. It's a terrible waste. There must have been an investigation."

"Not a very satisfactory one. It was regarded as a mystery, a freak accident."

"Didn't they get the whatsit . . . the black box ?"

"That's another mystery. You see, light aircraft don't have to carry flight recorders, but some do anyway. I'm sure Brandon said the one he flew had got a black box but, after the crash, the authorities said it didn't. I still don't think they took his death that seriously. Because the plane's so reliable, they put it down to pilot error."

Kyle did not have to respond. Between the two of them, there was a silent understanding. If YPI was worried that an ex-employee might go to the press with a scoop about an emerging biological weapon – even if it had been developed inadvertently – the company might want him conveniently out of the way. It couldn't be that difficult for someone who knew the mechanics of aeroplanes to sabotage a light aircraft. Suddenly, Brandon's accident had the smell of a cover-up.

Kyle was worried for a different reason as well. If the police and airport authorities were mystified by the crash, it smacked of a very professional piece of sabotage, a high-level conspiracy to suppress a thorough investigation, or both. A strong unseen current might be dragging Kyle rapidly out of his depth. In his mind, he heard again Ellie's words: *you share something with Brandon.* If he discovered the secrets of Lab 47 and chose to oppose or divulge them, would he share Professor Fleetwood's fate? He shivered uncomfortably.

11

Light had a kid sister once. She was sixteen. Sweet sixteen and never stopped being kissed. Oh, Shannon wasn't the only one. The world made new martyrs each and every day, an endless supply of innocent kids. No, there was nothing special about Shannon. The United States of America are full of Shannons.

Light's Shannon was bright enough at school, not too bright, not too stupid, kind of good-looking, a whole bunch going for her. Then she met a streetwise hustler and she was hooked. He was so Cool, a Real Man. A slick, easy talking, easy strutting, easygoing operator. Light saw him once. He was wearing IQ reducers: backward baseball cap and permanent shades. Of course, he was black and interested in only two things: dealing and bitches. By using all those young Shannons, he got both. He supplied Light's Shannon with cocaine and maybe other stuff. At first, he gave it away. He told her that snorting a little bit of this, injecting a little bit of that is what all the cool guys do. She fell for it. Next thing, the free samples had dried up and he was charging Real Big Bucks for the gear. Of course, she couldn't pay. By then, though, he'd got her on a chemical leash. So, how did she work off her debt to him? How did she keep her chemical lifeline? She worked for him, worked the street.

Before long she ended up not just working a downtown Atlanta street, but lying dead on it. What killed her? The drugs, a client who got carried away, a mugger, a dealers' dispute, a car, a gang war? It's different for every young Shannon but it's always that lifestyle, always that black hustler. He's always there, that cool gangster, dealing drugs, guns and girls. He's always there while the Shannons come and go, slipping through his careless ugly black fingers.

The way Light saw it, someone had to take a stand against the rising black tide of muggers, murderers, pushers and users. That was why he invented himself as Light. Someone had to say to all those politically correct liberals, "Enough is enough. To hell with your softly, softly, condemn-a-little-less-and-understand-a-little-more attitude." The niggers had swamped the country with crime and drugs, so Light had no ethical problem with turning the tables and inflicting violence and drugs on them. On behalf of all those Shannons, he saw no moral dilemma. Dammit. In the Land of the Free and the Home of the Brave, it was justice.

There's got to be some Light in this world.

In 1763, the invading British overcame the North American Indians by giving them blankets deliberately infected with smallpox. Now, Tristan Lockhart prowled around his nineteenth-floor office like a general who had unexpectedly developed the next generation of defiled gifts. He was the president of Yttria Pharmaceuticals Inc., the US side of Yttria Pharmaceuticals International, and his gift to the black American was going to be a high-tech cure for sickle-cell anaemia. Like those British blankets, though, the medicine concealed a weapon. This one was designed to pick out a specific ethnic group.

"I've sure got a moral dilemma here," said Tristan, looking out over Centennial Olympic Park and much of Atlanta, alive with early morning commuters.

His chief accountant stood patiently by the visitor's chair. "Shall I run down the dire state of finances again – and what our shareholders will think of it? Will that help?"

"I know it to the nearest buck."

"But you asked for me. That suggests to me you've come to a decision."

"I hear our Brit partners are carrying on, trying to use gene therapy to eliminate sickle-cell anaemia, but they're not going to waste the product they've already got."

The accountant smiled and nodded knowingly. "Of course not. They're going to diversify from pharmaceuticals into defence. It's potentially very lucrative."

"It's . . . regrettable but, yes, that's where they're headed." Tristan sat down heavily at his desk. "Defence is a much nicer word than weapons, isn't it? Anyway, I'm following suit so, despite our current deficit, I think

77

it's time to pay our insurance premiums again in case things get a little complicated – a little choppy, politically speaking – some way down this road."

The chief accountant smiled again. He knew that Tristan wasn't referring to real insurance premiums but to YPI's donations to political parties. "Very wise. We don't want to be exposed if we're steering towards the defence market. Senators aren't going to probe us too deeply when we're creating jobs, exporting medicines, and donating large sums to their election campaigns. You want to transfer the same amounts to the Republicans and Democrats as last time?"

Tristan said, "Hell, no. Haven't you seen the polls? Down here, we've got a big drift to the right. Take a million from the Democrat donation and put it on the Republicans. We've got to reflect the times."

On his way out, the chief accountant said, "Good luck with the product, Tristan."

"No problem," he replied. "It'll sell itself." Tristan had already received quiet enquiries from overseas governments willing to pay big money for the basic technology so they could try to develop it for their own particular ethnic challenges as soon as the human genome project revealed the tiny differences between other races.

And it wasn't just officials from India and Pakistan, Indonesia, Africa, the Philippines, Rwanda and Serbia. He'd been contacted by burgeoning home-made groups in the Deep South. The sickle-cell product that was nearing completion seemed to be of considerable interest to them all. But if Yttria stood at the dawn of an exciting and profitable venture, why did Tristan Lockhart dread the day?

"Happy New Year," he murmured cynically to himself.

12

The Hartswater labourers lived in a collection of small squalid houses out of sight of the beautiful farmstead. Some of the shacks had electricity, but none had a water supply. Rainwater was collected from plastic baths and large steel drums. Often, the children had to bleed precious water drop by drop from inadequate boreholes outside the village and carry it a long way home in buckets rather than go to the farm school. The landowner did not charge for the power or schooling, and he provided the village with sacks of vegetables. Because of this generosity, the workers' wages were a pittance. After all, the farmer had to take the rent straight out of the labourers' salaries or he would never have got it back. Sometimes, the workers got an end-of-year bonus as well. This year, the bonus was to be replaced with the provision of piped water in the village.

The Tap arrived just into the new year. It was a modest offering. It stood, small and rickety, under a tree, but it revolutionized rural life. It signalled a new era rather than merely a new year. The Tap would allow the workers to keep thirsty chickens and to grow pumpkins, watermelon, guavas, grapes, mangoes and paw-paws. The children would be able to spend more time in school. The Tap would also bring hygiene.

Water for drinking, cleaning, cooking and washing would no longer have to be shared with the pigs and donkeys.

With the coming of The Tap, the villagers thought they had it all. Luxury.

13

Stuart Urling-Clark had never seen anything like it. As soon as he clicked open the e-mail message, a countdown to self-destruct began. He was allowed three minutes to read the message, but warned that he would be prevented from storing or printing it, or cutting and pasting it into another document. In the message's short life, the computer's screen snapshot facilities would be disabled. After the allotted three minutes, the document disappeared from his screen, leaving only the sender's name and e-mail address. Four different YPI computer experts tried and failed to undelete the message. While they hunted unsuccessfully for a single trace of it, they told Stuart that they had come across self-deleting e-mails only in computer magazine articles. Up to that point, they had not met an autoshredder in the flesh. They were excited and impressed.

Stuart had to cope with the sender's guile rather than admire it. He was irritated that he didn't have a record of the message to show to the Management Board. Plainly, Knobel Industries of South Africa did not want to leave any evidence of its request to YPI for a biological agent that targeted black Africans.

Concluding his upbeat presentation to the YPI Board

in Cambridge, Stuart announced, "The prognosis is very good. Very good indeed. There's been an unprecedented level of interest in BF19 so I'm sure we're doing the right thing. Atlanta's had a lot of enquiries as well. Some have been from governments, some from non-government organizations. The strangest is a company in South Africa, listing itself as an ostrich farm among other things. Anyway, it sent an e-mail requesting a product like BF19. By the way, we're now calling it sickle-cell product 19, or SCP19 for short." Already, the biological weapon had acquired a harmless-sounding name and Brandon Fleetwood's part in its creation had been erased. "And there's an outfit in Australia that's concerned about an Aboriginal problem. They want to buy our method in case it can be applied to their own . . . difficulties."

"You could say the orders are pouring in already, then."

Stuart nodded. He didn't see much dissent around the table but, even so, he said, "It's no different from selling firearms or fighter planes to various regimes. Just because we supply a weapon, it doesn't mean we're encouraging its deployment. Weapons don't kill people: only people kill people. And we're not responsible for end use. Full stop. I'm sure we'd all agree anyone who knows the enemy's got a biological weapon will pull out of a fight. Mere possession will end a conflict. Besides, even if SCP19 were deployed, it'd *reduce* casualties. It's a smart weapon that eliminates collateral damage."

The managers sat back and relaxed over a coffee. They were safe in the ultimate refuge of the arms dealer. Their fingers were not on the triggers of the weapons that they sold. They could not be blamed. At least two Section Heads were wondering if their biotechnologists could come up with an antidote to SCP19. That way, they could double the profits. They could sell the weapon to one side and the antidote to the other.

The company's lawyer adjusted his tie and announced, "Right now, I'm looking into the legalities. There's the Biological and Toxin Weapons Convention to consider, but the good news is, I don't see any insurmountable barriers. The first step is an application to the Government for an export licence. As you know, there's a Cabinet reshuffle coming up and, if the rumours are right, I suspect that the new Trade and Industry Secretary will be someone we can do business with. I think, with an appropriate form of words, we can make a convincing case for our application."

Three men on the Board did have misgivings about the new direction. It seemed hypocritical to them that a manufacturer of health products should enter the weapons market as well. But they kept their doubts to themselves. Their uneasiness was overshadowed by economic considerations. The health of YPI always had to come first.

Abigail squealed in delight as she sped down the plastic slide. Coming to a halt on the soft carpet, she cried, "Again!"

Oonagh laughed. "As many times as you want. It's yours, Abi. Uncle Kyle's given it to you."

Kyle watched his excited niece climbing the steps awkwardly. In her bright eyes, he saw all that remained of his brother.

After tumbling on to the carpet again, she tottered to Kyle and gave him a big hug. "Thank you!"

"You're welcome."

She disentangled from his arms and, before heading back to her present, she glanced down at his hands. "Uncle Kyle's funny fingers!"

"No, Abi," Oonagh said sharply. "That's not nice."

"It's all right," Kyle replied.

Really, Kyle's mind was elsewhere. He talked to Oonagh, watched Abi and smiled, but he was thinking about the safe in Lab 47, Dwight Grant, and genetics-assisted genocide. Ellie Fleetwood had not confirmed that Lab 47 was making a sickle-cell poison but Kyle feared that it was.

On his way home, he called in at Addenbrooke's, where Dwight had begun the new year just as he had left the old one. He had dropped out of the normal passage of time altogether. Kyle told Dr Crear that her patient might have taken an experimental sickle-cell anaemia cure, based on gene therapy and delivered by a virus.

Helen did not dare to base a whole treatment on pure guesswork, but she thanked Kyle anyway. "I'll try another anti-virus treatment, just in case."

Since opening the *BAD Vibes* file, Kyle had tried to get in touch with the Black and Asian Defenders organization. It wasn't easy. But Helen Crear gave him a telephone number for someone called Linton Okri. When Kyle met the BAD representative that night in a city centre pub, though, he was disappointed. Linton had compiled an impressive list of boys at Westland who had been taken sick whilst on YPI drug trials. He also knew of some black prisoners in Atlanta, Georgia, who had become unwell after they'd volunteered for trials with Yttria Inc. But he had no irrefutable link between YPI drugs and the illnesses.

Kyle imagined that some of the volunteers had probably been unhealthy anyway and would have got sick even if they hadn't enlisted for the trials. Some might have been taking dummy pills: ones that didn't do anything. That was standard practice for clinical research. Other volunteers might have been faking sickness and fever because it got them out of Westland Young Offender Institution or out of prison in the USA for a few days. Linton could not prove that YPI was making its human subjects ill, deliberately or accidentally.

Kyle had to admit, though, that so much ill-health among YPI's black volunteers was an extraordinary coincidence. If people believed they got cancer by using mobile telephones and leukaemia by living near nuclear power stations, they would be utterly convinced by BAD's file. Yet Kyle had never seen anything about it in the press. He asked Linton, "Why don't you splatter all this across the newspapers?"

"We've tried, believe me. I even gave a copy to a journalist called Victoria Scates, but it's amazing what a business-friendly Government can gag when they claim it's not in the public interest. Victoria's story got pulled."

"What about the Internet?" Kyle said.

Linton uttered a derisory grunt. "Our website's trashed as soon as we get it up and running. You can thank your YPI computer wizards for that. They send thousands of requests for simultaneous access, overwhelming and crashing our server. Either that or they hijack the site, redirecting anyone visiting it to another website altogether. YPI doesn't like bad publicity. Make that BAD in capitals."

Kyle was running out of options. As someone on the inside of YPI, he realized that he was going to have to take some risks to find out for sure what lay behind Linton's statistics.

14

The way Shadow saw it, the United States of Kiss-My-Ass had sold blacks a dream of wealth and glamour but, for most blacks, the dream stayed a dream. They watched whites living the American dream while they got left behind. That's how whites always saw blacks: in their rear-view mirrors. A few blacks never gave up on the dream and tried to access it by getting some action on the streets. That didn't work either. Witness two million young black men filling American jails. That's no dream.

So, what did the future hold for the young Shadow? Joining his brothers in jail? No. The media, controlled by whites, called him reckless and foolish but he wasn't. More like the opposite. He was cautious and clever. As an arsonist, he was too cunning to be caught. He was going to enjoy himself, make his point, and stay free. And what was his point? He was going to make people realize that it's ludicrous for everyone to aim high for something that so few are ever going to achieve. It's stupid. It'd be better if everyone aimed lower. That was Shadow's thinking. He didn't hate whites – not in the way that some of them hated him – but he enjoyed the sport they provided. He enjoyed lowering their expectations. He enjoyed burning down their dreams.

In Memphis, the biggest white icon was obvious. Dead, but obvious. Shadow would strike at the icon's ridiculous monument. He crouched in the gloom of early evening, staring at those four majestic white pillars, waiting. All of the visitors had left, wrapped in thick coats. Now, Shadow counted the staff as they came out of the grotesque mansion and walked past the 1955 pink Cadillac. By his reckoning, there were still three workers to go. Even on his most ambitious venture so far, he had no desire to hurt anyone. He just wanted to see the flame bursting out of the gigantic windows, brushing the pale stonework, destroying the dream of Graceland, 3734 Elvis Presley Boulevard.

Shadow was invisible as he lingered among the trees on Elvis Presley's estate. He was into music – rap and blues – but not Elvis. Shadow felt nothing for the star's lavish home and grave site. It was an alien world. For Shadow, it was an example of the unattainable, a symbol of white supremacy, an insult on a grand scale. With its mirrored staircase, pool room with fountains, trophy building, and jungle den with a waterfall, it was perfect for cleansing.

The last three members of staff locked up and came down the steps in front of the overblown tourist attraction. Two left straight away and the third got into the pink Cadillac and drove it carefully into its garage for the night. When she also vacated the estate, Shadow's spine tingled. OK. The place was empty. He wiped the sweat from his forehead. "Shadowtime," he murmured excitedly to himself, coming out from behind the cover of the tree. Curling his lip, he sang softly and cynically, "Any place is paradise," as he made for the sumptuous door with the tools of his trade in his hands: a rag, a can of gasoline and a box of matches.

15

Standing stiffly in front of Stuart Urling-Clark, the
senior security officer looked like a soldier reporting to
his superior. "Proctor's been to Addenbrooke's to see
that sick volunteer and – you won't like this – he visited
Professor Fleetwood's widow for quite some time. They
must have had a lengthy talk. We spotted him with a
member of the Black and Asian Defenders as well."

"Did you have him bugged?"

"No."

Stuart's face crumpled with both disappointment
and admonishment. "Why did you put him on surveillance in the first place?"

"A technician noted he'd opened an unauthorized
e-mail from BAD. He's not supposed to do that,"
Wooderson answered.

"I see." Stuart wished that Security had done more
than a half-hearted job. They had a massive budget that
could buy all of the latest eavesdropping gadgets. By
now, Stuart should have had a transcript of all Kyle's
conversations. He sighed. "I guess the fact that he's
talked to all these people makes him leaky, irrespective
of what he actually said. Tell me, who else does he see?
Is he a family man?"

"No, but he seems to get on well with a little niece,
Abigail."

"Mmm. Family's so important, isn't it?"

Mr Wooderson uttered something that sounded like agreement.

"OK, thanks," Stuart said. "I'll take it from here."

Stuart assumed that a bitter Proctor was digging up dirt out of revenge for his missing fingers. Perhaps the most obvious action was simply to sack him. But that wouldn't be clever. It certainly wouldn't be the end of the affair. It could well be the beginning. Freed from worrying about losing his job, Proctor would be a loose cannon, firing off all over the place. No. Stuart's solution for dealing with Proctor would have to be much more subtle.

Before the security chief left the room, Stuart said, "And there's something else. Our homeless friend is still parked at the gates. He makes the place very . . . untidy. There must be a way of moving him on. Permanently."

For a moment, a frown flashed across Mr Wooderson's face. Then he said, "I'll see what I can do."

Kyle jumped when Stuart appeared suddenly at his side. "Sorry," Stuart said. "Engrossed in your work as always?"

Kyle shrugged. "You surprised me, that's all." He didn't want to appear to be enjoying his new job too much. He wanted to sound as aggrieved as he was – if not, a bit more.

"Well, Kyle, I've come with some good news. We've been monitoring you and we like the work you're doing."

"Oh?" Surprised, Kyle couldn't take the unlikely compliment at face value. "I've hardly done anything yet."

"Oh, that's not true. Anyway, this is more about potential."

"What do you mean?"

"When we took you on, we saw a great future for you in the labs. That didn't work out, unfortunately. Now, looking at what you've done here in your first month, we see great potential for you in computer modelling."

Still, Kyle could not believe what he was hearing. He waited for his manager's next move.

Stuart continued, "Yes, there's a promotion and training opportunity that's ideal for you, starting in February. I'd like you to take it up."

That meant Kyle should accept the place or face a future made miserable by management. "Promotion?" he queried.

"Yes. I thought you'd like the sound of that. Your salary can take a quantum leap."

"Really?"

"You've only got a couple of weeks, so I hope your passport's current. The opening's in Atlanta." Stuart paused for his revelation to sink in. "The salaries are higher in America. It's a great opportunity. We'll pay all your travel, of course."

Thinking of Brandon Fleetwood's accidental crash, Kyle muttered irrationally, "In a plane?"

Stuart laughed. "How else? Do you want me to see if there's a rowing boat heading across the Atlantic? No. I think you'll agree it's an offer you can't refuse."

"It's certainly. . . I'll have to think about it."

Stuart made a show of being astonished. "Not much time for thinking, Kyle, or the place will go to someone in Atlanta and it's too good to miss. Full stop."

"How long's it for?"

Stuart shrugged. "Six months in the first instance, then we'll review the situation. You might come back here – in quite a senior role – or you might want to try for an extension in the States."

Kyle took a deep breath. It was a clever tactic. In one sweet move, YPI was getting him out of the way for a while and buying his loyalty to the company with a bigger salary and an attractive trip. It was called bribery. Somehow, Stuart must have found out that he was rummaging around in YPI's dirty washing. Kyle guessed that, if the company's first-choice fix – a move to Atlanta with a hiked salary – didn't work, the second-choice fix would be an accident. With alternatives like that, Kyle didn't have any real option.

On Sunday, Kyle walked restlessly up and down his front room as he carried on the telephone conversation with Dr Crear. "So, you see, I wish I could help some more but I'm being disappeared, as good as."

Startled, Helen replied, "Disappeared? Atlanta sounds like a nice little earner to me."

"Maybe, but I bet that's not the main point."

"What are you saying? YPI's getting you out of the way?"

"Exactly."

"Do you have to go, then?" Dr Crear asked. "Promotion's not compulsory, is it?"

Kyle uttered a quiet, cynical laugh. "Guess what'd happen if I didn't take this job."

"What?"

"Well, I don't know for sure but I'm scared." He told the doctor about Brandon Fleetwood's fate and then added, "I don't want to end up like him, so I'm opting for the job."

Helen knew why Kyle was confiding in her. She had in her mind an image of a spent runner coming towards her, holding out the baton for her to grasp. "For Dwight's sake, I need more inside information on those YPI drug trials," she remarked.

Kyle paused. "I know, but it's hard, possibly dangerous. . . I'll try again before I leave."

"Thanks, but remember America's not as far as you think," said Helen. "If you get training on their computers, maybe you'll get on-line access to volunteers' files. And distance is no obstacle to an e-mail."

"It's a possibility," Kyle agreed. "When I'm settled in,

I'll see if I get clearance for drug trial records – but I doubt it."

"Something'll occur to you. You're a clever guy," Dr Crear said, trying to cheer him up. "And let me know if you find out anything interesting before you leave, won't you?"

"Of course."

"Good luck with the move. I hope it goes well."

"Yeah. Thanks."

The Urling-Clarks were regulars at their village church. They were uncompromisingly dedicated and devout. The last time they'd missed a Sunday service, they were abroad on holiday. On the way home, Mrs Urling-Clark asked, "What did you think of the new vicar, then?" There was an element of disapproval in her voice.

Smiling wryly, Stuart answered, "Well, at least he's not female."

"A bit soft, though."

After the pub, they took a right turn and strolled along the lane. "Let's wait and see," said Stuart. "He might work out all right." There was an orchard on the left and a row of luxury houses on the right. "Let's see what relationships he chooses to bless, who he agrees to marry, what he condemns and what he praises." Stuart was thinking of the gay couple who had moved in next door to them, the unmarried Catholics across the road and Muslims further up the lane. "It's a pity there's no such thing as a Catholic gene. Then there'd be something to work on. That way, we'd sort out a few problems. In fact, once we've got everyone bar-coded, who knows what we'll be able to do." He laughed. After all, he was joking.

Mrs Urling-Clark didn't see the humour. She just murmured, "Amen."

It was Sunday morning and, for once, Helen Crear was off duty. Putting down her phone, she stood in the bay window of her house and stared at the orchard opposite. The stark trees were still free of snow, but the ground was sprinkled white with frost. Inside, her central heating worked against the winter weather. Helen wasn't exactly depressed, but she certainly wasn't content. She was annoyed and frustrated. She could deal with tragic cases like Dwight Grant's as long as she had co-operation. She couldn't understand an organization that did not put human life at the top of its priorities. When that happened, maybe it was time for that organization to get out of the health business. She had no time for a business that put profit and shareholders before health and patients. Kyle Proctor's call seemed to confirm her dim view of the ruthless pharmaceutical company.

She watched a couple stroll unhurriedly past her property and glanced at her watch. They were probably walking home after the church service. They looked like a conventional married couple, in their mid-forties, wrapped up against the cold, arms linked in an old-fashioned, non-sexual way. They looked as if they were dedicated to each other, but any sparkle in their relationship had probably been extinguished some time ago. Now, they were merely stable.

Helen didn't go to church. She saw too much suffering to believe that above the medical profession there was a guiding hand looking after human beings. She'd heard plenty of patients mumbling a quiet prayer to themselves, but she was too busy stemming the flow of their blood to take the time to pray for them herself. In a way, she wished she had that couple's faith. She could use a miracle or two right now. There was something else about the couple that she envied. OK, maybe they didn't share blistering passion any more, but they each had companionship.

Helen's mind wandered back in time. Student days. The best days of her life. It was a time when she couldn't afford a decent house out in the suburbs. She shared a grubby flat in a cramped Cambridge cul-de-sac with Paul and two other students. It was a chaos of coming and going, a constant drain on student loans, a tip until someone took it into their heads to binge on cleaning. Back then, life was a soap opera and it had everything from the tragedy of failed relationships and failed exams to the comedy of extraordinary parties and extraordinary mix-ups. And it had romance that had since descended into farce.

Now that she was a well paid doctor in Cambridge and Paul was a secure academic in Coventry, Helen was reminded of characters in a comic play who constantly fail to meet each other or who constantly misunderstand each other. She'd been happier in that student tip, broke, not knowing if she was in love or not. She preferred those years when life was confusing, unlimited, and immense fun. Now, she had an immense mortgage, immense responsibilities and immense working hours. And Coventry was a world away.

She turned her back on the window, the orchard and the steady couple. On the table, she had laid out some pages from BAD's file on Westland Young Offender Institution. She had singled out three suicide cases, all carriers of the sickle-cell gene, all YPI volunteers, all death certificates signed by Dr Padley, all at about the same time. Helen knew Dr Padley. Well, she knew of him. He was one of an endless procession of doctors who had passed through her university course. And he had not been one of the impressive ones whose example she had immediately wanted to follow. She had assumed that he would have retired by now because, years ago, he wasn't just old but weary. Once, he must have had dreams and spirit, but an eternity of tackling human suffering had drained the energy from him.

She looked at her watch again. She thought that it was now a respectable hour to call him, so she picked up her phone again.

Two hours later, after grabbing a lunch in the village pub, Helen was drinking tea in Dr Padley's front room while half-hearted snow fell softly against the window. The old doctor dunked a biscuit in his drink. "We met four years ago, you say. I'm sorry, but you understand I see a lot of young medics. . ."

"It's all right," Helen replied with a smile. "I didn't expect you to remember me."

"After all this time, I dare say you haven't come to discuss the finer points of my classes, or just to renew an acquaintance. Unfortunately." He sucked on the soggy remains of the ginger nut as he kept his eyes on her.

Helen tried to ignore the way that he was looking at her. "No, it's these." She slid three pieces of paper towards him. "I'm interested in hearing any thoughts you had on this rash of suicides last year."

Dr Padley glanced at the documents and looked puzzled. "Why?"

"Because I've got a boy from the same place, not a suicide, but he's been in a coma for six weeks. His diagnosis is a mystery but he shares quite a few things with these victims."

"Victims! If anything, they were their own victims. I'm too busy with people who want the gift of life to expend much effort on those who spurn it."

"Were you told anything about the YPI drug trials they were on?"

"Not relevant." Dr Padley put down his cup. "One lad jumped to his death, two hanged themselves. One used shoe laces – quite ingenious – and the other tore up his bed linen and used that. Mind-altering drugs might have had something to do with it, I suppose, but the toxicity tests came back clean. Besides, YPI doesn't work with those sorts of drugs."

"You know the company?" Helen asked.

"No more than any other pharmaceutical company we get supplies from, or that helps the hospital out now and again."

"There was no doubt about the causes of death?"

"None whatsoever," Dr Padley answered, pouring out more tea.

"Nothing to suggest they were in a coma before-hand?"

"Dr Crear, in all my long years in medicine, I've come across some odd cases but never one in which an unconscious man hanged himself or jumped off the roof of a tall building."

Helen nodded and laughed quietly as she thought she was expected to do. Really, she didn't feel at all amused by the flippant remark that bordered on being unpleasant. "I meant, was there any evidence that someone had . . . assisted these suicides?"

"We all know young offenders are prone to suicide –

101

it's not unheard of in prisons and remand centres – and there was nothing special about these particular drop-outs. They dropped out of the community and then out of life." Seeing an expression of disapproval on his visitor's face, Dr Padley added, "As I said, I don't have a lot of time for these failures when other people are doing their damnedest to survive against all the odds."

16

It was Sunday morning and, for once, Tristan Lockhart was not at work. He was visiting his daughter in Memphis. He stood at the window of her house and stared across the wide avenue at the big white-washed house opposite, set well back in its lush garden. He wasn't exactly depressed but he certainly wasn't content. He felt uneasy and irritated. Once, as a fresh recruit to the Yttria management, he placed human health at the top of his priorities. Pressure from the previous president, the board and the accountants had soon shown him the error of his ways. To this day, Tristan remembered a conversation with the previous president. He'd said to Tristan, "It's always been more profitable to sell pills that help fat Americans lose weight than it is to develop drugs that'll help the starving poor to gain it. And it always will be."

Shocked by the old man's bluntness, the fresh-faced Tristan had argued, "I know we're not a charity, but we've got some responsibility, surely, outside the interests of our shareholders. After all, we get some pretty hot tax breaks and grants from *public* funds, don't we?"

The president had heard it all before and remained unmoved. "You're saying, if a poor man dies at twenty because we didn't supply a drug, there's no chance he'll be buying Coca-Cola at thirty. I can understand that. The country's lost a consumer and that's . . . unfortunate."

"It's not just that—" Tristan began.

"At thirty, he might have been adding to our profits by buying headache tablets and cold cures."

"No." Tristan had still tried to make his point, still tried to get the old man to take his blinkers off. "I meant it in a wider sense. What about our duty to alleviate suffering no matter how poor the sufferers are, even if they can't afford to buy—"

"What duty's that, Lockhart?" He'd never called his staff by their first names. "How are you going to persuade the shareholders to go down Humanitarian Avenue with you? There's no such road. They bought their shares as an investment, not to ease their conscience. No, if we have a duty to make cures for unprofitable diseases, it'll be for publicity – for the feel-good factor so folk'll want to buy Yttria drugs because our name's been in the news. *But*," he'd stressed, "it can only be done from a firm financial footing."

Still gazing out of the window, Tristan recalled every word of that lesson. He told himself that Yttria's need to make money today did not extinguish its commitment to health and humanity. It was just that only a thriving business could afford to be benevolent. With regret, Tristan would guide Yttria into the defence market until his accountants were satisfied with the bank balance. Then, health would float back at the top of the agenda and the profits from SCP19 would fund some fantastic new medicinal ideas.

Just down the road, the tarmac and a couple of leafless trees were still charred after the man called Shadow had burnt out a neighbour's Lexus. Tristan's mind turned to his daughter. She had married a black man. Gerald was a terrific guy, not at all like . . . some people thought. When she'd first moved into this Memphis house, the neighbours were cold and unwelcoming. They embraced Tristan's daughter on her own but, if she was with her husband, forget it. They seemed to think that Gerry was dragging the neighbourhood downhill and that a mixed marriage was unnatural. According to Tristan's daughter, there was still some prejudice and disapproval now, but the knee-jerk rejection had been replaced mostly by grudging acceptance. It wasn't like that back home in Atlanta. More liberal and less racially tense, Atlanta had been the first big southern city to elect a black mayor.

Tristan wondered if Gerry had the sickle-cell trait in his bloodline. If he had, he might have passed it on to his unborn child. In two months, Tristan might have a grandchild who carried the same faulty gene.

From the kitchen, Gerry called, "Dinner's ready!"

In the living room, Tristan's daughter struggled to her feet, groaning with the extra weight and the unnerving shift of her usual centre of gravity. Upright, her hands rested on the bulge that would soon become Tristan's first grandchild.

The inner city hummed, growled and pounded with Monday morning life. In the distance, a siren shrieked like an anxious animal alerting its family to the arrival of a feared predator. Nearer, two car horns blared and a street vendor shouted something indecipherable about his goods.

Much too close to Gerald, tyres screeched. A car was taking off from the lights at speed, faint blue smoke coming from its burning wheels. Still crossing the road, Gerald leapt out of the way, but the man behind him was not so quick, not so lucky. The crack of the speeding car hitting his legs was the sickliest sound Gerald had ever heard. The man was tossed up in the air. He rolled over the hood and smacked against the windshield in another nauseating thud. The broken body slithered across the roof of the vehicle and fell lifelessly into the road behind. This time, there seemed to be no sound other than the car's roaring exhaust. The man lay utterly still. There was no doubt in Gerald's mind that checking the victim's pulse was a waste of time but, even so, two people knelt by him. One woman nearby was screaming, her white eyes staring.

In shock, Gerald watched the accelerating car. The driver made no attempt to slow down. Out of the passenger's window, an arm appeared briefly and something fluttered from the gloved hand. In the confusion, only Gerald seemed to notice. Dazed, he wandered towards the small piece of paper, lying inert in the road like the victim himself. It was a calling card. Across the top, it was emblazoned, *Storm Force Brigade*. Gerald bent down and picked up the card. The only other words on it were: *Nathan McQueen RIP*.

"Nathan McQueen?" Gerald muttered to himself. He'd seen the black rights activist on television. And the man lying dead in the road was not Nathan McQueen. He was no one in the public eye but, to someone somewhere, he was everything.

That night it was announced on the news that there had been a deliberate attempt on Nathan McQueen's life but the messy hit had backfired because the assassin had chosen the wrong victim. Within minutes, a message appeared on Storm Force's bullet board. *Pity it wasn't McQueen. Never mind. It just shows they all look the same. Since you can't tell the difference between them, it doesn't matter which you get.*

17

The young Trade and Industry Secretary could not get over the serving of tea and biscuits. She had never seen so much silverware in an office before. She would have liked to dunk one of the biscuits in her tea, but it would have been out of place. Newly promoted to government minister, she thought that her dunking days were over.

She sipped some tea and then put the cup down. "I called you in because of this... difficult request for an export licence from Yttria Pharmaceuticals International."

"Difficult?"

"Given the Foreign Secretary's pronouncements on the ethical dimension to our overseas sales, yes."

Her adviser asked, "You're not playing the part of a new broom, then?"

The Trade and Industry Secretary smiled. "Not as far as the ethical dimension is concerned. I think people would find it unacceptable to go back on that policy and, besides, journalists and the opposition would have a field day, not to mention my enemies in the party. So," she said, "I need your advice. Fill me in on modern biological weapons." She had come straight from the Department for Education and Employment and, by tomorrow, she would need to be an expert on all aspects of trade and industry.

"And where would you like me to start?"

"At the beginning. The arms trade wasn't on the National Curriculum." She hesitated before adding, "And help yourself to biscuits. I recommend the ones in silver paper."

"Thank you." He sat back and took a drink. "Of course, biological weapons have got a long and dishonourable history. In medieval times, armies used to catapult dead bodies into besieged towns to spread disease. The Mongols hurled bodies of plague victims over city walls in the Crimea."

Interrupting, the Trade and Industry Secretary said, "Now you're trying to spoil my appetite."

"It's a few steps beyond battles with failing schools, I'm afraid, Minister," her adviser said, hinting mildly that he disapproved of government reshuffles that constantly moved politicians away from their areas of expertise. "Anyway, Germans used anthrax in the First World War. In the early forties, Japan conducted biological warfare experiments on thousands of human subjects: enemies and Chinese prisoners. They even dissected them while they were alive – not that they were alive for long. And I'm afraid it wasn't just down to nasty foreigners. Hand in hand with the Canadians and Americans, we developed an anthrax bomb for the Second World War but didn't get around to using it in anger.

"Here's something to think about. A hundred

kilograms of anthrax spores sprayed from a plane over a city on a clear, calm night will kill somewhere between one and three million people. That's the same – or more – than a one megatonne nuclear bomb, but it's eight hundred times cheaper for the same kill factor. Now you know why biological weapons are called the poor man's nuclear bomb. They're about as quick and easy to make as home-brewed beer. You need a small room and a few thousand pounds for equipment. That's it. Since World War Two, only a few countries and organizations are rumoured to have used germ warfare, though: the United Nations in the Korean War, white Rhodesians against black tribesmen and their cattle, the Soviet Union, cults in Japan and the USA. The old apartheid South Africa developed biological all sorts: chocolates filled with cholera, envelope gum with anthrax, and such party tricks. You name it, a man called Dr Bresson made it."

"OK. That's the history lesson. You're saying they're nasty weapons, they've been around a long time, but they're not widely used."

"That's a fair summary. The reason biological warfare hasn't caught on is, in a word, fear. It's an indiscriminate weapon of mass destruction. Let loose, it would move around unpredictably like any other bug at the whim of the wind and water, contaminating anyone in the area, anyone who breathes it, drinks it or comes into contact with it. That's your own side as well

110

as the enemy. It's like the nuclear option in another way. Why hasn't anyone used nuclear bombs since 1945? Because of fear."

The Trade and Industry Secretary said, "This is where you bring me up to date. YPI might have come up with the next generation of biological and chemical weapons, though they haven't said so in so many words. Reading between the lines of their application, though, that's how one could interpret it."

"Yes," her assistant replied. "In pursuing a cure for people with a particular genetic make-up, they seem to have stumbled upon a poison for blacks."

"By any common-sense definition, that's a racial weapon," she said. "But one could argue that it makes war more humane because it doesn't attack indiscriminately causing a lot of collateral damage."

"Yes, that's a spin you could use to justify it. But, in reality, a smart weapon removes the brake of fear. Anyone who's got it is more likely to use it because their own people won't be at risk. They'll contemplate military operations that they'd never have dreamed of before. The result'll be new campaigns, more conflict, and therefore more deaths, not fewer."

"What happens to blacks exposed to this SCP19? It wasn't clear to me even after reading the application."

"I think they skated over that bit, Minister. And I'm not sure they know exactly or, if they do, they're not telling." With a smile, he added, "After all, they're not going to get many human volunteers, are they? Even if they did somehow, they won't advertise the fact by putting the results of unethical trials in their licence application."

"Mmm."

"I could point out that a weapon's a weapon, Minister. I don't know if a smart biological weapon is more or less moral than a smart cruise missile. If I was going to be killed by some sort of weapon, I think the type would be a secondary issue. British companies export war planes, knives, missiles, guns, all sorts."

"Within our ethical foreign policy."

"Of course."

"Have another biscuit. There's still some chocolate ones left."

"Thanks."

"Aren't biological agents outlawed by the Biological and Toxin Weapons Convention?" the Trade and Industry Secretary asked. "Or am I being simplistic?"

"Maybe a touch, Minister. BTWC banned nations from producing, stockpiling, acquiring or retaining biological weapons unless they were for protective or peaceful purposes. However, it didn't provide a means of policing the agreements. There aren't any checks to verify that countries are living up to their obligations so quite a few rogue states flout the Convention. Since it came into force, the number of countries that're capable – or are trying to become capable – of waging biological warfare has doubled. Without controls, that's what I'd expect. There are certainly ten potentially unfriendly states that possess biological weapons right now. Maybe more. Take Russia as an example. Straight after signing the Convention in the seventies, they had more than forty thousand scientists working on their biological weapons programme. They had thirty germs set to be biological warfare agents, including huge stockpiles of plague, smallpox and anthrax ready to be loaded into bombs. That's some arsenal. And they might still have it." He nibbled at his biscuit and then said, "So, I think it's easy to decide for yourself if BTWC is doing its intended job."

"You're saying the easiest weapon of mass destruction to make is the least well regulated."

"Exactly so. And on top of that, BTWC is aimed at states, not individuals, groups or companies. Terrorists and criminals aren't going to lose sleep if they walk all over an international convention aimed at governments."

"Indeed."

"To try to get around this problem, the UK passed a law that makes it a criminal offence for individuals or companies to produce or trade biological weapons."

"I see." The Trade and Industry Secretary pushed away the YPI application and said, "It's been a most helpful session. Thank you. I've already had the Chancellor on the line, you know. He's a bit . . . er . . ."

113

"I think forceful is the word."

"He suggested that he would frown on fellow ministers who restrain a section of the highly profitable chemical industry."

"As I understand it, YPI is not exactly raking it in at this moment."

"It's employing a lot of people and its potential is vast, he tells me. And he doesn't want the wrong signals going out to other companies in the pharmaceutical sector."

"But it's not his head on the block."

The Minister smiled but did not comment.

"Here's something that might influence you," her adviser continued. "Yttria's an international company."

"What are you saying? If we don't let the British end of YPI do the supplying, someone else will?"

"Precisely, Minister. Not all countries have the . . . er . . . benefit of an ethical arms policy."

"And YPI *is* alleviating a lot of suffering through its drugs."

"Absolutely."

"The Chancellor's right that we don't want to stifle that sort of enterprise, so let me ask this," the Trade and Industry Secretary said, leaning forward and speaking quietly as if she were avoiding surveillance. "If YPI were to get an export licence to supply this company in South Africa, how likely is it that news of it will leak out?"

"We have ways of managing such things, and the

114

Home Secretary isn't as keen on freedom of information as she says. We're very accomplished at limiting damage these days but, having said that, the press is very accomplished at its job as well. We can't guarantee to be leak-proof."

"I appreciate your candour." She sat back for a moment while she thought up her carefully worded verdict. "I don't think I can let this one out as a weapon. I don't want my department to be seen to be colluding in suspect arms deals. In my judgement, YPI's current application contravenes BTWC, UK law and our own ethical stand on arms export."

"It would look odd when we bombed Iraq for not coming clean about its biological weapons programme."

"Yes, but that was different. We're not a rogue nation and neither is the new South Africa. Anyway, it's clear that the effect of SCP19 on humans is largely unknown. As yet, it's *not* a proven biological weapon so it's just a pharmaceutical product. In the interests of research and co-operation, I think we should allow YPI to seek overseas collaboration in the peaceful development of its pharmaceutical interests. After all, this product comes from the pursuit of a cure for sickle-cell anaemia. Export may allow the company to further its humanitarian ends."

"That's good," her adviser put in. "The Convention stops us developing, producing, stockpiling or otherwise acquiring, but it has nothing to say about researching."

"If the research reveals that SCP19 is harmful, capable of being made into an effective weapon, we'll need to know how to protect our own black community from it. The public would expect, and want, us to authorize that. We can only defend our own population if there's more research and knowledge about how SCP19 works. Agreed?"

"True, Minister. Put that way, it's a protective project so we wouldn't be violating our BTWC obligations."

"Quite. I'll instruct my Private Secretary to suggest that Yttria rewrites its licence application in those terms. Then I can be more positive. I'm sure I'll feel able to support the application and keep within the Foreign Office's ethical guidelines."

The adviser nodded. "Welcome to the Department of Trade and Industry, Minister. I think you'll enjoy your time here."

18

At the gate to YPI on Monday morning, Kyle wondered where the beggar had gone. Perhaps he'd moved to the city centre and joined the rising tide of homeless people who slept rough on the friendless cold cobbles of Cambridge and relied on a sympathetic student population for spare change. Leaving his hand in his warm pocket, Kyle let go of his coins.

Inside the fortress, Kyle settled in front of his computer. Glancing around, he noted with relief that no one was paying him any attention. Starting with Yttria's main menu, he clicked on the Medical Department. In an attempt to access volunteers' drug regimes, Kyle entered the site of the Clinical Trials Unit headed by a Dr Cameron Ingoe. On the screen, though, the sections under Ingoe's leadership were all listed in grey. That meant all of the doors into that part of the site were closed to Kyle. When Kyle double-clicked on them, bright red lettering splattered across his screen like a bloodstain. *Access denied*. He was allowed to view only the home page that catalogued the staff working under Dr Ingoe.

Turning to his neighbour, Kyle said quietly, " I've got to get into human drug trials but this stupid system won't let me. Have you got clearance?"

"I can't do that, Kyle. You know the rules."

"But I just—"

"Sorry. You'll have to see a supervisor."

Trying a different angle, Kyle entered the database that gave the current location of all chemical samples within YPI. The computer still regarded him as a worker in Lab 47 so it allowed him to see a list of everything known to be stored in that laboratory. Depressingly, *The Safe* was written in letters as grey as the metal box itself. Clicking on it elicited the familiar bloodstain. In frustration, Kyle hit the table with his left hand.

Back on the main page, he clicked on *Yttria Inc. (Atlanta)* and typed *human drug trials* into the search facility. After a few seconds, the site replied, *Finished search; there were no matches with your search terms.* Kyle shook his head. A pharmaceutical company with no reference to human drug trials? It was unbelievable.

"What are you doing?" Urling-Clark asked at his shoulder. The question was also an accusation.

"Nothing," Kyle replied, his false fingertip poised over the mouse button. "I was just trying to get some info on Atlanta. You know, since I'm going. I was just seeing what they get up to."

Frowning, Stuart asked, "Is anything wrong?"

"No. What do you mean?"

"You sounded . . . I don't know . . . uneasy." Stuart smiled slyly. "As if sir had just caught you playing Internet games in school hours."

Kyle tried to smile naturally. "No. It was all above board."

"Good."

"Did you want anything?"

"No. I was just passing, just saying hello."

Kyle nodded but inside he was panicking. Just saying hello! Stuart never just said hello. Perhaps he was reminding Kyle that computers were always monitored at YPI. Perhaps he'd already guessed what Kyle was really doing.

"I've been meaning to ask," Stuart said, leaning on the desk. "How's your family taking to your move?"

Kyle shrugged.

"Your mum and dad?"

"No problem there."

"Anyone else? Don't I remember you have a nephew or niece?"

"My brother's little girl, Abigail."

"Will she miss you? You'll miss her."

Kyle had no idea where Stuart was taking their conversation. "Yes."

"Who looks after Abigail now your brother's. . .? It must be hard for Abigail's mum, being a single parent."

Kyle nodded. "She works. Abi goes to a day nursery and my mum takes care of her the rest of the time. I chip in when I can."

"You'll have to make the most of her in the next few days. It's a pity she'll suffer because of your YPI activities.

Family's so important, isn't it?" Stuart looked away and called to another worker. "We must have words. Let's go to my office." Turning briefly to Kyle again, he said, "Sorry. Must dash. Just think on what I've said."

With a stormy expression Kyle stared blindly at his monitor. What had Urling-Clark said? Had he issued some sort of subtle, despicable threat against Oonagh and Abi? Had Kyle been warned to behave himself till he got on board that plane? Kyle wasn't sure. He sat back and shivered unpleasantly.

It was great. There was noise everywhere. Music was blaring from several sources, making a confused but fun sound. People were milling around, talking, shouting, laughing, screaming. There were thumps, bangs, screeches, squeals of delight. There were coloured lights and rides and sweets. Kyle was letting her do anything she wanted at the funfair, letting her have anything she wanted. Candyfloss, chocolate, any number of rides and games. He was spoiling her before he went away and Mummy was letting him.

"That one!" Abi shouted, pointing at the merry-go-round.

Kyle looked at Oonagh for guidance. "OK," he said.

"The bird!" Abi said. "I want to go on the big bird."

"All right." Kyle lifted her up and paid the fee. "Hold on tight now."

Abi didn't need to be told. Willing the fairground

120

ride to begin, she grasped the ostrich's long thin neck till her knuckles were white.

While she went round and round and round, the world blurring into a sequence of images and imagination, Abi lost track of Mummy and Kyle. But she knew they were out there somewhere, watching her and waiting.

"So, the time's come. You're really off?" Oonagh said.

"Yeah." Kyle had left his brother behind four years ago. Because of that ridiculous laboratory accident, he had also left the Short Cuts behind. His musical outlet for stress had been blocked off. Now he was leaving his fragmented family behind as well. He had not explained the real reason for his American trip to them and he didn't intend to do so now. Still perturbed by Urling-Clark's remark, he didn't want to involve them.

"Your mum and dad will miss you.".

"Will they?"

"Well, we will. I'm sorry. Your mum's still upset. . ."

"You just look after yourself – and Abi," said Kyle.

Oonagh nodded. "You'll love it over there. It's a super opportunity."

A few minutes later, the carousel slowed down and the children on their high horses, unicorns and bikes let out a communal groan of disappointment. When the ride came to a stop, Kyle looked around and for a moment panicked. "Where's Abi?"

"It's all right," Oonagh replied. Frowning, she put a hand on Kyle's arm. "She's stopped round the other side. That's all." While they walked round to Abi, Oonagh asked, "Are you all right?"

"Fine. Perhaps a bit nervous about going."

Feeling foolish, Kyle lifted Abi down from the merry-go-round ostrich.

"OK, love?" Oonagh said to her daughter.

Abi nodded, already glancing round for another ride.

Oonagh held out her hand. "Time to go home."

"No!"

"Yes."

"Oh." To punish her mother, Abi reached out for Kyle's hand instead. She knew that her luck would not last for ever.

At his parents' house, Kyle looked at his mum and remembered for a moment the way she used to be. He remembered a time when she had a life and two sons. She'd been impatient, lively, impulsive and confident. All that remained now was a shadow of that mother. And all that remained of Kyle's big brother was a permanent shadow that fell cold and long and dismal over the Proctor family.

Kyle could not replace his angelic brother, hadn't settled down with a family, couldn't do anything right according to his dowdy mum. When he set out to catch the train for Heathrow, next stop America, his dad shook his uninjured hand awkwardly and his mother kissed him coldly. She had no tears left for him. His leaving was no big deal. The important son had departed long ago.

19

Scattering the coarse vegetation around the yard for the flock of ostriches, Duma counted the demanding faces looking down at him. Once, in a scraggy schoolbook about other cultures, Duma had seen a picture of a Scottish man playing bagpipes. It looked as if he'd got an ostrich tucked under his arm: big, baggy body with long dangling bits everywhere.

The ostrich really was a ludicrous bird: bad-tempered, powerful and totally unable to fly. By far the largest living species of bird, its wings were ridiculously small, but its long thick legs could carry its chunky body at up to sixty-five kilometres an hour or deliver a very nasty kick. A fully grown ostrich would tower over the villagers with its tiny but arrogant head, wide stubby bill and extravagant eyelashes. Still, it could go for long stretches without water and it served several purposes on the farm. The female birds laid eggs that weighed thirty times more than a chicken's egg. The ostriches' stumpy wings and tails yielded big feathers that were still prized by the American fashion industry. Their skins made good leather for shoes and bags, their meat could be eaten or dried and salted for storage, and their bones ground up for fertilizer.

Duma checked his counting of the flock and watched the birds scrambling for fresh food. They were amazing eaters. They'd swallow almost anything. To help digestion, they swallowed stones, rusty nails, gravel, bits of wood, almost anything. Inside that small head there wasn't much room for a brain.

The ostrich might be a laughable bird but it wasn't as laughable as human beings. It was a myth that, when it wanted to hide from a world that frightened it, the ostrich buried its head in the sand. In the new South Africa, that activity was the preserve of certain white people.

Duma ran back to his house and announced, "One of the ostriches is missing."

"Missing?" his dad echoed.

"Missing."

"Are you sure?"

"I counted twice."

His dad sighed angrily. "Who tended them last?"

His mouth firmly shut, Duma turned away.

"Who was it?" his dad demanded to know.

Duma knew perfectly well. It was Sisters 3 and 4 but it suited him to appear to be unwilling to blame the girls. He simply glanced in their direction.

"I see." Lazily, Duma's dad rose and reached for his belt. Under his breath, he muttered, "Girls!"

Defusing the situation, Sister 1 shouted, "Come on. Time for school."

Their father grunted. "Huh! School." But he didn't stop them leaving. It saved him the effort of a thrashing.

Duma followed his sisters out of the house. For once, he didn't want to miss school. Outside, the sound of crying still came from the next cottage. At the weather-beaten door, several women were standing, talking quietly and seriously. Duma knew that, inside the shack, the fourth member of the family to have sickle-cell anaemia was dying slowly and painfully. It wasn't the only family to be blighted with the illness. A lot of the villagers carried the disease but didn't suffer from it themselves. When they married each other, though, many of their children died from it. Duma didn't know if he was a carrier or not. He didn't want to know really.

In the classroom, something amazing was happening. The place was a complete mess. Several of the rickety wooden desks had been overturned. Tattered books were scattered across the floor. Many of the pages were screwed up, torn, half-eaten. The two cardboard boxes that used to contain sticks of chalk, rulers and pencils had disappeared and so had most of the chalk and all of the smaller pencils. Wooden letters and word-cards littered the floor. The teacher had been cornered by an ostrich that looked accomplished, determined and angry at the same time. Obviously, the bird had been enjoying the scholarly aids to digestion and did not approve of the teacher's intervention. Its long neck stretched, the teacher quaked and the word-card in her hand disappeared into the audacious bird. It looked decidedly pleased with itself.

"Children!" she called. "Come and guide him out. Don't all come at him the same way or he'll get scared and kick someone. Just walk him slowly between the desks and out towards the yard."

The girls looked worried, the boys tried not to grin too openly. In particular, Duma worked hard to stifle a laugh. Like lambs at last turning on a sheepdog, the children herded the unruly ostrich out of the classroom and Duma ran ahead to open the gate to the yard so the bird could rejoin the flock inside. As it pranced shamelessly past Duma, it seemed to exchange a knowing look with him.

Back in school, the teacher was still smarting. "Tell me this, children. How do you think an ostrich got inside a closed room? How could it?"

There was no response, just an uneasy shuffling of feet.

"Have they learnt to turn a door handle now, these clever birds?"

There were a few giggles, mainly male.

The teacher continued, "Someone must have opened the door on purpose and driven him in. Now, who'd do that?"

Every single child in the school turned and looked at Duma. His own four sisters wore the most accusing stares.

Duma held up his hands. "It wasn't me."

"Mmm."

Spitefully, Sister 3 said, "He tried to blame us."

One day, Duma vowed to himself silently, he would succeed.

"Duma," the teacher called out ominously. "Come to the front of the class. I've got something for you to do."

20

At work, everyone knew Tristan Lockhart. For one thing, his photograph adorned the foyer that he walked through every morning. He regretted that he did not know by name everyone who wished him good morning and respectfully got out of his way as he made briskly for the elevator. Of course, Yttria was a big organization. He hadn't got a hope of knowing all of the staff who relied on his decisions and judgements for their livelihoods. Tristan prided himself, though, on his ability to recognize each grade of staff. In the art deco foyer, the smart woman with her hair piled up, holding a blue file, was a secretary. She probably thought that her boss was absolutely useless without her and she was probably absolutely right. The nervous looking man, who had not been one hundred per cent successful in shaving this morning, was a scientist or computer specialist. The woman in her forties with an immaculate suit was in Human Resources. No doubt about it. Then there was the man with outsize sideburns, aged thirty-something, who gathered in his briefcase when it threatened to brush against Tristan in the doorway of the elevator. He was a science technician and probably an Elvis Presley fan.

All of these people would make way for Tristan. He was used to deference but the technician's reaction was exaggerated. It seemed to Tristan that he wasn't trying to avoid catching his president's legs embarrassingly with his briefcase, but shielding something inside his bag from a bump, something precious, delicate or dangerous like a bomb. Of course, it couldn't be a bomb or anything else harmful. To get this far into the building, the technician's case would have been searched by Security or scanned by X-rays. Tristan relaxed as the elevator door closed smoothly and almost silently.

Light was angry. Incredibly angry. He'd logged on to the Storm Force website and read about Shadow's latest atrocity in Memphis. Attempting to burn down Graceland! That really was the limit! Elvis was untouchable. Shadow had to be stopped.

Light looked carefully around the lab. There wasn't much activity now. There was another technician over by the computer room, but she was concentrating on her own work. Quickly, Light took the box of eggs from his briefcase and slipped it into the airlock. There was the hiss of the vacuum sucking out air, then the chemical sterilization spray, and finally clean air piped back in. From outside the sterile box, Light slipped his hands into the giant gloves. Now he could open the interior door to the air lock and manipulate the box of eggs safely inside the sealed cabinet.

After checking again that no one was watching him, Light took a hypodermic syringe and pulled into the glass barrel a small sample of SCP19 virus. Holding one of the ordinary hen's eggs in the other hand, he pierced the shell with the ultra-fine needle and injected some of the virus. Replacing the first egg in its cardboard nest, he took hold of the second.

Viruses were not always easy to work with. Outside a living host or a nutrient material, they did not last for long. Eggs, though, were perfect incubators for a virus. Injected into the nourishing yolk, SCP19 would thrive and multiply until it had made a billion copies of itself inside the handy and innocent container. Six eggs, six billion viruses. In theory, that was enough to infect every person on the planet. Of course, the viruses would affect only blacks like Shadow and they would spread only a short distance from the place where he smashed each egg so they wouldn't harm everyone. But they were ideal for Light's purpose.

Both Elvis and Shannon would have been proud of him.

As far as Tristan was concerned, Yttria's move into the defence market was a simple contest between financial necessity and right. It was simple because a financial necessity was exactly that: necessary. Right was a matter of opinion and debate. That made the contest hope-lessly one-sided. Even so, in the back of his mind, an alarm was sounding. He could hear it best in the quiet of sleepless nights.

131

Tristan also made another decision. Wanting to be more personable to the ordinary worker, he decided to get to know staff better by meeting and shaking the hand of every new employee, and sharing a first coffee with them. And he really meant it. He wouldn't delegate the greeting to some secretary or deputy manager in Human Resources when things got busy. He would do it with his own hand, starting now. The Head of Human Resources told him that the next recruit would be the young man from Cambridge, UK. "Kyle Proctor. You know, the one the Brits sent us a file on."

"Ah, yes," Tristan replied. "The awkward one. Interesting. When's he coming?"

"Flights permitting, tomorrow."

"Well, sort me out a coffee room for morning break tomorrow. I want Proctor – Kyle – there, along with his Section Head and anyone else you can rustle up from Computing. Maybe a couple of people who'll be his colleagues."

Kyle Proctor was a skinny guy with a clumsy handshake. When Tristan extended his right hand and said, "Welcome to the United States of America," Kyle offered only his left. "And welcome to Yttria Inc. Got yourself a coffee?" Tristan could see that Kyle would make a computer technician – he looked the part – but the British man – still a kid really – didn't look like the troublemaker he'd been made out to be by his file.

132

Tristan asked a series of polite questions. "How was the flight?" "Have we got you somewhere to live?" "Have you been to the States before?" "Is the Section treating you well?" "Have you ever seen Stone Mountain?" "Is it still impossible to find a parking space in Cambridge like when I was last there?" "Do you know anyone this side of the pond?" Kyle was reserved, answering each question briefly. Plainly, the new arrival was overawed by the occasion, as if he didn't expect to be received by the president of the company. "I do this with every new employee," Tristan reassured him, making it sound like a lifelong habit, the American way of doing things.

"I see." Kyle paused and then added awkwardly, "It's . . . good of you."

Tristan put Kyle's reticence down to jet lag. "You'll go down well here. We're suckers for an English accent. Everyone'll ask you if you're related to the Queen." With a grin, he added, "You're not, are you?"

"No, I'm afraid not."

"Well," Tristan said, glancing at his watch, "I bet you're itching to crack on."

"Yes."

"Yes?" The president laughed. "Round here you're supposed to say, 'I sure am!' You'll get used to us pretty soon. Anyway, you have a good time with us and share in our success. Right?"

"Yes."

133

Tristan slapped him on the arm. "Remember to say, 'I sure will!' That's the enthusiasm we want to see." And with that, Tristan left to deal with the e-mail messages, the phone calls, the faxes, the people that he had missed while he was welcoming Kyle Proctor.

It wasn't like Cambridge. Atlanta was the place where the Olympics were held in 1996, where gigantic figures of Confederate war heroes carved on Stone Mountain formed the world's largest sculpture, where Coca-Cola was invented and sold on Peachtree Street in 1886, where Martin Luther King was born and buried. *Free at last, free at last, thank God Almighty, I'm free at last.* It was a fast city. Rising from a surface of asphalt and concrete, the brick and steel forest was tall and bright and compact. From a distance, it looked as if it had been built by an overambitious child with an expensive Lego set. In summer, Atlanta's sidewalks, buildings and asphalt absorbed so much daytime heat that the city itself could trigger thunderstorms when it let go of the warmth at night. By comparison, Cambridge was dull, quaint and sluggish. The university city in Britain valued charm above convenience, but the commercial Goliath of the New South had it the other way round. If someone were to import Cambridge into Atlanta, it wouldn't have made a single difference to the jagged towering skyline. The only thing that the two cities shared was a real sense of their own histories.

134

Kyle found himself living on the thirteenth floor of an anonymous block of apartments in the city. The man next door was obviously a country music fan, judging by the slide guitar's cloying calls that penetrated the wall. The people above him were into something noisy. Perhaps they worked out a lot or maybe they were decorating or dancing or. . . Kyle decided to rein in his imagination. Still, it was crime-free and the view was amazing. He looked across a wide road straight into the apartments of the skyscraper opposite.

Work was exactly as he expected. For Kyle, the job had been transplanted into an alien land, but it was identical to his new role in Cambridge. Even the computer's operating system and programs were the same. When Kyle focused solely on the screen, he could have been back in England, except that the American system automatically corrected his spelling of centre, sulphur and colour. When someone spoke to him in an unfamiliar accent or when he looked around, he was reminded that he had been shunted into a remote siding where he could not be such an embarrassment. He felt lonely and out of place.

He typed an e-mail to Helen Crear. Assuming that the American technicians were as watchful and paranoid as their English counterparts, he made his message brief and almost innocent. *Dr Crear, I've arrived safely and bedded into a flat. Started work just like Cambridge. All the best with your patients. Kyle.* As soon as possible, he would set up a computer in his new home and, freed from surveillance by Yttria staff, exchange more e-mails with Helen. He wanted to know if she had discovered anything that was helping Dwight Grant.

21

Distracted for a moment, the passing junior doctor knocked into the drugs trolley and then leapt to one side, narrowly missing a nurse. "Sorry," he muttered as he continued his dash towards Ward 17 at Addenbrooke's.

The nurse shook her head and, seeing Dr Crear on the telephone nearby, smiled wryly. Helen Crear was the eye-catching reason the male doctor had not been paying attention.

Men liked the way Helen looked. She was beautiful and slender, although she hadn't made a conscious effort to stay slim. She'd always been a chubby child, yet an adult life of taking scraps of meals on the fly, rushing from bed-to-bed and ward-to-ward kept her in shape. For her, it was almost certainly artificial. Her parents always worried that she had lost weight and would never put it on again. If she ever relaxed and ate properly, though, she would soon find out what her natural figure really was.

Helen wanted to believe that human beings were more, far more than vulnerable bags of bones, soft tissues and fluids. She wanted to believe that they were more than the sum total of their ailing body parts, but that was how she defined the people that she met at work. To her, they were broken femur, thirty per cent

137

burns, lacerations to hand and wrist, brain tumour. She was too busy curing them to get to know them by anything other than their medical conditions. But then there was Dwight. She didn't really know his medical condition. It was a coma with an unknown cause. Since she couldn't define him by his condition, she had to get to know him as a person instead.

On the phone, she had got hold of Linton Okri. She was saying hurriedly, "I just haven't got time to do it myself. My pager's buzzing me right now. Yes. That's what I want. There must be a few offenders who've just been released from Westland. They're not locked up for ever, are they? Yes. If you could find one or two who were in Yttria's drugs trial, I'd be interested, especially if they signed up at about the same time as Dwight. Then, chances are, they'd be in the same drug programme. And, no, that's not all. Sorry, but can you put me in touch with the families of the most recent suicides? What they say might be quite helpful. Yes. That's right. As soon as possible. You've got my number, haven't you? No, there's no change in Dwight, I'm afraid. That's why I want to speak to these people. Got to dash. Thanks for your help." Having accepted the baton from Kyle, she was determined to run with it.

The BAD rep was late. On her own in the bar, Helen was drinking orange and lemonade because she would be on night duty soon. She shrugged off the second

138

insistent offer to buy her a stronger drink and, just as she was glancing anxiously at her watch, Linton Okri made his entrance with a couple of young men. Helen breathed a sigh of relief as the three of them joined her at the table.

The two young men – boys really – had recently been released from Westland Young Offender Institution and, yes, they both knew Dwight Grant. Eager to get information from them, Helen asked straight away, "What sort of boy was he?"

"Football crazy," they both replied at once.

Suddenly, Helen understood. "That's why he went on the drug trial."

One of the lads seemed more willing to talk than the other. He said, "Most of us checked our release dates, you know, before we signed up, but not Dwight. He said he'd do it if he could get into the footie team. Daft sod."

Helen nodded. "So, both of you were in the trials as well?"

"Yeah."

"At the same time as Dwight?"

When they both hesitated and looked longingly towards the bar, Helen realized that she was disappointing them. She dug in her handbag for some cash and gave it to Linton so he could go to the bar and buy drinks for himself and the boys while she carried on talking to them. "So," she continued, "did you start at the same time as Dwight?"

"More or less."

"What did YPI tell you about the drugs you took?"

"They'd got no effect on the brain, you know what I mean, so if we nicked them we couldn't sell them to the junkies at Westland."

"Is that all? Didn't you ask what they were for?"

Both of them shook their heads. The second boy chipped in, "We was offered good rooms, OK jobs, maybe even early release. Who cares what they were for?"

"How did you take them? By mouth, patches or what?"

One said, "I had jabs."

The other replied, "Pills."

"Did they make you ill at all?"

"No."

"Not even a bit dizzy?"

"No."

"How about depressed?"

"Depressed? Have you ever been in Westland? You don't need no pills to make you depressed."

"Do either of you know if you carry the sickle-cell trait?"

"The what?"

"Look, would you do me a favour – do Dwight a favour – and come to the hospital tonight so I can take a blood sample from you both?"

They both looked like they had spilled some blood

in their time, but not their own. Immediately suspicious and bashful, they muttered, "Blood sample?"

Smiling, she told them, "You won't feel a thing."

They looked at each other, took a drink of beer and then the more talkative one replied, "If it's for Dwight, all right."

"Did Dwight take anything else?" All of the toxicity tests had confirmed that he had not taken any of the common drugs, but Helen was wondering if something new and unusual, not covered by the hospital tests or Paul's work, was doing the rounds. She was also wondering if a combination of drugs had knocked her patient out.

"Like what?"

"Anything," Helen replied. "Drugs, booze."

"We wasn't allowed them."

"Right," Helen said. "Since when have rules stopped anyone getting their hands on that sort of stuff?"

"Well, he might have done a bit of booze. Nothing else. He wouldn't do nothing that'd make him a bad deal for footie."

"Did you two combine the Yttria trials with booze?"

"We might have."

"Meaning you did."

They nodded. "Inside, you got to get off your head sometimes, you know."

"And you still didn't feel ill or dizzy?"

"There weren't that much of it floating around."

141

"OK." She encouraged them to finish their drinks so she could take them both to the hospital with her. She was sure that, if she let them out of her sight, she'd never see them again.

The blood tests on Dwight Grant's friends came back negative. Neither of them had the sickle-cell trait. If they had been given an experimental treatment for sickle-cell anaemia, the smart drug would have had nothing to get its teeth into. It would simply have been flushed out of their systems. That would explain why the two young men had not experienced any side effects: they would have been totally immune to YPI's medicine.

Helen was disappointed, but at least BAD had found her a mother who was willing to talk about the suicide of her son in Westland Young Offender Institution. Mrs Davis was in her early forties, heavily made up, with narrow hips and shoulders, and a curved spine. She moved slowly as if her joints were painful or she was tired. In her left hand she clutched a ragged handkerchief. Over a coffee, Helen said to her, "I'm sorry but let me ask you this. Do *you* think your boy committed suicide?"

"Sean was tough as old boots. Know what I mean? He wasn't going to let the system grind him down." While she spoke she grimaced and clutched a hand to her large chest. Her words were interrupted by short gasps for air.

"But the doctor confirmed that he'd taken his own life."

"That's medicine talking, not his mother."

"What do you think happened?"

Rain pounded at the window as if trying to break in to the hospital through the leaky frames.

"You hear all sorts about what goes on inside, don't you? I don't know but. . ." Mrs Davis let out a cough and then carried on. "But I do know this. Someone or something's behind him dying. He wouldn't kill himself. And definitely not like they said."

Helen caught sight of a swelling of the soft tissue of the woman's left hand behind the handkerchief and realized her condition. Sympathetically, she asked, "Are you on iron supplements and hydroxyurea?"

Mrs Davis nodded.

Even with hydroxyurea, the outlook was not good for someone with advanced sickle-cell anaemia. In a few years, complications in her heart, spleen, lungs or kidneys would lead to her death. "What about Sean?" Helen enquired.

"Before I die, I want to know what happened to him."

"I meant, did he suffer from sickle-cell anaemia as well?"

"Yes, they'd got him on penicillin. But he didn't die from it – if that's what you're getting at."

"I'm sure he didn't. The doctor would have noted it. It seems he died from a fall."

Mrs Davis looked down at her hands for a few moments. Then she gazed at Helen. "Sean was only scared of one thing, Dr Crear."

"What was that?"

"It sounds silly – a brave boy like him – but he was scared of heights."

"Heights," Helen repeated, deep in thought.

"He kept it to himself as much as he could. He was ashamed of it."

"So, no one knew?"

"No. He wouldn't go near tall places, high windows."

"Interesting."

With her wheezing voice, Sean's mum said, "You got to ask yourself, would someone like that go up on the roof of a tall building and throw himself off? Know what I mean?"

22

In Memphis, drive-by shootings were not uncommon, but drive-by egg throwing? And at a downtown homeless centre? It was crazy. It didn't make sense. Mitch could not believe his good luck. He reached up and, like an expert baseball player, plucked the single egg out of the air, cushioning it in the soft skin of his palms. Usually he got his free meals from the back of McDonald's or the restaurants around Beale Street and Union Avenue, or from the city bins, but today he intercepted an egg before it smashed against the wall behind him. Shaking his head in wonder, he examined the gift from heaven and then laughed. Jabbing a finger into the shell, he broke it, put it to his lips and in a couple of seconds sucked the raw protein straight into his mouth and swallowed the nourishing slime. His teeth crunched a few fragments of the eggshell, but he didn't care. It was all food.

Later that day, Mitch could not believe his bad luck. He felt sick and dizzy. The egg must have been off. It hadn't come from heaven after all. He collapsed on the sidewalk and everyone who passed him by thought that he was sleeping rough, probably after he'd been swilling too much dodgy booze.

23

At the farm school, Duma learned to read, write and do sums. At least, he would have done if he had paid attention. What use were words and numbers in the South African prairie? He needed to mend leaky roofs, to spend long hours tending sheep, pigs, ostriches, goats and donkeys, to drive a tractor in a straight line across the vast plains of wheat and corn when there were no landmarks for reference. He'd seen that a bent furrow earned a beating from the farmer. Duma knew exactly what he should be learning at school. It was nothing to do with words and numbers. He should be learning how to make his dream come true. One day, he wanted his own house, maybe even with its own water supply and electricity, and he wanted to tend his own animals, plough his own field.

Now, the Afrikaner farmer owned everything that Duma could see. The land, the school, the workers' ramshackle homes, the farm animals, the machinery, the crops. The labourers worked everything and owned nothing. Most of the children, like Duma's sisters, wanted to flock to the cities but not Duma. In his dream, *he* owned a plot of land. Nothing on the white farmers' scale, of course. Just a small area where he could grow enough of his own crops to feed himself and his family. He didn't even fantasize about finding diamonds or gold on it. He wanted to be a farmer, not a prospector. He wanted food and fun, not riches. But the schoolteacher could not teach her pupils how to realize a dream. It was outside her experience. To her, ownership of land seemed much less attainable than the skill of reading and writing.

It was the end of the month – the worst time of all. As always, the men's meagre wages had disappeared into bottles from the general store and into the greedy hands of dagga dealers. It was the time when the farm workers would refuse to work. The sheep, pigs and ostriches were neglected. That was the time when the farmer would shout recriminations and withdraw what he called privileges, like miserly gifts of vegetables. He tolerated only those villagers who asked for little and stole nothing. Everyone was on edge. The women and children in the farm shacks would be beaten by their frustrated men. Duma's dad would rant and rave and strike out along with the rest of them. Then, to avoid the bruises, Duma spent even more nights sleeping in the sties and stalls of the animals that he tended.

At the end of the month, one of the farmer's many animals would disappear from his stock. A labourer would hide it, as insurance against inflation and a perk instead of a decent wage. Later, if the baas found it, the worker would be fired for theft and frequently jailed. Then, when the labourer got out, his family would hide from him till his anger subsided. Duma learned that it wasn't wrong to steal from whites; it was wrong only to get caught.

On the night of the village barbecue, impala roamed the desert as silhouettes against the gorgeous orange sunset that followed a flaming February day. The stolen pig was brought to the centre of the village and placed on the spit. With the smell of a good roast, the fact that no one had been caught yet, the arrival of The Tap, and the clear cool evening, everyone was in good spirits. The daytime temperature still topped 30°C so the twilight plunge of 15 degrees came as a welcome relief. Unusually, there had not been any rainstorms for several days so the village, the track and the homes had been baked by the relentless summer sun.

When the Land Rover halted on the dirt track at the edge of the workers' quarters, everyone froze. The farmer got out and strode purposefully towards them. He had a walking stick in one hand, a rifle in the other and a snarl on his face. Pieter hissed, "I can smell a barbecue from miles away." He stared at the roasting animal and demanded to know, "Who stole my pig?"

The motionless band of workers and their families were struck completely dumb.

Duma knew who had swindled the farmer out of an animal. It was his father. And he knew that if his dad was punished, *he* would be punished afterwards by a father who, to preserve his pride, would have to take

148

out his anger on someone. To protect his dad – and to protect himself – Duma stepped forward. After all, he was used to taking the blame for things in the village and it was unlikely that the Afrikaner would have a young boy jailed. "I did it, baas."

"You?"

"Yes, baas."

"How old are you?" he growled.

"Twelve, baas."

"Twelve. What's your name?"

"Duma," he mumbled, staring at the dusty road.

"Have I seen you driving one of my tractors?"

Duma nodded.

"Even after I give you a tap for water, you still steal from me." Pieter shook his head and then shouted, "Someone fetch me a chair. I want to talk to this specimen and look into his eyes."

Eager to please, at least three of the statues came to life and dashed towards three different hovels. The first seat to arrive was sturdy but basic.

"Call that a chair?" Pieter muttered disdainfully. "Oh, well." He rested his bulk and laid his rifle across his rounded knees. He positioned the weapon slowly and deliberately, making sure everyone could see it.

The baas had a reputation for talking calmly then erupting into violence. The villagers held their breath and Duma gulped. What had he got himself into?

"Now, boy. Do you know what I've done to thieves?"

"Yes, baas."

"Speak up."

"Yes, baas."

"Yes, you do. You've heard. I've put them in barrels and towed them down the road behind my truck. I've put them in prison – where horrible things happen that you don't want to know about. I've torched their houses. Which is your house, boy?"

Silently, sadly, Duma pointed.

"Mmm. Hardly worth the effort." Pieter Fourie ran his fingers through his considerable beard. "Do you know what I'm going to do to you, urchin?"

"No, baas."

"I'm going to tell you a story about a pig."

Astonished, Duma dared to glance momentarily at the farmer's shaggy face – after all it was a free country now – but immediately he resumed his downward gaze.

"Yes. That's right. A story about my favourite little pig. He was a remarkable animal – more like a pet, one of the family – but there was something odd about him. Do you know what it was?"

"No, baas."

"He had a wooden leg. Yes, a wooden leg. I fitted it myself, with my own hands. Didn't trust it to one of you slackers because he was a special pig and he deserved the best. People would come to me and say, 'Why's your pig got a wooden leg?' and I'd say, 'Let me tell you

150

about that little pig. He's a hero.' You know what he did?"

No one said a word. They were all waiting anxiously to see where the farmer was going. They feared the worst.

"Last winter, when my wife heated the oil up on the stove too much, that little pig ran a mile across the plain to warn me that the kitchen was on fire. I raced back in the jeep just in time to put the flames out and save the house. All due to that amazing pig. A hero, that's what he was. 'Is that how he lost a leg?' people ask. 'Did he hurt it in the run?' No. I'll tell you more about him. When my daughter was little, younger than you," Pieter said to the boy who was quaking in front of him on the scorched road, "she once went swimming in Harts River. It was summer and she was very unwise, very silly, but she wanted to cool off. Well, the river was swollen after some storms and it dragged her out of her depth and into big trouble. But that little pig knew. He charged off to the river, dived in, risking everything, grabbed her leg in his snout and pulled her out of the water. He saved her from drowning, saved her life.

"People say, 'Incredible. Is that how he lost his leg?' But it wasn't, no. There's more to tell. When my son got out of the Land Rover one time, he didn't put the handbrake on. He was working at the bottom of the slope when the jeep hurtled towards him. My brave pig saw it all, though. He was ready to sacrifice himself for any of us. He dived in front of the Land Rover's wheels and brought it to a stop with his own body. That way, he saved my son's life as well. He was a treasure, that poor pig. 'That *must* be how he lost his leg. It was crushed by the jeep.' That's what people think but they're wrong. He was badly injured, my favourite pig, but in time he recovered, I'm glad to say, with all his legs intact. Then everyone asks, 'So, how *did* he lose a leg, then?' And I tell them. 'When you have a pig that good,' I say, 'you don't eat him all at once.'"

The baas rocked back in the unfamiliar chair, his large frame shaking with laughter. When he saw that Duma and the others were staring at him, bewildered, he stopped roaring at once and glared coldly at them. Dutifully, everyone began to laugh. Thankfully, Pieter smiled, nodded and then continued to hoot until it pleased him to end the amusement. "You see, boy, I understand hunger," the huge farmer said in the quiet that followed the crowd's nervous laughter. "I know that any pig, no matter how good, will end up on a plate. That's just the way it is. It's nature. Now, bring me the one you've just barbecued."

"Yes, baas."

When Duma was ten steps away, Pieter stood up and called after him. "Is it good and hot?"

"Yes, baas."

"Then bring it to my jeep in your bare hands."

Duma hesitated and swallowed before replying in a hushed voice, "Yes, baas."

After the baas had left with his ready-cooked meal and the wise woman of the village was applying healing herbs to Duma's hands, the talk was all about the Afrikaner. Why hadn't he exacted a more terrible revenge for the stolen pig? After all, Duma's hands would be cured in a couple of weeks. Normally, that wouldn't be enough to satisfy the fiery farmer. And then there was The Tap. He'd provided them with their own supply of water. OK, the tank up at the farm was the highest so, if the water level dropped, their supply would dry up first. Even so, they didn't need to worry that the rain was reluctant to show now and, in the coming winter, they wouldn't have to worry that the boreholes might dry up. Was the baas at last swimming with the tide of emancipation that was sweeping across South Africa?

They didn't realize that Pieter needed them all alive and living in the village – at least for the moment. They didn't realize that he needed them all to be making good use of the gift of The Tap.

24

The rain was so frenzied that it almost obliterated the view. On the streets, umbrellas didn't stand a chance against the furious wind. Some took off like balloons, some turned inside out, others were torn apart. The rain bounced on the surface of the road, creating a thick grey carpet of mist that the wind drove along like a layer of smoke. The wet carpet lashed the tyres of crawling cars, the ankles of brave pedestrians, the cardboard and rags of the homeless.

Kyle looked down into the miserable street from his warm apartment. Above his head, there were three sharp thumps. He wasn't startled any longer. In the last month, he had got used to the plaster-trembling sounds of the people living upstairs. He turned back to his computer and continued to pour out his heart to the grey screen. As soon as he had finished and clicked on the *Send* function, his feelings would be scrambled into a telephone signal and beamed across the Atlantic to the only person he could trust with them.

Dr Crear,

Any news of Dwight? You can e-mail freely to this address because it's my home computer. Not that an apartment block is really home, of course. I am 13 floors up and that does not come close to scraping the sky in Atlanta. I dread the lift not working. It's a hell of a climb up 13 sets of stairs. The weather is appalling at the moment – a wet and windy gale just like home.

At work, I can't do much investigating because the computers are heavily supervised. That's like Cambridge as well. They say the monitoring is done to stop us accessing unsuitable websites but it might have more to do with policing internal secrets. They even have clever mice helping with security. When you are working at a computer, there's a window on the side of the mouse where your thumb is. The computer takes your thumbprint through the window so it knows who is operating the computer all the time and locks out files that you don't have clearance for. For me, they could not convince the computer that a lump of silicone without any distinguishing marks was really a thumbprint. I have to put a sticky dot on my thumb and the daft computer thinks the little circle is my print. Anyway, it means I can use any computer but never get above my security code. I can't figure a way round this cunning device. Still, I am taking an interest in the drug trial part of the business to see if I am cleared for those sorts of files one day. If so, I will e-mail you straight away.

I suppose there is one good thing about being here. I am not so self-conscious about my fingers.

Shape is in the hands of plastic surgeons, not nature, over here. Noses, hips, breasts, stomachs, skin and everything seems to have been reconstructed to make it flatter, less wrinkly, bigger, smaller or whatever. Americans seem to be obsessed with redistributing flesh around the body. If you have not had a bit of cosmetic surgery done, they think there is something wrong with you because you don't care about how you look. Or, even worse, they think you are poor. With my fingers, I fit in OK.

Looking forward to any news from you.
Kyle

Before he transmitted the e-mail to Helen Crear, he wondered if there was a risk. Yttria had got him this flat. Could they have installed any surveillance equipment? Did they already know the content of the message that he had written? He looked around the room and then, with a wry smile, told himself that he was becoming paranoid. YPI was a pharmaceutical company, not an espionage outfit. Besides, there were greater issues at stake than his own livelihood. All those years ago, he had not been able to help his brother as he lay on life support, but it wasn't too late to help Dwight Grant. He tapped the button with his silicone forefinger.

Your message has been sent successfully.

Helen's reply decorated Kyle's monitor like the chilling preamble to a horror film.

Kyle,
Thanks for the message. I have nothing to report on Dwight but I do have evidence that he was not the first hiccup in Westland drug trials. I think something similar has happened before. The suicide rate at Westland might be down to YPI as well. At least one of the suicides was probably not suicide at all. I think a boy called Sean Davis died under the drug trial, possibly going into a coma like Dwight, and it was covered up by faking his suicide. I suspect he was taken up on the roof and pushed off. I do not stand a chance of proving it but the doctor who signed the death certificate is not trustworthy. I guess he has been paid off by YPI.
Be careful,
Helen

Kyle shook his head in exasperation. He could see the company as a monster that had him firmly in its claws. If it really was testing a biological weapon against the black races, he could carry on working for Yttria, taking its tainted money in his salary, only if he exposed the conspiracy and somehow halted the project.

Tristan had long since grown tired of being devious but it came with the job. He should have reported the deaths of black prisoners during the SCP19 trial to the National Institutes of Health but the NIH had the power to shut down the company's gene therapy experiments and the whole sickle-cell operation. He had decided not to inform the NIH because the deaths might have been caused by factors that had nothing to do with gene therapy. At least, they were easily made to look like they had other causes. Besides, occasional fatalities from unexpected side effects were inevitable in drug trials. They were a regrettable but accepted part of progress in medicine. The research into sickle-cell products had to continue because a colossal pharmaceutical prize was at stake.

Tired of manoeuvring around the regulations, Tristan watched the rain obscuring the view from his elevated office and wished that he had been able to make different decisions about SCP19. A blood test on his unborn grandchild had just revealed that the baby would have the sickle-cell trait.

25

Outside the confines of his Westminster office, the Defence Secretary leaned on the top of the wall and surveyed the drab Thames. The Head of the Department of Trade and Industry pulled her coat around herself as protection against the cold wind.

"I just wanted to jog your memory about our arms export policy," the Defence Secretary said. "You know, the Prime Minister's keen to ensure that we're all singing from the same hymn sheet. And you being new to the ranks, he didn't want . . . you know."

The Trade and Industry Secretary frowned. "I'm well aware of all our policies, I assure you."

"It's just that I heard about an export licence for Yttria Pharmaceuticals."

"Oh?"

His eyes on a barge approaching Westminster Bridge, the Defence Secretary said, "To me, it looked faintly concerning."

Plainly, the wily politician had been doing his research into the DTI's business. The Trade and Industry Secretary responded, "It's all perfectly legitimate, I assure you. It's part of an important research project into sickle-cell anaemia."

"That's all right then. As long as you're convinced you're acting in the spirit of our ethical policy, you won't embarrass the Government." He straightened up but still didn't look her in the eye. "There's a related reason for asking to see you. The Prime Minister wants us to take a lead in the push to tighten up biological weapons treaties. He wants Britain to be out there in front, the good guys."

The Trade and Industry Secretary raised her eyebrows. "That's a lonely place to be. Anyway, what push is that? There won't be one because, as I understand it, no government's keen to close loopholes in the biological weapons treaty."

"And, as you understand it, why not?"

"Because tightening up would mean on-site inspections to verify who's making weapons instead of medicines. Pharmaceutical and biotechnology companies would be first in line and they won't have it. They can't be inspected because they have to keep their commercial secrets secret."

"Are these companies dictating to governments now then? It'd be consistent with our ethical policy to force inspections on them."

"No government's going to do that. You know, and the Prime Minister knows, how rich and powerful the multinational drug giants are. You know how much money they bring into the country. They're untouchable. It'd be financial suicide to throttle them with regulations. Then there's the emerging pharmaceutical companies like YPI – the giants of tomorrow – they've got too much potential to put obstacles in their paths. If we saddle them with unnecessary administration and inspections, they'll just uproot and go somewhere else. Somewhere that's not so fussy over regulations. It's my job to promote trade, and protect income and jobs. We don't want to captain the *Titanic*, do we?"

Finally, the Defence Secretary turned to look at her. He smiled. "I'll leave you to explain that to the Prime Minister, then."

26

The water delivery system was in place. By the farm-house, alongside the whites' tank, there was now a blacks' tank. A long, long pipe led to the workers' quarters and the village tap. All that Pieter Fourie and Eugene Knobel needed to begin their experiment was the weapon.

Hot and sweaty, Pieter had deposited his mass in an armchair and was dwelling on his favourite topic. "You know what I hate most about them? Their eyes, all white and staring, especially when they get angry. That white in a black face makes them very threatening, you know. It's not right. No wonder they get us going when they look like that. It's their own fault for being built that way."

Eugene was not really listening. Having been holed up in Pieter's house for three months, he'd already heard everything Pieter had to say. He'd heard the entire repertoire. That was the difference between the two men. Pieter talked a lot and acted little and, when he did act, it was an explosion. Eugene talked little but plotted calmly and effec-tively. No explosions of anger at all. He planned mass murder like a sly schoolboy plans practical jokes. Eagerly, he took a hard copy of the e-mail from the printer and began to read it, his bright eyes sparkling.

"This is what we've been waiting for: a reply from YPI in England."

Pieter sat upright. "What's it say? Good news?"

His eyes still scanning the paper, Eugene beamed. "Very good. But, according to them, we're not buying a biological weapon at all. We're just helping them to develop a product. They say they're hoping to produce a smart cure for sickle-cell anaemia but, if it turns out by accident to be a poison, we're not so much using it as investigating the effects for them. If that's their terms, so be it. We're YPI researchers now!" Eugene laughed mischievously. "These people do like to play their little games with words." He put the letter to his nose and said, "I smell the work of a politician."

"I hate Brits. You can't trust them, but on this occasion. . ." Eager for the day when he would become a biowarrior, Pieter put aside one of his prejudices. "When do we get the stuff?"

"No promises on a date, but soon," answered Eugene, handing him the message. "When I worked on bacteria that only attacked blacks I could never get the little devils to do what they were supposed to do. That's the bacteria, not the blacks," he said with a charmer's understated smile. "Though the old government couldn't get blacks to do what they're supposed to do, either. Anyway, it looks like at least one multinational was ahead of me, but they've still got to work out

163

how to package, preserve and deliver the goods safely. We need to be patient awhile."

It was March and the two men had forgotten that it would soon be Human Rights Day in South Africa.

27

As soon as Paul had wound up his tutorial on Friday afternoon, he made for the door. With a heavy heart, he clambered into his car that already contained his suitcase, packed with everything he needed. Driving south from Coventry on the M45, he could have made a long list of everything that was bugging him. His latest research proposal had been turned down. He had not got any conclusive results from the final tests on Dwight Grant's blood sample so he was going to have to admit to Helen that he had failed. The tutorial that he had just given was more like a lecture because the university had enrolled too many students to teach in small groups. His house needed cleaning, his computer needed a good kicking, his desk needed organizing, his administrative load needed thinning, his credit card needed changing because a hacker was running up astronomical debts through on-line shopping, his life needed an injection of good fortune. He'd finished his teaching for the term so he'd decided to take an early extended Easter vacation.

The M1 did not give him a break. Roadworks near Watford Gap held him up for three-quarters of an hour. Still, he rolled up on to Helen's drive eventually and gazed at her home. It was one of the smaller properties in the exclusive lane, but it was very stylish.

Things hadn't always been like that. Once, Paul and Helen hadn't been able to afford even an old rusty car between them and that slummy house they shared with other students... It wasn't like the detached property that she owned now. But, back then, they were chaotic, poor and happy. Now they were merely chaotic.

Helen was not ready to provide him with a break either. There was no answer to his ringing of her bell. Standing by her front door in increasing darkness, Paul called her mobile number and found that she had also run into a delay. She was helping to treat several victims of a fight between rival gangs, but she promised to get home as soon as the situation was under control. Paul locked his car and strolled unhurriedly to the village pub at the end of the lane.

Back at home in Coventry, Paul's video was merrily recording the wrong TV programme.

When Helen eventually joined him in the bar, she looked haggard and exhausted. The hug with which they greeted each other was half-hearted and awkward. It was not a passionless formality nor was it a lovers' embrace. Neither of them knew where this encounter was leading and the uncertainty made them restless. At first they kept the conversation easy. "It looks like you could use a drink. What do you want?" "How was the journey?" "Are all your days at the hospital like this?" "How many research students have you got now?" "How are you really?" The more troublesome questions had to wait till they were alone in Helen's house.

"So, tell me," Helen asked over some bland microwaved convenience food and good red wine, "did you get any more results on Dwight's sample?"

"Not that you'd want to stake your life on – or his."

"You got something then."

Paul replied, "Not really. I told you before by e-mail there's no sign of any kind of drugs, but we had the bright idea of trying a DNA profile."

"And?" Helen prompted.

"Well, I don't know what's normal for your Dwight but one segment looked abnormal."

"In what way?"

Paul shrugged. "One strand didn't correspond to any known sequence."

"As if it had been altered?"

"I guess so, but how?"

"What if he'd received gene therapy?"

Paul did not hesitate. "Yes, that would make sense. But . . . I don't want you thinking I'm on firm ground here. We tried to reproduce the analysis and failed. Perhaps we were imagining it – or the experiment was contaminated."

Helen nodded. "Perhaps. But gene therapy's looking more and more likely. Gene therapy and then the body reacting badly to it."

"If that's right – a big if – was his reaction the intention or a side effect?"

"Ah, that's the crunch question," Helen said. "Only YPI could answer it and they're staying totally bloody mute."

"Do you still shout at people down the phone?"

"Only when they deserve it," she replied with a smile. "Anyway, thanks for giving it a go, Paul."

"Pleasure. It gave me an opportunity to come over and give you the final report – for what it's worth."

"You could have e-mailed or faxed it, like the earlier results you got for me."

With a wry smile, Paul said, "It wouldn't have been the same, would it?"

Helen shook her head. "Why have you really come, Paul?"

"I wanted to see you. It's been a long time."

"Too long."

"Have you got some sort of relationship in the offing?" Paul asked. "I think you know what I mean."

"Who with? How would I fit it in?"

"I'll take that as a no," said Paul.

"The question is, 'Do I want one?'"

"What's the answer?"

"We're good at questions, not so good at answers."

Across the table, Paul took her hand in his. "You'll just have to tell me to back off if that's what you want me to do." By the light of the scented candle between them, he looked into her face and saw no reason to let go of her hand.

Abruptly, Helen Crear sat up. Unexpectedly, she was fully awake. "Hey."

Paul screwed up his sleepy face and groaned. "Uh? What?"

"Could you do that same DNA profiling on some suicide victims?"

"You what?"

"If the pathologist kept tissue samples from some suicide cases, could you do a DNA analysis on them?"

Lying in bed, Paul mumbled, "Not right now, no."

"But you could."

"Yes, but. . ." He rubbed his eyes. "What are you saying? This gene therapy makes people prone to suicide? What time is it?"

"No. It's a long story. And it's three-thirty."

"Well, I'm not going anywhere," said Paul as he turned on to his back. "That includes not going back to sleep, if I'm not mistaken." He let out a long breath.

The bedroom smelled faintly of blueberry from the scented candle that Helen had lit earlier in the evening. She explained her theory about the Westland deaths. She believed that the young blacks had slipped into a coma like Dwight's and then died. Their deaths were disguised as suicide to avoid any question of corporate manslaughter or even murder. Dwight Grant

169

was the one who got away because he had disintegrated in front of a small audience during a football match. Helen guessed that, if he'd collapsed and died quietly in his cell, he might have apparently jumped out of a window, hanged himself, or taken an overdose by now. "If I'm right," Helen said, "if they're victims of YPI's drug therapy, they'll have the same DNA anomaly as Dwight."

"Is medicine always this exciting?" Paul muttered with a tired grin. "I've been missing out all these years."

"There's no need to miss out from now on," Helen replied. "I can drag you into this as much as you like."

"All right," Paul agreed. "I wasn't thinking of getting YPI to sponsor my research anyway. Besides," he added, "it sounds like a good cause to me."

"Thanks. You're a good 'un really."

"You haven't heard yet what favours I'll demand before I take it on."

Helen snuggled down beside him, saying, "I can guess."

28

To Kyle, it didn't look far on a map. Just a few centimetres between Atlanta and Memphis. But it was 550
kilometres – the same distance that separated
Cambridge and Edinburgh. In some ways, Memphis
was a whole world away, so why was Kyle staring with
such interest at the website of the *Memphis Flyer*? He'd
been trying to track down unexplained deaths in the
southern states when his search engine had turned up
a newspaper article on the strange case of a homeless
African-American called Mitch. It made Kyle feel so
sad. According to the report, no one knew anything
about Mitch. Not even a surname. He was just Mitch
of Memphis. Now, he was just a statistic, a nothing
really. His only claim to fame was a mysterious death in
Grady Memorial Hospital. Of course, he could have
succumbed to almost anything out of the ordinary – an
uncommon virus, a new street drug, an unexpected disease – but Kyle saw only parallels with Dwight Grant.
Two weeks ago, Mitch had slipped into a coma for no
obvious reason and then died for no obvious reason
before he could be revived. Because his condition was
so bizarre, the hospital had isolated him from other
patients.

Even if Kyle was right that there was an unlikely

connection between Mitch and Dwight, six and a half thousand kilometres apart, he had no idea what to do about it.

At Yttria Inc., Kyle had been introduced to a large number of colleagues. He would not have called any of them friends, though. Not really. He felt more like an object of curiosity than a friend. When he went up to the sixteenth floor for a talk on genetic engineering, he found himself sitting next to a man with extraordinary sideburns. He was about ten years older than Kyle, he looked a bit like Elvis Presley, and he spoke in the now familiar southern drawl. "Are you new around here?"

"Yes, I'm from. . ."

"England!" the man exclaimed, immediately attuned to Kyle's accent. "Don't tell me you're related to the Queen."

"No, I'm not."

"Shucks." Just before the talk started, the American said, "Anyway, I'm Max, biotechnology technician."

"Kyle. I'm a chemist, but I do it all on computers these days."

Afterwards, they chatted about the lecture and then took lunch together in Yttria's extravagant canteen. Max crammed a considerable number of chips into his mouth and asked, "So, Kyle, what're ya doing here in little ol' Atlanta?"

"I guess it's all about widening experience."

Max bit off a large chunk from a fat hamburger and chomped on it noisily. "You homesick?"

Kyle shrugged. "It's just that everything's different here. It takes a bit of getting used to, I suppose."

To Kyle, the American looked like a loner. The thought made Kyle smile inwardly because in America he felt like a loner himself. Perhaps that's why it was inevitable that the two of them would meet. Two sad cases together.

"You got a whole bunch going for you here. You got your land of the free, home of the brave, and your American dream, you got your high standard of living, you got the best scenery going, you get to do whatever you want, you got your Coke and Big Macs, you got the greatest music in the world. . ."

"Really?"

"Sure have. You want to go to Memphis for the real thing: Elvis, the undisputed king of music. Everyone knows he's the King. No one can replace him. You've got that lily-livered Cliff Richard in England." He laughed. "Christ, he's a joke. Elvis is your man. I impersonate him some – you may have guessed, even though I don't have my blue suede shoes on today – but no one can take his place. Not Elvis."

Mitch of Memphis came to Kyle's mind more easily than did Elvis Presley. "I'm into music all right but Elvis isn't really my style. You know, I want to look forward, not back."

"There's no point when Elvis's already done it all, said it all, sung it all."

"Mmm."

"You don't sound convinced."

Kyle smiled. "I sure don't. Rock, pop and country, it all comes out so soft and saccharine here – apart from rap, of course – they all sound the same to me. Easy listening."

"No accounting for taste," Max replied, stuffing more chips into his face. Realizing that he wasn't going to convert this strange being from England, he changed the subject. "I got to admit, living in the US, you got a few downers as well. You got your cultural divides, you got some crazy kids on the streets with no respect, you got your drug dealers, you got a whole lot of murders. That's your cost of freedom. You don't get freedom for nothin'." Not lingering for long on the negative, he asked, "What do your folks think of you being over here?"

Kyle shrugged again. "I guess they think it's a good career move."

"Girlfriend?"

Kyle shook his head.

"Brothers or sisters?"

"I haven't. . . No, not now."

At last, Max Levine stopped eating. He put down the remnants of his hamburger and gazed into Kyle's face. "You too, eh?"

"What?"

"We've got something in common, you and me. That's maybe why we found each other. I lost a kid sister," he said solemnly.

Max seemed to expect a response so Kyle replied, "It was my brother."

Max shook his head in sympathy. "How?"

"A car accident." Kyle paused before asking, "What about your sister?"

"It was. . ." He looked down at his messy plate and then back to Kyle. "Dammit if she didn't die on the street as well. On a God-forsaken street."

Kyle was not sure how to interpret Max's remark. Did he mean a traffic accident? Perhaps. Perhaps not. Anyway, he realized that it would not be a good idea to pursue the topic. "What do you do in biotechnology?" he enquired.

For a few seconds, Max did not answer. In those moments, Kyle wondered if Max was going to burst into tears, fly into a rage, or storm out without a further word. Instead, he took a long drink of Coke and then smiled. "OK, it don't do your teeth much good but it's a hell of a drink. An icon in a bottle." He put down the glass, resumed the mopping-up operation on the scraps of his lunch, and said, "I work in genetic modification. You Brits don't go for it much, do you? We heard about all the protests over genetically modified food. You'll soon change your minds when gene technology's

175

curing cancer, muscular dystrophy, Alzheimer's, and then some."

"And sickle-cell anaemia?"

"You know about that?"

Kyle saw a door suddenly swing open in front of him. "Sure. I worked on it for a bit in Cambridge."

"Really?"

"Yes," Kyle replied, wondering where the conversation would take him. He tried to appear casual, as if his heart-rate were not taking off.

"Me too. That's three things we've got in common."

"Three?"

"Music, losing a sister or brother, and SCP19."

"What are *you* doing with SCP19?" asked Kyle, as if SCP19 meant something to him.

Max hesitated. He put a finger to the side of his nose. "All hush-hush." His gesture was comical but his comment was cautious and deliberate. Clearly he was keeping to company policy on secrecy.

Deciding he could probe just a little more without overreaching himself, Kyle said, "Pity about the side effects."

"Yeah." Quietly, Max added with a smile, "But it depends what you want to use it for, doesn't it?"

Kyle nodded. "Sure does."

Helen,
    Bingo! I've spoken to someone here about

genetic modification and sickle-cell anaemia. He admitted there is a treatment and it's got side effects. I think we are after something called SCP19. He hinted that the side effects could be useful. Surely, that can only mean YPI is thinking of using it as a weapon.

Kyle

29

The pathologist looked up from his notes on the Westland suicides and gazed at Helen and her companion over half-moon glasses. "No. Officially, the bodies were sent back intact to the relatives."

"So, officially, you haven't got any samples at all. How about unofficially?" Helen prompted.

He looked back at his records, turned a page and then said, "Research kept a few bits and bobs – mainly liver and kidneys – because the men were sickle-cell carriers and one day the hospital might do a bit of work on it."

"Research. Thanks."

Walking with Helen to the research block, Paul smiled wryly. It was a peculiar way to spend a fortnight's holiday, delving into body organs and listening to what Helen had learned from her YPI mole called Kyle Proctor, but he was happy just to be beside her.

Dwight Grant was still in a world of his own, somewhere between life and death. In the real world, he showed no sign of life at all. It was as if he'd left his body behind and his spirit had gone through a secret door into another universe. Perhaps he was enjoying himself too much in that other place to return to a dreary life in a young offender institution. Perhaps, on the other side, he could not find the hidden door that would allow him to return to his body. Obviously, he was not being guided by sounds. From wherever he was, he could not hear the bedside anguish of his parents and Uncle Akoda, the frustration of nurses and doctors, the outrage of the Black and Asian Defenders, and the cassette that played at least four times a day. It had been Dr Crear's idea. She had persuaded Arsenal's leading goal scorer to record a message of encouragement. But it was useless. Nothing. Obviously, Dwight was not being guided by sight either. From wherever he was, he could not see the authentic signed Arsenal shirt waiting for him or he would have emerged by now. And after two months of antiviral treatment: nothing. No change at all. If he'd had a virus, it had delivered its payload and already done the damage.

No matter who spoke to him, no matter who appeared at his bedside, no matter how many drugs Dr Crear tried, Dwight slept on, oblivious to it all.

Uncle Akoda slouched in the seat beside the hospital bed, listening to the Arsenal striker's voice. "That's right," he said as if the footballer were really in the room and needed Akoda's support. "That's right. Hope you listening, Dwight." When the tape finished, Akoda sighed and pulled himself up to the bed, avoiding the tubes that were Dwight's lifelines. "You gotta listen. He's a mean striker and he drives a mean motor. When police stop him in his car and see who it is, they let him go. Respect. That's what you gotta have in this life, Dwight. Respect." Even in the subdued indoor lighting, Akoda wore sunglasses. "You don't get it lying around. You gotta be up, putting yourself about. You gotta be noticed."

Really, it was easy to see that Dwight wasn't just asleep. He didn't move at all and his breathing was controlled by a machine. Under his lids, Dwight's eyes were utterly still. It was unnatural. It looked like death but it was something else. Something much less certain.

Akoda said, "You're destroying your mam and dad, Dwight. Why don't you wake up?" A tear rolled out from under Akoda's shades. He wiped it away quickly and looked round to make sure no one had seen it. With a desperate shake of his head, he slipped another tenner under Dwight's pillow and left the waxwork model that Dwight had become.

The ball looped over Paul's head and fell, dead, into the back corner of the court where he had no hope of doing anything with it. It had lost all momentum and he had nowhere to swing his racket.

He picked up the ball and handed it back to his opponent. "What are you trying to do, Helen?"

"What do you think? Beat you at squash."

Before she could serve again, he replied, "I can see

180

that. And you're succeeding. No. I meant, what are you trying to do with this result on the suicide's kidney sample?"

Helen turned towards him, surprised. "What do you think? Help a patient, of course."

"Really?" said Paul. "I got a positive. Almost certainly I found a trace of the same DNA abnormality that Dwight Grant had. All you get out of that is a link, sort of, between your patient and a suicide case. That's it. It doesn't tell you what happened, it only suggests Dwight and the suicide are connected, presumably through the young offender institution and the drug trial they were both on."

Helen let out a long breath. "They both had the same abnormal gene. That tells me they've both probably been through the same gene therapy."

"The probably's an important word."

"You'd find it hard to come up with another explanation."

"Coincidence, experimental error, the same glitch in both analyses. Need I go on? It'd take a lot more work to *prove* what you're saying."

Helen put in an explosive, unreturnable serve. "Five–one." She paused and changed the subject slightly. "Before you ask, I'm not going to claim you've discredited the suicide verdict, just because the victim might have had dodgy gene therapy, but you've got to admit there's another explanation of his death now. A possible explanation anyway. The drug might have got him before someone thought of faking his suicide."

"You've stepped down from probable to possible now," Paul noted.

"I know what you're saying but your work's the only solid thing I've got. It's good enough."

"Good enough for what? Helen, the cynic would think it's got more to do with your campaign against Yttria than helping a patient."

"What campaign? I don't know what you mean."

"Come on. You're gunning for Yttria, big style."

"I'll tell you what your result's good enough for." With the same determination that she applied to the game of squash, Helen said, "It's good enough to present to Yttria. Tomorrow, I'm going there in person to confront them. You're right, the result's not foolproof, I know, but it's OK. It's threatening enough to get some co-operation for a change. Maybe YPI's got an antidote or just more information or some ideas on how to treat Dwight. Maybe they wouldn't give me them before because it would be admitting liability as well as giving away their industrial secrets. When they see I'm close to the truth anyway, they'll help me out because, if they don't, they know I'll dig deeper. They wouldn't want that." She was about to serve again but stopped. "That's not a campaign against them, Paul. It's a way of prising information out of a tight-lipped organization. Perfectly legitimate under the circumstances."

"All right," Paul replied. "I surrender."

"Not in the game, you don't. I don't take prisoners." Her racket hissed through the air again.

30

The masked gang snatched Nathan McQueen as he left a radio station in the evening. Overpowering him, they bundled him quickly into the back of a van and pinned him down while they bound and gagged him. Then they left him alone, trussed up in the claustrophobic vehicle, for several hours before they returned and drove him away. At no time did they blindfold him. Nathan realized that either they were confident he would not be able to identify them because of their masks or they were not going to allow him to live long enough to talk about his ordeal. That was when Nathan started to sweat.

What was the ordeal going to be anyway? He knew that he wasn't going to get away with a few hours locked inside a van. They were going to do more than dump him in the middle of the Tennessee countryside to face a long walk back. They were after more than simple humiliation.

The answer came after a short journey. The men dragged him out of the van and pushed him roughly into the darkened loading bay of a tall, modern building. With the speed and chaos of the operation, Nathan did not recognize it at first. Yet when his captors dragged him into the semi-darkness of a large indoor arena and gave him the opportunity to look around, he knew exactly where he was. He was standing inside one of the world's largest pyramids, the home of the Memphis State University Tigers, down on Wolf River Front. Only the Pyramid's security lights remained on. According to the glimmering stadium clock, it was two-thirty in the morning.

Nathan McQueen was sweating like a prize fighter. Whatever the men had in mind, it was going to happen right there and then. He was surrounded by five jokers in masks – only they weren't joking. They were white, though. He didn't need to see skin to work that out. Two of them, one in a Bill Clinton mask and the other a rubbery George W Bush, had him by the arms. They had removed the shackles from his ankles but his wrists were still tied tightly in front of him. The parcel tape covering his face from chin to nose pulled at his skin as his throat formed cries that his sealed mouth could not utter. Even in the gloom, his eyes were wide and staring, revealing his fright.

Right in front of him, the man in the Jack Nicholson disguise who seemed to be the leader squatted down and extracted a hammer and large nails from a bag. He did it slowly and deliberately, laying the nails out in an orderly line on the Tigers' turf.

Nathan frowned, puzzled and scared.

"Trying to work it out, boy? It ain't that difficult. Just think what day it is. Heh, heh."

He was right. It all became horribly clear when two

185

more members of the gang appeared out of the darkness carrying a large wooden cross.

Several of the men laughed when they saw that Nathan had realized what they were going to do to him.

"What did you expect, boy? It is Easter after all." The fake Jack Nicholson spoke in a low menacing whisper.

"Not that we're suggesting you're Jesus," George Bush said. "Nothing like."

"Shush," someone else said.

They put the heavy cross down on the ground and four of the other men forced Nathan to his knees beside it. He tried to kick out, to struggle, to fight, but it was useless. There were too many of them and they were too strong for him. He felt powerless, just like he had when the police had beaten him up. Then, there had been nothing he could do but roll himself up into a protective ball, clutch his head in his hands, and submit to it. This time, he was denied even that. The four men had untied his hands and stretched him out flat on the grass. A phoney president on each arm, Arnold Schwarzenegger on one leg and Frank Sinatra on the other, they were manhandling him, edging him closer to the cross. All that Nathan could do was jerk his body, but it was wasted effort.

"Keep your staring eyes off me, nigger!"

"Don't worry none about his eyes," Jack Nicholson ordered in his quiet but commanding voice. "Just concentrate. This is more than a $500 job. By morning, we've got ourselves an easy $10,000. Maybe more for a spectacular like this."

When Nathan felt the wood bruising his back, he panicked and lashed out with all his remaining strength. He wrenched one leg free and kicked Schwarzenegger in the face, but in the next moment he felt a dead weight fall across his loose leg as another man dropped mercilessly on it.

"Dammit! This is ridiculous. . ."

"Just because you got a boot in the face. You should've hung on, Arnie."

"No arguing. Come on. Let's get it done."

Nathan twisted his head to the left. He saw Jack Nicholson with the hammer and nails kneeling beside George W who was holding Nathan's arm and hand firmly against the wood. If Nathan could have shrieked, he would have done. The muffled cry tore his throat.

"Remember, don't go through the hand," Bush said. "That's not how it's done. It's not strong enough. Put the nail through his wrist."

"Thanks for telling me my job." Jack Nicholson took a giant nail in his left hand and the hammer in his right.

Nathan's whole body juddered. No! Somehow, the inability to scream made it worse. He yanked on his arm, trying to wrest it from his torturers, but failed. Anticipating Nathan's reaction, George Bush had his entire body weight on it. There was no way to stop what was about to happen. Bracing himself, Nathan felt the cold metallic point scratching his wrist, the perspiration rolling down his cheeks, the warm urine soaking into his pants. He saw the hammer rising. Then he saw nothing else.

He was blinded by sudden floodlights from every corner of the stadium. All he could do was blink in the brightness.

Someone was shouting, "What's going on down there?"

The stab of pain never came. Nathan heard the white men gathered around him jump up in confusion at the same time. He heard them running towards the loading bay, the slamming of doors, the roar from the getaway van. But he saw nothing. His eyes were open but somehow his brain couldn't make sense of it all. He was stunned. He couldn't even move. He lay there immobile on the cross as if he had been nailed to it.

Blotting out some of the bright light, two figures in uniform appeared above him. Nathan wanted to roll up into a ball again and protect himself, but his body refused to budge. He waited for the barrage of blows.

Yet it didn't happen this time.

"Are you all right?"

"That's a dumb question," someone else said, kneeling beside him. "Can't you see the man's petrified?"

The first security guard replied, "I'll call 911."

188

Nathan cringed as he felt a touch on his arm and a voice, "You're going to be all right. You're lucky. I thought I heard something so we decided to do an early patrol. It's all over. They didn't have time to do nothing. Do you hear me?"

Nathan continued to stare silently even after the security guard had ripped the parcel tape from his mouth.

A Storm Force Brigade calling card lay on the pitch. Its message was brief and inaccurate: *Nathan McQueen RIP*.

For the second time in his life, Nathan had survived a racist attack. But the mental battering, the trauma of this night would take longer to heal than the bruises, cuts and broken bones inflicted last time by police batons.

31

It was the other side of the Easter break before Helen Crear had an opportunity to go to Yttria for a meeting with the Head of Clinical Trials. Before she was allowed on YPI's premises, she had to pass through a security lodge where she gave her name and assured the guards that she was an official visitor, having arranged the meeting with Dr Cameron Ingoe by telephone. While she filled in a form about herself and her business, the guard called Dr Ingoe to confirm the appointment. Only then was she allowed on to the site.

Waiting for Dr Ingoe in the foyer, she sat and watched people coming and going. It was nothing like the swarming crowds in a hospital. It was much less disorderly. In Addenbrooke's, half of the people milling around were lost or emotionally shaken. Here, everyone was striding purposefully to wherever they wanted to be. In hospitals, though, there were few barriers to movement. Hospitals had been built on the idea of openness because they belonged to the community. In YPI, Helen was fascinated by the door into the inner sanctum. Every employee pushed a pass into a slot next to the door. Then, before entry was sanctioned, they stood still for a moment and seemed to be staring at a blank patch on the wall. Afterwards, the pass reappeared and the door could be opened. On top of all that, there was a closed-circuit TV camera above the entrance.

Helen found the premises intimidating because she was not used to high security. At the hospital only the maternity ward had a security alarm, to stop strangers wandering off with someone else's baby, but it was nothing compared with the system here in the pharmaceutical fortress. Helen thought it odd that the nation protected its drugs and industrial secrets more than it protected its infants.

Eventually, a man came towards her and held out his hand. "Urling-Clark." It was a formal greeting, lacking any friendliness.

Reluctantly, Helen indulged in a half-hearted handshake. To mirror his frosty introduction, she said, "Crear." She also frowned because she thought that she recognized him. He looked familiar, but the memory was so vague that she did not comment on it. Perhaps she'd seen him visiting the hospital or perhaps he just reminded her of someone else. As she stood up, she said, "I was expecting Dr Ingoc."

"I'll take you."

Beyond the security door, Urling-Clark escorted her along two lengthy corridors, much brighter and narrower than those in Addenbrooke's, up a flight of stairs and into an office that bore the inscription, *Dr S J Urling-Clark*.

Inside, he waved towards a seated man and said, "You've already spoken to our Head of Clinical Trials."

"Ah, yes," Helen replied, this time not encouraging a hint of a handshake. When she had talked to him on the phone, she had envisaged him as a slight man, but in reality he could have been a rugby player.

"Cameron Ingoe," he said for himself in his soft, reassured and strangely unsettling voice. He made a movement as if he was going to get to his feet but he didn't. He sank back into the chair. "The last thing you told me to do was to go to hell." His wide smile was as ominous as his tone.

"Yes, well. That was because you deserved it." Helen was less intimidated by the two middle-aged men in suits than by the security arrangements with which they surrounded themselves. She was cornered and outnumbered but not dispirited. "I've come to see if your attitude's changed."

Helen took a seat. She felt the scientists' eyes on her. It wasn't the look that she was used to. They were not sizing her up in the way that a lot of men – especially middle-aged men – did. They were trying to gauge her mood, her degree of determination, her motives, the extent of her ability to cause them a headache.

"Let's see," Cameron said, glancing up at the ceiling as if he were really trying to recall their last conversation. "It was a boy from Westland, as I recall. He was a participant in one of our trials and, rather unfortunately, collapsed and went into a coma, possibly because of something that happened on a football pitch. A nasty fall, perhaps."

It was going to be a dry meeting. The atmosphere bristled with tension and there was no offer of a drink. "He hardly sustained a bruise," Helen retorted. "You've got to look somewhere else for an explanation."

"I don't have to look anywhere, Dr Crear. But, yes, you were worried about our experimental drug. Apparently I didn't put your mind at rest because you seemed to get rather upset when I told you that the law doesn't require drug companies to reveal their results to doctors, volunteers or the public. If you have a problem with that, you should be writing to your MP about the law of the land, not meeting us here." The biologist paused before asking, "How is the young man, by the way?"

His eyes told Helen that he already knew. He had guessed that she would not have come if Dwight were better. Ingoe's eyes also told her that he didn't really care about Dwight himself. Cameron Ingoe wanted the boy to recover only to get Yttria off the hook. "His condition remains unchanged." She made it sound like a cold hospital bulletin, then she launched her first wave of attack. "Dwight Grant was carrying the sickle-cell trait. Is that why you were interested in having him in your trial?"

"As always in a drug trial," he replied in a flippant

voice, "we wanted a good cross-section of characteristics. We gave him a medical and didn't find any factors that made it unwise or dangerous for him to join. I dare say you've done much the same tests and I imagine you've come to the same conclusion. He was a very healthy boy."

"So, you did know he had the sickle-cell gene."

"Our blood test showed it up but that didn't disqualify him."

"You seem to have enlisted far more blacks than whites. That's hardly a good cross-section."

Cameron smiled again. "Perhaps you're aware of the people we recruited from Westland Young Offender Institution, but clearly you're not aware of the volunteers drawn from other sources, like university students wanting to top up their loans. Our overall profile of subjects is fair and well balanced for the aims we have in mind. We had permission from the Medicines Control Agency for the study, and a licence from the appropriate government committee. I'd be happy to show you it but it contains details of our drug design. You'll understand why it must remain a confidential document."

Helen didn't doubt for a moment that Yttria's operation was legal. "Just what is the drug designed to cure?"

"As I said by telephone, our drug development programme must be kept from competitors. Secrecy's an integral part of the process. It wouldn't be appropriate for me to discuss our next big medicine with you."

"I'm not a competitor."

"No, but—"

"Look, I'll sign anything you want, guaranteeing not to pass on any information you give me." Helen looked closely at Cameron Ingoe and said, "What did you call it on the phone? A no-publicity clause."

"Not good enough," Urling-Clark put in abruptly and dismissively. "Signing a piece of paper doesn't stop you letting the cat out of the bag. It only allows us to sue you afterwards."

"That licence you mentioned," Helen said. "Is it from the Gene Therapy Advisory Committee?"

Drily, Stuart replied, "No comment."

"OK. Just tell me this. If Dwight's condition was caused by—"

"It wasn't."

Ignoring Urling-Clark's intervention, Helen carried on. "If your drug's got something to do with Dwight's coma, can you give me some ideas on how I could reverse the effect – without telling me all your precious secrets?"

"Hardly," Cameron answered in his uncanny voice, far too small for such a big man. "Given that the drug is almost certainly irrelevant to his condition."

"How about an antidote or vaccine?"

Both men reacted for a split second. They glanced at each other fleetingly and then recovered. Urling-Clark said, "Being a medic, you're not going to use that

195

term loosely. By asking for a vaccine, you're suggesting that your patient's got a bacterial or viral infection. Do you know that?"

Helen was edging into the driving seat, exactly as she had intended. "I've done lots of tests on him. Believe me, I've got a lot of resources at my disposal. You might be surprised what I can turn up."

"If you're so well informed, why haven't you improved Grant's prognosis? Why are you here?"

"Because I want you to confirm what I already know."

"And what's that?" The two men were not treating her as a lightweight any more. They sensed that she had discovered more than they had anticipated. And certainly more than they hoped she would ever discover.

"Let me put it this way. You're experts in drugs and biotechnology. What would you think if a volunteer on a drug trial turned up with an abnormality in his genes?"

In his lazy style, Dr Ingoe said, "I'd wonder what it had to do with the drug trial at all."

"But if it was a gene therapy trial?"

This time their faces remained fixed. "Well, depending on exactly what sort of gene therapy we're talking about, it might explain an alteration – a correction – in gene sequence. And so might technical errors in your analysis."

"Dr Ingoe. I don't make mistakes. My patients' lives

depend on it." She decided not to reveal Paul's part in her reasoning and she did not reveal his reservations in the results either. It suited her to be absolutely certain, or at least to appear to be absolutely certain.

The YPI men did not respond to her remark. They were not going to volunteer any more than the bare minimum. Helen could tell that they were waiting for her to show all of her cards before they decided if they had a trump to play. They still looked confident and smug.

Chipping away at them, Helen continued, "Dwight Grant's been through gene therapy, delivered by a virus, presumably in an attempt to repair the sickle-cell gene. That's all very worthy. I'm glad someone's working on it. And mistakes are part and parcel of any medical advance. But, when it does go wrong, you have to put up your hands, admit it, and help me put things right. Without that help, my patient's stuck in limbo without a hope in hell of recovery."

"All this is conjecture," Ingoe muttered.

"OK," Helen responded, getting impatient. "Explain this. Another of your Westland volunteers – another black offender with the sickle-cell trait – had exactly the same gene abnormality."

Using almost exactly the same words as Paul had done, Cameron replied, "Coincidence perhaps. More likely an experimental error that was common to both analyses."

"Checked and dismissed," Helen stated as if she

really had checked and dismissed the possibility of errors. "This abnormality doesn't appear when white people's blood is analysed in the same way. And it doesn't happen with blood from blacks without the sickle-cell trait. If it was an experimental error, we'd see it all the time, with any sample."

"We?"

"The analytical department in the hospital." Helen was settling into the role of rebel. She was beginning to enjoy the intrigue, probably because she saw herself edging ahead of the opposition.

"Who was this other volunteer?" asked Dr Ingoe.

"Now there's a funny thing," Helen said with relish. "Like a suspicious number of Westland lads, he committed suicide. Isn't that strange?"

"Not especially. Young offender institutions can be depressing places."

"Not that depressing," Helen snapped. "Now, will you help me before I extend my studies to other so-called suicides and make my findings public?"

"There's a very serious accusation – a very unwise accusation – lurking in there, Dr Crear," Ingoe warned her.

Helen decided to try a bluff. "Working in a hospital, I have access to an extensive bank of samples, going back months and years. I'd have no reason to analyse more of them and compare the results with Dwight Grant's if Dwight was on the road to recovery."

198

The man with the faintly familiar face wore a righteous look of disapproval. "Have you discussed your findings with anyone else?" he barked.

She still didn't want to drag Paul into the pharmaceutical quagmire. "No. But that doesn't mean I'll always keep my conclusions to myself. It depends on the level of your co-operation."

"I thought we'd made our position very clear," Stuart Urling-Clark stated. "We have nothing to say about any of our drug trials. We still don't. We're not required to do so and we won't. End of story. Full stop."

What had happened to him? A holiday, two weeks in Cambridge, two weeks with Helen, a few drinks and meals with her, a tour around the old haunts, a game of squash, some contract work in Addenbrooke's, and he was a different person. What had caused it? Paul was supposed to be an intelligent man. It didn't take him long to figure it out, even if he couldn't find a scientific explanation for his feelings. He knew only that Helen had affected him to an extent that he had not anticipated when he set out from Coventry. It was as if, in returning to Cambridge, he had found a vital piece of himself that he had left behind before. He had not realized that it was missing until he rediscovered it. Now, he did not want to leave it behind again.

When he'd left her last time, she'd been feeling optimistic about the prospect of a long and successful career in medicine, caring for those who needed her attention more than Paul did. This time, she was angry and depressed that someone was blocking her attempts to treat a patient.

Paul held her by her shoulders and her hands rested on his waist. "You send me more samples and I'll get them analysed straight away, but I'm not sure. . ." He paused, annoyed that he couldn't find the right words without sounding heartless. "Maybe you've got to drop this YPI thing. You've done your best, you could hardly do any more, to help that lad. You've just got to keep him going, hoping one day he'll suddenly wake up and wonder what all the fuss is about."

She shook her head. "I saw it, Paul. Those two YPI men – Stuart Urling-Clark and Cameron Ingoe – they've both had an ethics bypass operation. They know exactly what's going on. I could tell. But they won't say. And I can't . . . I can't understand them."

"I guess you've got to keep trying different treatments."

"That'd be a needle in a haystack job."

"I just don't like the idea of you messing around any more with these YPI heavies. If you're right, they've pulled a lot of strings. I don't want them pulling yours."

Having no intention of behaving herself, Helen said, "Yes, OK, I'll behave myself." She smiled. "And don't turn possessive on me all of a sudden. It doesn't suit a man who's ignored me for years."

"That's not true," he exclaimed. "I sent you a Christmas card every other year."

She moved into his arms and kissed him.

Paul said, "I've got to go – I hear the distant thunder of the new term – but I'll be back as soon as I can. It'll be different this time. Promise. OK?"

"Yes. Sure." There was the beginning of a tear in Helen's eye. It was a combination of frustration at work and, she had to admit, Paul's departure. She would miss him. She would miss his help, his support, his affection.

"You hear about a job for a brilliant chemistry lecturer in Cambridge and I'll be on to it like a shot. Let me know."

She nodded.

"And Helen?"

"Yes?"

"You're looking good."

She shook her head. "I don't feel it."

"I know."

"Go on," she told him. "Get going before I. . . Anyway, get going."

Paul had learnt something. He had gained more from being with Helen than from any academic achievement in Coventry. He squeezed her and whispered, "Love you." Restlessly, he turned away, leapt into his car and closed the door before she saw his weakness. As he drove away he felt like a patient in need of Dr Crear's care.

Paul did not have a lot to smile about when he got home, but he smiled when he saw his most recent e-mail message. It had been sent soon after he'd left Cambridge and it read, *Love you too, H.*

That same night, a dark anonymous figure with fine silvery hair laid a trail of petrol. It wasn't a hot evening and there was no rain. Perfect. The shiny liquid fuse did not evaporate and it didn't get washed away. Twenty metres from the building, the man stopped and put down the empty petrol can without a sound. A cigarette lighter flared briefly, a tiny source of ignition, and the cleansing began. The flame danced silently towards the building along the glistening stream of eager fuel. Like a visitor, the glow loitered for a few seconds in the doorway before stepping into the petrol-soaked interior.

Outside, the dark figure waited. He was itching to make his escape before the world woke to his handiwork, but he could not. He couldn't leave until he was sure that he had done his job.

Simultaneously, flames appeared at the windows on either side of the door as if someone inside had turned on lamps, but this light was unsteady, alive. It lurched, flickered, leapt and grew. Then it happened. Flash point. The glass in the windows shattered and the greedy spectral visitor fed on oxygen from the cold air. The fire swelled, filling the rooms with colour and life. Joyous and unstoppable, it began to roar.

Feeling the unnatural breeze of heat, the watcher knew that his work was over. He walked away unseen, slipping easily into the darkness between buildings.

The sound of sirens descended on Addenbrooke's Hospital. Three fire-engines raced past the ambulances, heading for the research block and mortuary where the hospital's tissue samples were stored. Before the fire-fighters could do anything, the extensive bank of samples would be destroyed for ever.

It wasn't the only emergency in Cambridge that long, dark night. Dr Crear's central heating system developed an unexpected fault. When the automatic timer switched on the heating in the early morning, there was a blockage in the water pipe. The flames in the gas boiler popped into life and started to warm the water. Instead of surging away, carrying heat to the cistern, the sizzling water could not go anywhere. It just got hotter and hotter and it expanded and expanded until it could not be contained within the blocked unit any more. The boiler burst apart in a deafening explosion, blowing out the side wall of her suburban house. Helen Crear's bed fell through the collapsed floorboards into the kitchen where the gas pipe still delivered its flammable load into the space where the boiler had been. There was a wild whoosh as flame gushed from the broken pipe, spraying the bed and what was left of the room with flame. Bright yellow fingers clawed out of the ruined kitchen through the hole in the wall, up the blackening brickwork, pushing aside the darkness before dawn, illuminating the damaged house and empty sky.

32

"What happened to you?" Kyle said with a sly smile, gesturing towards Max's black eye. "That's a beauty. You went over to Memphis for Easter, didn't you? Did you get walloped by a rival Elvis impersonator?"

"Very funny," Max retorted. "Actually, I had an argument with a door, dammit, that's all."

Kyle wasn't sure how a door could give Max a black eye without bruising other parts of his face as well, but he let it drop. It was clear that Max didn't want to talk about the injury. They ate their lunches at the same table but said little. When Kyle stood up to go back to work, Max asked him, "Are you wanting to come over to Memphis next time I go? It's a good place to look around, even when Graceland's closed for repairs."

"Yeah. Sure. That'd be nice."

"I'll be in touch," Max replied.

"Thanks."

Back in the computer room, Kyle was presented unexpectedly with a golden opportunity. The colleague on his left jumped up and said, "Keep your eye on the computer, will you, Kyle? I'm a bit. . ." She held her stomach, indicating that she suddenly felt sick.

"OK."

Kyle watched her race towards the toilets. The orders were to turn any computer to standby if it was going to be left unattended even for a short while. Then, the next user's thumbprint would dictate the clearance level when the system was activated again. But Kyle found himself sitting next to a terminal that was still being used by an operator with high-level security clearance. The trouble was, if he tried to take advantage of it and inherit her access, the computer would lock him out because it would detect the change in thumbprint. Or would it? Kyle had an idea. He wondered if he could beat the security system after all. He peeled the sticky red dot from his thumb, shuffled into the empty seat and placed his artificial thumb, devoid of any fingerprint, on the mouse.

The computer did not show a sign of registering a new print at all. The poor thing was confused. Plainly, someone was using it. Plainly, someone was moving the mouse around and clicking away, opening files on prisoners in drug trials, but there was no thumbprint and that persuaded the in-built security device that no one was using it at all. Occasionally, Kyle looked up furtively, making sure that the original operator was not returning and that a pack of supervisors was not bearing down on him, but no one took any notice. It was just Kyle tapping away at a keyboard as he always did. He did not dare to hardcopy anything because a supervisor walking past would see what he was printing. He might even be searched on his way out of the building – the guards seemed to pick on him more often than anyone else – so keeping any paperwork would be foolhardy. Instead, he remembered as many of the facts as he could. Among the prisoners volunteering for an SCP19 trial, there had been five deaths. Officially, there had been three suicides, one freak allergic reaction to the virus, and one heroin overdose. Unofficially, it felt exactly the same as the fake suicides at Westland Young Offender Institution.

Maybe an artificial thumb that couldn't play guitar had its uses after all. Without a pause, Kyle logged on to the British YPI site and opened the inventory of all chemicals stored at the Cambridge branch. On the list of everything stored in Lab 47, *The Safe* was written in black letters. This time, clicking on it did not elicit a bloodstained rebuke. This time, he got exactly what he wanted.

Code name	Originator	Properties	Location
BF19, renamed SCP19	B N Fleetwood	Harmless in mice, rats, dogs, monkeys; toxic in humans with sickle-cell gene (see Westland trials)	Locked safe, Lab 47

It was tempting to sit back and stare open-mouthed at the screen. *Toxic in humans with the sickle-cell gene. See Westland trials.* He had to fight the impulse to freeze. If he'd had more time, he would have gone into the documents on the Cambridge drug trials, but he'd already seen everything he needed to see. Before anyone got suspicious, he returned the machine to its original status and slipped back to his own monitor. It was only then that he could afford to think about his find.

Any feeling of celebration and triumph over the system was banished by horror. As Kyle suspected, the safe in Lab 47 housed a smart biological weapon, a barbaric weapon against the black population, and it had been tested on Westland inmates. The entry in the database stunned him because there was a big difference between suspicion and certainty. For so long, he had hunted a link between the Westland trials and a treatment that had gone horribly wrong and now that he had it, he was overwhelmed and could not think what to do.

Claiming a crushing headache, he walked away from the building and towards his apartment. In the open air, his brain cleared slowly. He decided not to create a scandal by contacting the press. Besides, that BAD activist, Linton Okri, had told him that the British government could gag such a story and Kyle imagined that much the same would happen in the States when a powerful and influential company came under threat. No. Kyle's first duty was to inform Dwight Grant's doctor. That was the humane thing to do. After that, he would work out how to sabotage the deployment of SCP19.

Carefully, Kyle composed an e-mail message to Helen Crear but, a few minutes after transmitting it, it was returned, undeliverable. He tried again with the same mysterious result. Somewhere between his computer and hers in Cambridge, there had to be a breakdown. Kyle cursed his bad luck. Then, when he tried her home telephone number, he got the number-unobtainable drone. The howling in his ear meant that Helen Crear was in serious trouble.

33

Helen had moved in with a female friend while her own house was being rebuilt. She still shuddered about last night. The fire officers had told her that if she had been asleep in the bed at the time of the accident, there would have been no chance at all of her survival.

Partly, she had Paul to thank for her life. She had gone to bed around midnight and failed to get to sleep. Alone and restless because Paul had returned to Coventry, annoyed and baffled by Yttria Pharmaceuticals, she'd tossed and turned for well over an hour. She'd switched on her bedside radio and, after hearing the local news, decided to get up, get dressed and go into Addenbrooke's to see the damage to the research block for herself. While she was in the hospital, she'd volunteered for the night shift. The extra work had kept away loneliness, frustration and death.

The morning after, in shock, Helen had asked the police if there was any evidence that someone had interfered with her central heating system. Once its parts had been salvaged from her lawn, the road and the next-door's garden, and examined by engineers, the verdict was vague. There was no evidence for sabotage and no evidence against it. The unit had been damaged too much to reach a definite conclusion. Yet, on her mobile to Paul, Helen had to admit that sabotage was still a possibility.

"YPI's ruthless," Paul said, making up his mind straight away about who was responsible. "It's because big money's involved. You think they've already covered up some deaths by—"

"Hang on. You didn't believe that."

"I didn't believe the evidence. I didn't say it didn't happen." He made no attempt to disguise the agitation in his voice.

"Well, there's nothing to say YPI fixed my central heating to explode either, but you seem to think they did. Pipes do get blocked on their own sometimes."

"But—"

"You're just emotional, Paul."

"Oh, and I'm supposed to be calm when I leave you alone for a couple of minutes and you're nearly incinerated in your own bed."

Helen smiled to herself. Paul was a typical scientist. He could assess facts coolly and logically, but when there was personal involvement, he was just as capable as anyone else of getting hysterical. She found his passion reassuring. "You shouldn't have any trouble believing YPI's been experimenting on young offenders with gene therapy. At least we've got a bit of evidence for that."

"You're ignoring the fire at the hospital. You said that

211

was arson. It's too much of a coincidence, Helen. The same day you threaten YPI with analysing tissue samples, those same samples go up in smoke and your house falls apart when you were supposed to be in it. OK, it's not going to convict anyone, but it sounds to me like a two-pronged attack to put you out of the picture. You must have really rattled them when you went to see them."

"You think they've moved on from fiddling with death certificates to attempted murder. That's heavy."

"If they're into weapons of mass destruction, death's the name of their game from now on, so what's one or two extra casualties? Nothing."

"I still live in hope that they're just testing new treatments for sickle-cell anaemia, covering up embarrassing mistakes, and that the rest is coincidence."

"Forget the coincidence, Helen. It's a counter-attack."

At the other end of the phone, Helen didn't respond for a few seconds.

"Helen?"

"You might have put your finger on it."

"What?"

"A counter-attack." Thoughtfully, Helen said, "The virus they use to deliver the treatment must be safe, but if it was carrying a drug that latched on to volunteers' sickle-cell gene, their immune systems might have launched a massive counter-attack against the foreign

212

bit of DNA – the abnormal piece you found. Instead of sending repair chemicals, the body sends out its soldiers. All hell could break loose then. A ruthless immune system could destroy a whole number of organs. That'd explain the problems. The drug turns the body's defence against itself – in the case of sickle-cell carriers. There'd be no effect in other people because the drug's not going to stick. That might be it, Paul."

Typical of Helen, Paul thought. She was considering her patient more than the threat to herself.

Carried along by her enthusiasm, Helen continued, "In Dwight's case, maybe some white blood cells got into his brain. They could have swollen a tiny part – too small to spot on a brain scan – and destroyed some nerve endings, making him unconscious."

"Would that be permanent?" asked Paul, fearing for the boy.

"Not necessarily. His brain might've gone into hibernation to fix itself. Anyway, I'm jumping to conclusions."

"What are you going to do next, then?"

"That's a good question."

"Meaning, you haven't got a clue?"

There was another pause. Then Helen said, "Of course. The Black and Asian Defenders have got a whole file on YPI guinea pigs with a variety of minor ill-nesses. Maybe they're just like Dwight but nowhere near as severe. I bet that's the order of things: level 1, depression; level 2, feeling dizzy; level 3, fainting; level 4, full coma. Dwight got to level 4 and the suicides made it all the way to level 5: death. I need to test the lads who only got to the lower levels. The first call's got to be Westland's doctor. I assume Westland's got an in-house medic."

"All right." Paul bit his lip because it sounded as if he'd just given her permission. Helen was an intelligent woman who would make up her own mind. "I mean, that sounds sensible. I just don't want you getting into any more . . . you know . . . trouble. I couldn't bear it if you . . . OK?"

"You sound more like my dad every day."

"Just take care."

"All right. Promise." She put her phone away, eager to get on. Suddenly, she was feeling much more upbeat. Parts of her life might be ragged or ruined, but it was OK if she could see a way ahead.

Stuart Urling-Clark sat back in his chair and concentrated on his files. Before YPI started to ship its product, he needed to confirm that all of the paperwork was correct and up to date. In gene therapy drug trials, the company was required to report the death or deterioration of any volunteer to the Gene Therapy Advisory Committee. Stuart smiled with satisfaction. GTAC had agreed that the deaths were due to unforeseen suicide. Dwight Grant's case was still pending. For the moment, the committee accepted that the likely cause of his condition was a blow to the head during a football match. There was no evidence to the contrary. The minor illnesses suffered by Westland's black volunteers were of unknown cause and were being dealt with adequately by an on-site doctor who put them down more to institutionalized living than to a drugs trial.

The doctor at Westland Young Offender Institution wasn't obstructive, but he wasn't very obliging either. He said that he couldn't do anything immediately, but he promised to put Helen in touch with YPI volunteers who were willing to speak to her about their health and who might agree to having various tests. When Helen stood up, she glanced around the walls of his surgery and realized that every single poster came from Yttria Pharmaceuticals International. She nodded towards one display and, while she buttoned up her coat, said, "You have close contact with YPI, then?"

"They're very generous to Westland. My practice is partly sponsored by them."

"That's good," Helen replied, keeping her true feelings hidden. In her rush to make progress, she hadn't thought that this doctor's loyalties might be split between his patients and his sponsor. "Anyway, thanks for your help."

Unbeknown to Helen, the doctor picked up his phone as soon as she closed the door.

Helen Crear did not believe in superstition. She knew that bad things had a reputation for coming in threes but, because she wasn't superstitious, she wasn't expecting the third. She'd already lost a valuable back-catalogue of tissue samples and a sizeable chunk of her house. Walking back towards Addenbrooke's, she didn't expect to lose her life to a speeding motorist.

Something was wrong. Paul did not bother to try Helen's e-mail address – her computer had been destroyed by the explosion at her house – but her mobile was not responding either. Three times, the recorded voice announced, "The number you have dialled has not been recognized. Please check and try again." He called Addenbrooke's instead, but the hospital authorities refused to tell him why Dr Crear was not on duty any more. Finally, when he got through to someone he'd met in the hospital's analytical department, he couldn't believe the news. He was totally thunderstruck.

"Are you sure?"

"Yes, I'm afraid I am."

"Helen? No. Are you absolutely sure?"

"Yes. Look, are you all right, Dr Turrell?"

All right? Of course he wasn't all right. He dropped the receiver without a further word and stared ahead blankly. He saw the rest of the world rushing headlong into the future – just as it always did – but now it seemed to be leaving him behind. He felt as if he had ground to a halt, abruptly dropped out of life, unable and unwilling to catch up with everyone else. The last time that he'd felt anything remotely similar, he had gone into hospital for an operation after a sports injury.

The general anaesthetic went into his left arm and almost straight away the limb went cold from the wrist, as if it had been plunged into freezing water. Coldness crept over him as his life became suspended. Just before the top of his brain felt the same icy effect, he had the sensation of the world carrying on without him. Then, suddenly, there was nothing.

The anaesthetic had knocked him out for several hours. This time, the numbness was not so long-lived. It was pushed aside by anger and outrage. The woman he'd almost ignored all those years, wasted years, the woman he'd just rediscovered, had been snatched from him. And what had been snatched from Helen? A career, the ability to heal, a life of her own. Paul had witnessed an awakening in her also. And he had seen it in her last short e-mail message. She had been denied the option of sharing some part of her life with Paul. She had been denied any hope of love. And some other doctor would have to step into Helen's shoes to take care of her patients. But it wouldn't be the same. If Dwight Grant woke up one day he would not even know the doctor who had battled so hard on his behalf. There was no one to live Helen's life for her. It had gone for ever.

And it was all supposed to be at the whim of a speeding motorist, possibly drunk, possibly joyriding, possibly high on drugs. Rubbish. Paul stood up and took a deep breath. It wasn't a whim at all. It was a cold, calculated assassination. Helen was making herself a nuisance at YPI and YPI eliminated that nuisance. Paul could hear his own voice when he talked to Helen yesterday. "If they're into weapons of mass destruction, what's one or two extra casualties? Nothing." Helen's death convinced Paul that she had been right about YPI. Maybe Helen hadn't built a watertight case, but the "accidents" she had suffered were proof enough. The person behind the wheel of the car that killed Helen was not a drunken joyrider, but a skilled, well paid professional who knew exactly what he was doing.

Paul swore that he would avenge her death. He would drop everything to avenge it. Immediately, and with only one thought in his head, he made for his car.

Paul Turrell had always regarded himself as a calm, rational man, but he burst back into Cambridge like a hurricane. His first stop was YPI. Yet he didn't get any further than the gatehouse. If he hadn't got an appointment and no one was expecting him, he was not welcome. When he continued his protest, demanding to see Urling-Clark, Ingoe or anyone else in charge, thumping the desk in frustration and anger, two guards appeared either side of him.

"What's your name?" they demanded to know.

"None of your business," he snapped.

"Have you been drinking?"

Paul shouted, "You're killers. All of you!"

At that point, the two formidable guards had had enough. Believing him to be drunk, they grabbed an arm each and escorted him roughly from the security office. They dumped him well away from the entrance in a quiet alley where they had once beaten up the homeless man who used to sit outside the gates with an upturned hat in front of his crossed legs.

Paul tried the hospital instead. He wasn't manhandled in the same way, he wasn't expelled from the premises, but he got nowhere at all with Helen's stand-in. "I've been told you've taken over from Helen Crear," he began.

The new doctor said, "Not entirely, but yes, I've inherited a few of her cases. Why?"

"What happened to her?"

"She was run over."

Agitated and stressed, Paul replied, "Yes, but what *really* happened?"

"Look," the doctor said, obviously anxious to get on. "I'm picking up some of her duties. I hardly knew her."

"But you *must* know—"

"I'm sorry. Sorry about Helen, but. . ." He shrugged.

Paul still had a wild expression in his eyes. He seemed to be on the point of grabbing the medic by the shoulders and attempting to shake an answer out of him.

"Who are you?" the doctor asked. "Her brother?"

"No. I'm her. . . I *was* her boyfriend. Paul Turrell." Normally he would have offered his hand, but he was too distressed for niceties.

"You're upset, I can see, but I can't help. The only thing I can say is that I've just had a call from someone in the States – Kyle, he said his name was – asking after Dr Crear and telling me what he thinks happened to Dwight Grant. I'm grateful. It might help with his treatment."

Calming down at last, Paul stood, hands on hips, and sighed. The doctor's comment reminded him of Helen's ally in the enemy camp. At once, Paul knew that he had to contact Kyle Proctor. "Did he leave his number or e-mail address?"

"No. I'm sorry. Now, you'll have to excuse me. My patients. . ." The doctor slipped away.

Paul wandered out of the ward. On his way through Reception, he did not notice the young woman in worn, pale blue denims who was also trying to prise information on Dr Helen Crear from the hospital authorities. Determined to stay in Cambridge until he had some answers about Helen, Paul checked in at a city hotel. Then he went to the hotel bar to anaesthetize himself from the pain.

"Poor Dr Crear," Stuart Urling-Clark murmured, shaking his head and putting down the newspaper. "First, we find out she lives – she lived – in our village. We

221

even heard the explosion just down the road. Now. . ."
He ground to a halt.

"We might have met her or at least seen her," said Mrs Urling-Clark. "Did she go to church, I wonder?"

"I don't think so. When she came to see me at work, I didn't recognize her. A couple of times, she looked at me as if she knew me, though. Perhaps she'd seen me in the village. She didn't say anything about it."

"It's sad, a professional young woman like that. Was she married?"

"I believe not," Stuart answered. Nodding towards the newspaper, he added, "It says here she lived alone. And in my office she told me she hadn't discussed her patient with anyone else. I think she must have been something of a loner."

"Dedicated to her work perhaps."

"Apparently so," Stuart replied.

"Very commendable," said his wife.

Stuart sighed. "I wouldn't have wished this on her but, I have to say, from a YPI perspective, it's worked out pretty well. Dr Crear was threatening all sorts against us, just because she'd got a bee in her bonnet about one of our drug trials. She could have crippled our health programme."

"Every cloud has a silver lining," said Mrs Urling-Clark. "But I still think it's a pity with a dedicated doctor, someone so caring."

"Caring *and* misguided."

"We all need guidance some time, Stuart. Anyway, do you want a cup of tea?"

Picking up the newspaper again, he said, "Yes. That'd be nice. Thanks."

35

The receptionist at Addenbrooke's was very cagey. She wouldn't tell Kyle the whereabouts of Dr Helen Crear. "I can't give out information by phone," she said. "I'm sure you understand. You could be anyone. I suggest you contact her family."

"I don't know them," Kyle replied from his flat. "I'm a professional colleague. I'll tell you what. If Dr Crear's not around, can you put me through to the doctor who's looking after a patient called Dwight Grant in Intensive Care? It's urgent."

"Yes. Hold, please."

When the doctor revealed Helen's accident, Kyle was aghast. He stared in horror at the apartment block opposite without seeing anything at all. His mind was occupied with unbearable images of his own brother, Professor Fleetwood's plane plunging from the sky, and Helen Crear's attractive face.

"Mr Proctor?"

"Er, yes. I'm here. That's . . . awful." Kyle hoped that Helen Crear had been mown down only by a joyrider. The alternative was much, much worse. Yet, he could not bring himself to believe that, like his brother's accident, it was entirely innocent. Helen had been a thorn in Yttria's side and the key to Dwight Grant's treatment and now. . . Her accident was suspiciously convenient to YPI. No doubt Urling-Clark would prefer life without either Helen Crear or Dwight Grant. To Kyle, Dr Crear's death had the same smell, the same stench, as the removal of Brandon Fleetwood. This time it involved a car and not an aeroplane, but it was the same imagination behind the same conspiracy.

In that moment Kyle felt utterly alone. He was in a foreign country and he no longer had anyone to talk to about his darkest fears, not even a distant Helen Crear. He had new information on black American prisoners and Westland inmates who had been subjected to the toxic SCP19 and the responsibility for using this knowledge now lay solely with Kyle. Holding himself together, he explained the Westland drug trial to the Cambridge doctor in case it shed any light on Dwight's treatment and then he hung up. Kyle didn't really know what else to do but, to scupper the weapon, he thought that he ought to confront someone with the facts. He had already met the man at the head of Yttria Inc., but. . .

Kyle jumped when the phone rang. "Hello. Kyle Proctor," he answered.

It was Max. "Are you all right? You sound a bit . . . jittery."

"I'm fine," Kyle lied.

"Good. How about this weekend for that trip to little ol' Memphis?"

"Er, yes. OK," he replied absently. Under the circumstances, it was much easier to agree than to explain a change of heart.

"It's a deal."

"Max?"

"Yeah?"

"Do you know Tristan Lockhart?" Kyle asked.

"I nod when I see him but no, I don't *know* him. Not really. Why?"

"No, I met him but I don't know him either. I was thinking of going to see him."

"You've got to be joking. He moves in a different galaxy. What d'ya want to see him for anyway?"

"Well," Kyle said, "there's something going down with SCP19."

"Like what?"

"I can't say on the phone. It's . . . sensitive."

Max didn't reply immediately. After a pause, he said, "Sensitive, eh? Then you don't want to see Mr Lockhart. Drop it."

"Why?"

"Because. . . Think about it. If you're wrong, nothing's going down, you'll look a fool," Max said. "If you're right, he's not gonna give you a medal, is he? He's not gonna be happy a whole bunch if you stir things up. Either way, you're shot. You listening to me?"

"Yes, but. . ." Kyle stopped. Max had a point, of course. "No, you're right. Thanks."

"I'll see you at work – to arrange the weekend. Cheers."

Kyle put the phone down and let out a long breath. He was still unsure, still alone.

And he was still struggling to absorb the shock of Helen Crear's death.

"I heard you had some excitement – and some good news – yesterday. A grandson, granddaughter?"

Tristan smiled broadly. "A little boy, arriving a couple of weeks late." In the back of Tristan's mind, a quiet voice added, "A little boy with the sickle-cell trait."

"And how's Mum?"

"Doing fine. We talked some on the phone. They're both doing just great."

"Ah, I knew there was a reason for that smirk on your face. A grandson or a superdrug. One or the other."

At his neighbour's party, Tristan Lockhart was chatting to the host while his wife had been taken away to see some new acquisition. It was that sort of area: downtown in the exclusive Buckhead district where the big earners of Atlanta lived. It was an affluent and trendy neighbourhood of large houses, rolling lawns and neat lines of well proportioned trees. It housed the best shops, the hip art galleries, and the hottest restaurants where it was normal to wait two hours for a designer meal. In Atlanta it was *the* place to see and be seen in.

227

Tristan's neighbour was a talkative and argumentative lawyer. "Thinking of babies, is Yttria still tinkering with human genes?" The way he pronounced *tinkering* indicated disapproval. As an evangelical Christian, he believed that Tristan's work trespassed on land that belonged only to God.

"We're in on the human genome project, sure. We've got to be. It's the future of health."

"And, in that future, can people like your daughter ask for their babies to be free of cancer?"

"Yes, we'll deliver that soon."

"And how about making a baby into a genius or top-flight athlete?" asked the lawyer.

Tristan hesitated. He was about to move from the shallow end into the deep. "Like it or not, that'll come as well. At least, it'll come as an ethical issue. Me, I'm happy to manipulate genes for medical reasons so our grandchildren won't have cancer or whatever, but I'm much less comfortable with tinkering, as you put it, for cosmetic reasons. There's nothing abnormal about being smarter, stronger, dumber, weaker than other people, it's all within the normal range – but something like cystic fibrosis *is* an abnormality. It should be laid to rest with gene therapy." He avoided using sickle-cell anaemia as an example so that he gave no hint of Yttria's current direction.

"OK, Tristan, fixing cancer's obviously medical. I can see that. It's a good thing, you say. At the other end of the street, making a baby into a blue-eyed blond is obviously cosmetic. You say that's a step too far. How about something that's somewhere in the middle? How about ageing? That's partly medical, partly cosmetic. What would you say if I wanted my grandchildren to live for ever and always look young?"

"The technology's not impossible," Tristan answered, knocking back the rest of his beer. He needed it if he was going to get through this conversation. "Science will learn how to switch off the ageing process, one way or another, one day. That's for sure. Maybe in ten years, almost certainly in a hundred. Then immortality beckons."

"Now, here's something that really bothers me, Tristan. More beer? Immortality's not for humans. That's God's prerogative."

"Here's some good news for you, then. It's not my job to make the decisions. I'm only a scientist. I just find out what's feasible and what isn't."

"Any tampering with nature's an insult to God. You're trying to make science the new religion."

"No, I'm not," Tristan said. "It's not a case of one taking over the other. We need both. If you want to know how a brain works, you don't go to the church. You go to science. If you want to know how the owner of that brain should react to a neighbour in need, you sure don't ask a scientist. You call the church. See? They don't tread on each other's toes. As far as gene therapy's concerned, it's your job – the public's job – to draw the line between what it wants and what's a no-go area. That's where ethics and religion come in."

"Mmm. OK, but who's going to be chosen to live for ever and who isn't? I'd say anyone who wants immortality should immediately rule themselves out. They must be nuts."

Trying to make light of it, Tristan smiled. "You've got a point there." It was supposed to be a relaxing party and not an ethics meeting, but Tristan felt as if he had to justify his business.

The lawyer was warming to his theme. "There's another thing with all these new cures. Who can afford them? I can, you can. The Buckhead and Bill Gates types. Who else? Good men in India, Pakistan, Ethiopia? No chance."

"That's another ethical issue for the public, for politicians, to solve. Sure, it's starting in rich nations. We're the ones with the resources."

Interrupting, Tristan's next-door neighbour said, "It'll widen the gap between the haves and the have-nots. Your grandchildren or great-grandchildren – and mine – they won't get cancer and they won't get old. People in poor countries will be cursed with cancer, crippling old age and the rest of it because they can't afford our technology. Right now, thousands die every week in the tropics from curable diseases because they can't afford the drugs we take for granted. The expensive ones that'll come along next, they'll just make matters worse. And what are our drug companies doing about it? They're working out how to give well paid Americans designer babies." He waved a hand dismissively, as if disgusted, and nearly spilt his drink.

"I've got a lot of sympathy with that," Tristan replied. "But it happens because, in the cold light of economics, there isn't a viable market in poor countries."

"But there's a need."

"Oh sure, there's a need," Tristan agreed. "No one's going to argue with that. Speaking for the drug companies, though, we've got to get a good return on our research investment otherwise we're out of business and that doesn't help anyone, rich or poor. Governments and charities will have to cough up to make it worthwhile to market our products in developing nations."

The lawyer slapped Tristan on the back. "Sorry. You come round for a drink and a chat and I lecture you. But it's not you I'm getting at, you know. It's the system. Now, don't get me started on politics or you'll be here all night."

The two businessmen laughed politely.

Behind the new grandfather's laugh, though, there was a tangle of thoughts. His company set out to find a cure for a worldwide disease. In England, they were carrying on that search. But, on the way, they'd stumbled on a highly marketable biological weapon. How would Tristan feel if one of their future customers actually used SCP19? Who could hate people with the sickle-cell gene that much? Where does their hate come from? Newborn babies don't hate anyone, that's for sure. So, somewhere along the line, they learn to hate. Who teaches them? It must be parents and other adults who teach the young to hate. And if one of those adults deployed SCP19, would the company and its clever technology be to blame? No. You can't blame inanimate objects. You've got to point the finger at the people who decide to use them, the people who hate, not the people who sold the smart weapon. If gun manufacturers could sleep easy in their beds, Tristan should be able to do the same.

36

Paul sat anonymously at the rear of the chapel. Occasionally, some of the mourners at the front would turn furtively and glance at him. One of them looked exactly – eerily – like Helen but thirty years older. Presumably she was Helen's mother. Anyway, it was obvious that they were wondering who he was. But Paul did not feel like introducing himself or speaking at all. For Paul, it was a time for silence, for thinking, for regretting.

He was on official leave from the university. There had been an unexpected death, he'd explained to the Personnel Manager, and he was the one who had to make the arrangements and sort out all of the repercussions. He also needed time to grieve. Perhaps he'd led the university authorities to believe that the death had happened in the Turrell family, but he had not actually lied. The university had declared itself to be in sympathy with his request for leave and granted him the time and space he needed to put things in order.

At Helen's funeral service, someone said something inadequate and the plain wooden box rolled automatically through the curtains that separated the chapel from the crematorium. It seemed so mechanical, so cold. No one escorted her, no one held her hand, no one even looked at her. Concealed inside the coffin, her body slid out of this world on a conveyer belt like an obsolete commodity. It was as if everyone was ashamed of her death and could not bear to look upon it. Paul wondered if any staff from Yttria were present. They were the ones who should be most embarrassed and ashamed.

Slowly, the chapel emptied of its mourners. They left to view the floral tributes outside, leaving Paul alone to stare at the place where Helen had lain. He tried to avoid thinking about what was happening to her behind the curtains, tried to remember her as she was when he last saw her. Affectionate, frustrated, compassionate, and beautiful. After five minutes, or maybe half an hour, he got up and walked away.

Outside, he knocked accidentally into a woman who was standing by the door, gazing intently at the funeral party. She was in her early twenties with cropped dark hair and frameless glasses. A camera hung down in front of her chest.

"Sorry," Paul muttered.

"No problem."

As he walked away, Paul glanced at her over his shoulder, wondering what the woman was doing at the crematorium. She certainly hadn't come to pay her respects to Helen. She was dressed from head to foot in inappropriate light blue denim.

Usually the police force co-operated with Victoria

Scates. She got the information she needed to write a good story and they made sure her article contained only the information they wanted in the public domain. This time, though, she was getting nowhere. Straight after the funeral, she asked the press spokesman, "Did Dr Crear ever work in gynaecology?"

"No."

"How about research?"

"No."

Victoria rested her elbows on the counter. "Hey, let's play a different game. You don't want me standing here guessing all day. Why don't you just tell me if she had anything to do with Addenbrooke's . . . difficulties?"

"Ask Addenbrooke's."

"I did," Victoria responded. "They're tight-lipped about it all."

"Aren't you supposed to be an investigative journalist?" the policeman responded with a grin. "So investigate."

"Come on. You know what I'm getting at. A doctor's house keels over, she dies, and a load of samples go up in smoke. Ten-to-one on, it's about the hospital's little problems."

"No comment."

"When it's about babies dying it's always sensitive, I know, but surely you can give me something."

"Obviously the hospital didn't. Neither can I. Not this time."

Victoria sighed. "Are you really going to say 'No comment' to everything?"

"You got it."

"All right," Victoria said, walking out. "I guess this time we can't do business."

37

While Max drove, window wound down and elbow resting casually on the lip, he asked, "What's this thing with SCP19, then?"

Distracted from the Tennessee flatlands, a sea of cotton, corn, tobacco and bean fields, Kyle said, "Well . . . nothing really." After all, Kyle was not sure how far Max could be trusted.

Max looked at his passenger. "Nothing?" His eyes back on the long, straight road again, he added, "That's not what you said before."

"No, but. . ."

"Do I look like a company spy?" said Max with a wide grin, fingering one of his sideburns. "Or a reporter?"

They were on State Road 57, heading west, closing in on Memphis and the Mississippi. Max was a new friend and Kyle did not know much about him, but he was sympathetic and Kyle was desperate to offload on someone. Kyle was very grateful for Max's friendship in this land of strangers. Besides, Kyle was convinced that Max wasn't the type to shop him to the company hierarchy. He could not take an Elvis impersonator seriously as a YPI agent. While Max had to be intelligent to hold down his Yttria job, Kyle assessed him as a harmless fool. "I . . . er. . ." Kyle breathed deeply, cleared his throat and confided his worries about SCP19.

"Wow," Max said, "that's hot stuff. Have you been to Mr Lockhart about it?"

"No."

"I still wouldn't if I were you."

"What do you think? You've worked on it. Is it a weapon?"

Max shook his head. "Far as I know, it's a cure for sickle-cell anaemia."

"But you knew about the side effects."

"That's why it's not out there on the market, that's why it's still being improved. A few black prisoners is one thing, a rogue drug on the market is a different ball game."

"When I first met you, you implied the side effects might be useful."

"Over here, we don't have the same squeamishness as you Brits."

"What does that mean?"

"It means I don't have a problem if Yttria *is* selling it as a weapon. Christ, we live with guns, missiles, a whole bunch of things. It makes us feel secure. If we've got a biological weapon as well, I'm even more secure. Fine."

"But what if you had the sickle-cell gene?"

"Being as white as they come, that's not very likely, is it?"

"That's just an accident of birth. What about all those Americans who *have* got it?"

Max glanced across at Kyle. "I don't see your point. If you've got a full arsenal, a full range of different weapons, you've got flexibility. That means you're gonna have the right tool for whatever job, doesn't it? In any society with weapons, you just got to trust they're used properly. Freedom and security with responsibility: that's the American way, not banning everything in sight." He nodded ahead and said, "Anyway, that's what you've really come for."

In the distance, Memphis loomed. Even from several kilometres away, Kyle could see that it was another city that reached for the sky.

"Nearly there," Max announced.

Kyle did not try to resume the conversation. He'd heard enough to know that Max's viewpoint was radically different from his own. Kyle felt just as isolated, and just as alarmed.

At the edge of downtown Memphis ran Mulberry Street where the Lorraine Motel had been transformed. Clearly it wasn't a motel any more. "What's that?" asked Kyle, the tourist. "Half motel, half something else."

Keeping his eye on the road, Max responded halfheartedly, "It's a museum." He pulled over and then, when traffic allowed, he backed up to the National Civil Rights Museum. He couldn't bring himself to say that since 1991 the building had become a shrine. "It was where what's-'is-name got shot. Nineteen sixty-something."

"Ah, yes. Martin Luther King."

Max replied, "Yeah."

"I've seen some of the speeches he made, I mean, on video. Amazing." His voice full of admiration, Kyle gazed at the strange museum. "He was into defiance, breaking bad laws, without using violence. No wonder he got the Nobel Peace Prize. "

Grinning, Max joked, "But he's not the real King in Memphis."

"Now, how did I know you were going to say that?" Kyle thought that he could understand Max's coolness. If Kyle were showing Max around London, he'd find it hard to sound excited about Buckingham Palace. Familiarity blunted enthusiasm and sometimes bred contempt.

"Want a Coke and stuff?" Max asked. "Grab the cans and lunch boxes on the back seat, will you?"

Kyle opened the first plastic container and smiled. "Not exactly a feast." He showed the contents to Max.

Max glanced down at the single egg. "Oh, sorry. Wrong one. That's been in the car for ever. I should've chucked it ages ago. The food must be in the other one."

While they tucked into sandwiches and Coke, Max looked round for a waste bin. Spotting two police officers instead, Max gave his can to Kyle, stuffed the rest of his food into his mouth and put the car into gear. Pulling away, he said, "Time to move on before I get done for parking. We'll go to Beale Street, home of the blues, a couple of blocks north of here." For some reason, he let out a nervous laugh.

When they cruised down Beale Street, Kyle recognized it instantly, even though he'd never been there before. The place oozed music and creativity. Kyle listened at the open window. Thankfully, it was too early in the year to experience the true heat and humidity of Memphis, but it was not cold, despite the breeze. Kyle loved the easy feel of Beale Street. Almost every face was black. The moody sound of blues burst from the open doors of bars, clubs and barbecue joints. In the park on his left, a small appreciative crowd had gathered round a guitarist who was putting a new spin, a rap, on a blues tune. Kyle couldn't see the boy's face but he guessed that he was about sixteen or seventeen years old. To Kyle's ear, the music sounded good and earthy. The whole area thrilled Kyle. "Great songs," he said. "You won't agree, but it spawned so much, the blues."

Max cringed visibly. "Great songs? Aw, you're joking. Totally tuneless music."

Kyle shook his head but did not argue. Seeing a statue in the park, he asked, "Who's the big guy with the trumpet?"

"He's a blues man called Handy. He wrote 'Memphis Blues' here in Beale Street. That's why the place's called Handy Park."

Max pulled over opposite the statue of W.C. Handy and finished his Coke. Then he took the plastic container with the egg in it and turned to his British passenger. "Are you a good shot?" He nodded towards a bin in the park on Kyle's side of the car. "Do me a favour and chuck it."

"I might miss."

"Go on. It's no big deal."

Kyle stopped tapping his foot in time to the teenager's blues. "No chance. I'll hit someone or make a complete mess."

"Oh, all right." Opening his door, Max muttered, "I'll get rid of it."

Distracted from the young black singer, Kyle watched Max walk across to the waste bin and tip the egg into it without touching the shell itself. He dropped the egg from such a height that it must have broken in the bin. Then he strode back to the car and jumped in. "That's better." As soon as there was a gap in the traffic, Max accelerated down the street. More relaxed, he said with a smile, "Now I'm gonna teach you proper music, the real reason for coming to Memphis. First, we're going to Sun Studio up on Union, another two or three blocks north. It's where Roy Orbison, Jerry Lee Lewis, and, of course, Elvis cut their sound. You'll see. Then

242

we go to Graceland to see how the repairs are doing. Some of it might be open. On the way," Max added, "you can see a whole bundle of history. It's all here, from civil war to civil unrest."

Kyle looked askance at Max. "Haven't you got past civil unrest yet?"

Max grunted. "On the surface, yes, but there's an undercurrent. . ." He said no more.

In the Beale Street Bar-B-Que, wallpapered with the photographs of celebrities, Nathan McQueen was trying to unwind over a beer and barbecue. Two officers, his armed bodyguards, sat either side of him and competed with each other to name as many of the stars as possible. Nathan didn't join in. His troubled mind was still absorbed with ugly images from that night at the Pyramid.

Armed bodyguards were no protection for the assassin that swept unseen into the bar on a restless breeze. There, it did what fists, batons, nails and a hammer had failed to do to Nathan. Guns and muscle were useless against it. They couldn't stop Nathan becoming the first victim, the first to be rushed to hospital.

38

After getting the Yttria Inc. telephone number from the Atlanta company's Internet site, Paul tried calling Kyle Proctor for the third time. After a few minutes, he was gratified to hear an English accent. "Is that Kyle?"

The response was full of curiosity. "Yes, speaking."

Assuming that someone might be eavesdropping, Paul chose his words carefully. "The Kyle who used to work with Dr Helen Crear?"

"Yes." The tone was even more inquisitive.

"I'm Paul Turrell, speaking to you from Cambridge. I'm an analyst who also worked with her."

"Ah, yes. I think she mentioned you to me, ages ago."

"Then you remember what I was working on?"

"Yes, but. . . It's difficult here at work. . ."

"Yes. I understand you're busy. If you give me your home number, I'll call you this evening – or in the early hours over here."

"OK."

At one o'clock in the morning, Paul called back and introduced himself as Helen's boyfriend. He told Kyle everything he knew, and everything he suspected, about the central-heating explosion that had wrecked Helen's house and the hit-and-run accident that had finished her life.

In return, Kyle told Paul what he had learned in America. This time, Paul noticed that the young man's voice conveyed relief. Plainly, Kyle Proctor was eager to share his thoughts. Perhaps it made him feel less isolated. Perhaps Kyle hoped that Paul had a formula for ridding the world of SCP19.

Sprawled on the hotel bed, Paul said, "So, as far as you're concerned, what Helen thought is all true?"

"No doubt about it."

"Thanks. That's what I wanted to know, even if we can't prove anything. We can't, can we? There's nothing solid to take to the police, is there? It's just what you and Helen have seen and heard. No print-outs or hard evidence."

"'Fraid not."

Paul didn't have a quick fix for corruption on such a grand scale, but at least he now had the confidence to go for YPI's throat. It was easier for Paul because, unlike Kyle, he didn't carry a lot of baggage. Kyle worked within the organization and drew his salary from it. That made him very vulnerable. Paul was not so encumbered. Yttria did not even know who he was, although he guessed that it would not take the managers long to find out. In fact, he hoped that they would soon find out who he was.

As a prominent academic researcher in analytical chemistry, Dr Turrell was welcomed by the scientists when he gatecrashed the forensic department. As an outsider, though, he could not get near the car that had mowed Helen down. He was told that forensic evidence could not have led the police to the conclusion that joyriders were responsible because there was no forensic evidence. All of the fingerprints, hairs and fibres belonged to the car owner.

Paul was amazed and annoyed. "Doesn't that speak for itself?" he asked.

"What?"

"No evidence. This wasn't an amateur!" Paul declared. "Since when did joyriders avoid leaving evidence? Since when did they know what sort of clothes avoid leaving fibres?"

"We just gave the police the facts. We didn't tell them what to deduce. I suppose, without evidence, they just went with the obvious: a joyriders' favourite car was nicked from a place where joyriders nick cars and it was abandoned on the A14 where joyriders abandon cars. Police like it simple."

"Yeah, simple. Naïve would be another word. They've been led by the nose to the result a professional wanted."

"You may think that. I couldn't possibly comment," she said wryly.

It was the same story with Helen's house. The lack of evidence led the investigating officers to the conclusion that it was an innocent accident. Yet Addenbrooke's research wing hadn't gone up in flames by sheer bad luck. The stench of petrol was too conspicuous. The scene-of-the-crime team did not need sophisticated methods, just good noses, to prove that it was arson. But who had done it? Yet again, there was no evidence.

"The police are making an assumption," the forensic scientist told him in a quiet voice, as if someone was listening to her dissent.

Paul sighed. "What's that?"

"There's been a bit of a scandal up at the hospital."

"Oh?"

"Yes. Some parents are on the warpath. Their babies died there, all perfectly innocent and natural, but, when they got the bodies back, they weren't told some organs had been removed. They buried or cremated what they thought were whole babies. Wrong. Some parts had been removed for research, but someone forgot to ask permission from the mums and dads. Now it's come out, there's a right old rumpus going on."

"So, the police reckon the parents got their own back by setting fire to the place. That's ridiculous!" Paul cried. "If they want their children whole for a proper burial, why would they destroy the organs? It doesn't make sense."

"No, it doesn't," she replied. "So they came up with another idea. Some embarrassed member of staff at the hospital decided to destroy the evidence of their forgetfulness."

"Does that make any more sense?"

"Not to me," she admitted. "No one's going to ruin all that research to protect their own part in a scandal."

"No. And burning some evidence wouldn't stop an inquiry anyway."

The next day, Paul went to Westland Young Offender Institution. He was not put off by three wardens and one very obstinate secretary. He insisted on seeing the doctor and barged straight into the surgery. After all, Paul thought that the medic might have been the last person to see Helen alive – apart from a killer through a windscreen.

As soon as Paul saw the posters advertising Yttria's drugs, as soon as he introduced himself as Helen's boyfriend and saw the doctor's wary expression, he realized that this man knew more than he was going to admit. There was a degree of guilt, hidden just below the surface of his hard face. At once, Paul guessed what had happened and worked out his strategy. He didn't care that it was exceptionally dangerous.

"What did Helen – Dr Crear – ask you?"

"Well, I think she thought she was going to walk in and run blood tests on some of our lads who volunteered for YPI drug trials. Just like that."

"And it wasn't possible?"

"No."

"So, how did the two of you leave it?"

"I said I could have words in the right ears and put

her in touch with offenders who were willing to talk about their health. It'd be up to her to get their consent for any tests, or back off if they wouldn't agree to it."

"And that was it?"

"As far as I recall."

Paul asked, "She didn't persist or say anything else?"

"I don't think so."

"Did you tell anyone she'd been putting her nose into Yttria's business?"

"Look, Dr. . ."

"Turrell."

"I don't have to say anything to you. I'm only helping because of her unfortunate demise. I sympathize but I certainly don't have to put up with your innuendo."

Paul ignored him. "Did you tell anyone at Yttria about her visit here?"

"What are you trying to accuse me of?"

Paul leaned on the doctor's desk, getting uncomfortably close to him. "I'm accusing you and YPI of engineering her death."

The doctor's mouth opened but not a lot came out. "That's. . ."

"Don't you medics take the Hippocratic oath?" Paul asked. "Doesn't it say you'll never harm *anyone*? That'd include patients *and* other doctors."

"Yes. And I haven't—"

"Doesn't it tell you never to give advice that'll cause death?"

"Look, I'm not standing for this." His hand reached for the telephone.

On top of the phone, Paul clamped his strong hand over the doctor's. "And doesn't it say you'll only prescribe beneficial drugs?"

"That's exactly what I've done. Now, I'm warning you. . ."

Calculating every move, Paul let go abruptly and stepped back. "Thank you. You've told me all I want to know. At least, your face has." He turned and left.

Just as Paul hoped, the doctor picked up the phone as soon as his unwanted visitor closed the door.

For Paul, it was now a matter of patience but, while he waited for the storm to brew, he did not see any merit in suspending his stubborn pursuit. He was quite content to make himself more of a pest to YPI.

Helen's MP was a junior minister in the Department of Defence and she held a surgery for her Cambridge constituents every other Wednesday. Paul sat down on the other side of her table and, like a father talking to a teacher at a school's Parent Evening, he was given ten minutes of the politician's precious time.

Paul began, "I thought you'd like to know how a prominent member of your constituency, Dr Helen Crear, met her death."

To prove that she kept up to date, or that at least she read the local newspaper, the MP said, "A road accident. It was awful. I'm so sorry. I'm still encouraging the local authorities to install more traffic calming—"

Paul was having to get used to butting in. "I don't think a few humps would've stopped an assassination."

"A what?"

Succinctly, Paul filled her in on Helen's murder, YPI, SCP19, Brandon Fleetwood's accident, the Westland deaths.

It was clear that the politician was struggling to believe Paul. Yet an MP had a duty to listen and take note. She also had a right to be sceptical. She had to think about YPI's commitment to employment and sponsorship in the area, and she had her own career to consider. Listening intently to Paul, at least she had the good grace to become quite pale. Trying to steer a middle course between gullibility and disbelief, she said, "This is all very serious. Very . . . sensitive. You'd better leave it with me so I can look into it, and ask the police to double-check their findings." Then she glanced at her watch.

Paul did not expect much more. The politician might do something about it and she might not, but she had served her purpose. If anything happened to Paul in the next few days, this MP would be in a position to raise questions. If anything happened to Paul, this MP would know exactly why. If anything happened to Paul, YPI was finished. At least, he hoped so.

Next, he sweet-talked his way into the Cambridge University Chemistry Department in Lensfield Road. He offered to share his analytical expertise with both staff and students in return for the occasional use of some of their facilities. Once he'd struck a bargain, he walked back to his hotel. It was an easy ten-minute stroll.

He searched the telephone directory in his room without success. Neither S Urling-Clark nor C Ingoe were listed. Presumably they did not want calls and visits by animal rights groups and opponents of genetic modification, so they remained ex-directory. Pity. In his drive to make himself as big a nuisance as possible, Paul would have gone to each of their homes to insult and, if necessary, assault them. Instead, he plugged his laptop into the phone line and visited the Yttria website where everything was rosy and all manner of health issues were being resolved. Finding Urling-Clark's and Ingoe's e-mail addresses, he left each of them a terse electronic message requesting an urgent meeting to discuss Helen Crear's death, Dwight Grant's health and SCP19. That, Paul thought, should get their attention and elicit a response.

Paul uncoupled the computer, turned it off, and went to the bar downstairs. He had already struck up a useful friendship with the barman. Ordering a whisky, he said, "Have one yourself. How are things?"

"Thanks. Could be worse."

"You haven't heard Cambridge United's result, then?"

"Ah, now that couldn't be much worse," the barman replied, handing over the drink and adding the charge to Paul's bill.

"Any news of that staff vacancy?" Paul asked.

"They're interviewing someone tomorrow – a man, I think – but I don't know anything about it, or when he'll start if he gets the job."

Paul nodded. Lifting up his glass, he said, "Cheers. Let me know, eh?"

"Sure. Thanks for the drink."

"You're welcome."

Later, with an unwise volume of alcohol sloshing in his bloodstream, Paul went back upstairs. He switched on the television and promptly ignored it. In his empty room, he stood by the window and, turning his back on the empty bed, stared at the empty night-time sky above Cambridge.

39

From the window of Kyle's empty apartment, there did not seem to be a night-time sky above Atlanta. Tall, illuminated buildings punctured the darkness and pushed nature away. Kyle's mind was in turmoil. Behind him, the TV news station was broadcasting continuously from Memphis. It was like watching a war unfolding, the body count mounting. In this war, though, all of the dead and injured were black. An activist called Nathan McQueen had been the first to die. Now there were a few more deaths, tens unconscious, hundreds dizzy and fainting. No one knew exact numbers but, depressingly, everyone knew that the numbers were rising. Memphis was in the grip of a new version of the Black Death.

The television commentators were speculating on a mystery bug, a bad batch of beer in the Beale Street bars, a leakage of a toxic chemical from some laboratory, food poisoning, an outbreak of legionnaire's disease, mass hysteria, a foreigner with a contagious disease flying in to Memphis, anything they could think of. The more outrageous the theory, the higher the ratings. They were interviewing anyone they could pin down in front of a camera for more than thirty seconds. Police officers, witnesses, paramedics, passing crackpots, politicians, victims, community leaders, psychologists, and a born-again Christian who had foretold that the wrath of God would visit Memphis. Really, none of them had got the faintest idea.

If Kyle Proctor had been there, in front of the cameras, he would have come up with a different theory. In shock, he would have related how some racist could have released a smart biological weapon aimed exclusively at blacks. Of course, the audience would have listed him among the passing crackpots with more imagination than sense.

The awful events in Memphis made him think about Max Levine and that egg. As far as Kyle could tell from the news broadcasts, the outbreak was centred on Handy Park where Max had dumped it. Could it be. . .? No, surely not. Kyle hoped not. Then again, Max had tried to persuade him to dispose of the egg, perhaps in an attempt to shift the blame. Thinking about it, Max might have cracked it outside the National Civil Rights Museum if those cops had not been on patrol. And it was another location that was important to the black community.

And what was an egg anyway? An egg was nature's device for nurturing new life. A sealed shell for protection, packed full of nutrients – protein, water and fat – for healthy growth. OK, Max's egg was designed for a chick embryo, but perhaps it would have provided an effective nursery for the SCP19 virus as well. The needs of a growing embryo and a multiplying virus

255

were much the same. Yet how could the virus have got inside a chicken's egg? Only by deliberate spiking. Kyle's stomach was as tight and painful as it was when he woke in the middle of the night with his brother on his mind.

He had to get a message to the authorities. They had to check everyone in the area for the sickle-cell gene. If the sick and dying all carried it, Kyle probably had the answer. If people who remained healthy did not have the faulty gene, Kyle definitely had the answer. Someone had released SCP19 in Memphis.

The Storm Force website was buzzing. On its Bullet Board, there was no talk of a crisis. There was only delight. Amid the false claims of responsibility and credit, amid the wild enthusiasm, one simple chilling message stood out. *I told you I could do it. Feeling good, Light.*

On-line, Kyle looked up the telephone numbers of the Regional Medical Center and the police department in Memphis, Tennessee. When he tried the numbers, though, they were engaged continuously. Frustrated, he could not get his message about the sickle-cell gene through to the authorities. When emergency telephone numbers appeared on the TV screen, he tried those as well, but again all that he got was the engaged signal. Until he fell asleep, fully clothed on the bed, he heard only the sounds of heated TV commentators and the tiresome tone of jammed telephone lines.

The authorities in Memphis were 544 kilometres away. When Kyle woke up early in the morning, television still on, he had little choice but to try the telephone again. He got through at the third attempt. But the police officer who recorded his name, address and ideas about a smart biological weapon in an egg did not take him seriously. Oh, she took notes, as she had been ordered, but she had been up most of the night listening to wild claims, ranting and raving, and devastated relatives. She was tired and cynical. In his Atlanta apartment, Kyle could imagine her entering his theory into a folder under the heading "Farfetched in the extreme". He could imagine how his message would end up in a large document that would be examined when all of the plausible lines of investigation had been exhausted.

Now he knew what he had to do. He hung up and hurriedly got ready for work. If Max Levine was behind the Memphis disaster, then Kyle should do exactly what Max had advised him not to do. Suspecting that the emergency services would sooner listen to the president of Yttria Inc. than to a young visiting Brit, Kyle decided to confront Tristan Lockhart. He would convince Mr Lockhart to contact the authorities and admit that one of his products might be causing the crisis. It was a bold, brave and probably foolish move, but then again it suited Kyle's style and mood.

The president's secretary presented a considerable barrier. Screwing up her nose she murmured, "Kyle Proctor. I don't think. . ."

Kyle had thought about this. He interrupted. "When I started here, Mr Lockhart said if I ever had a problem I should come and see him personally."

"Really?"

Kyle nodded. "Sure did." He thought that he'd get away with the lie because it sounded like the sort of thing a caring president might have said to a new employee over a first coffee, even though he wouldn't have meant it. Neither Tristan Lockhart nor his secretary was likely to remember if he had actually said it.

"Well, I can't promise. . . What shall I say it's about?"

"Memphis."

"Memphis?"

"Yes, Memphis."

Intrigued, the secretary walked into Tristan's office.

Fifteen minutes later, against all the odds, the company's new young recruit found himself in front of the president in a spectacular nineteenth-floor office. Out of the window, the huge CNN TV Center towered.

"How you enjoying the States, Kyle? Settled in OK?"

Kyle was tempted to reply, "I sure am," but he wasn't in the right frame of mind. "Yes," he said. "It's fine."

"And work?"

"Work's fine as well," he answered, anxious to get on with the real topic of conversation.

"Good. Now what's this about Memphis?"

Of course, Tristan had never told the English boy to come and see him but he admired the kid's nerve. That was why he'd agreed to see him for a few minutes. There was another reason as well. Tristan had a vested interest in Memphis. His own daughter and her family were there. At least, they had been there until the news broke last night. Tristan had got on the phone straight away. No matter what was causing the health scare, it was no place for a newborn baby. That was for sure. It didn't take much for Tristan to persuade his daughter and Gerry to evacuate and drive to his own house in Buckhead, Atlanta. The place was easily big enough for all of them.

Inviting the British boy to sit down, Tristan asked, "What's this about Memphis?"

"I meant the outbreak there."

Tristan nodded. "What about it?"

"Doesn't it sound familiar to you?"

"Familiar? No. What do you mean?"

The Brit took a deep breath. "It looks like the side effects of SCP19 to me."

"SCP19?"

"Yes."

Tristan drew a breath, but his discomfort was barely

259

noticeable. "You know about that?" His colleagues in Cambridge hadn't told him that their troublemaker was so well informed.

Kyle was beginning to loosen up so he answered, "I sure do."

"Well, my bucks are on food poisoning. Salmonella perhaps, in one of those chicken barbecue joints."

"The last time I saw those symptoms, it was in a file on black prisoners who fell ill during Yttria drug trials."

Tristan sat upright. No wonder Cambridge wanted to get rid him. He was hotter than he looked, definitely major league. "How did you come by that information?"

Kyle shrugged. "I saw it on someone else's monitor. But how I know's not important."

"I think you'll find big differences with this Memphis outbreak."

"Like what?"

"For one thing, we don't recruit in Memphis. They weren't on a drug trial so they couldn't have come into contact with SCP19 or any product from this company."

"What if someone took SCP19 from here and released it in Memphis?"

"You're joking!" Tristan kept a sceptical expression on his face but, inside, his stomach churned. He'd had the same horrifying thought last night just before he pulled his daughter, grandson and Gerry out of the

260

danger area. "That can't happen," he declared. "Our security's too good for anyone to smuggle it out."

"Do you know Max Levine?"

"Max Levine." Tristan hesitated and then, by intercom, asked his secretary to dig out Levine's personnel file. "The name's familiar maybe, but . . . no. Not really. What are you saying?"

In silence, Tristan listened to Kyle Proctor's opinion. The young chemist painted a believable and frightening picture. Tristan would have to rely on the company's technical experts to tell him if an egg was a realistic container for SCP19, but it sounded feasible to him. Yet, if Kyle's guesswork turned out to be true, what were Max Levine's motives? When Kyle had finished, Tristan the grandfather wanted to say one thing but Tristan the president of Yttria had to say another. "That's quite a spin you're putting on it. All very imaginative."

"But—"

"Listen," Tristan said, leaning forward, "no one can get SCP19 out of here. Do you hear me? It can't happen. I'll check out this Max Levine for you but. . ." He sat back with his hands behind his head.

Kyle looked desperate. "That's not enough."

"What are you suggesting? Do you want me to have him arrested on no evidence at all?"

"No."

"What then?"

"You could find out if he was in Memphis the day a homeless man called Mitch went into a coma."

Tristan frowned. "Mitch."

"I heard about him on the news. He died – it'd be about two weeks ago – with the same sort of symptoms. And there's something else. You could get the hospital to test these new victims for the sickle-cell trait. That'd tell you straight away if it's SCP19."

Tristan nodded thoughtfully. "OK. That's sensible enough, I guess. When some of them don't have the gene, it'll put your mind at rest."

"And if they all have it?"

"They won't."

"But if they do?"

Tristan asked, "What are you driving at?"

"You'll have to go public with SCP19," Kyle replied.

"I'm glad it won't come to that. Anyway," Tristan said, ending the interview by standing up and holding out his big hand, "leave it with me. Thanks for sharing your thoughts. It's appreciated."

"Here, Dad – or maybe I should say Grandad – you hold him."

Back at home in Buckhead, Tristan said, "It's not diaper time, is it?"

Tristan's daughter laughed. "No. I've just changed him. You'll be all right."

Tristan was out of practice with babies. Awkwardly,

but carefully, he took his first grandchild in his arms and looked down into the boy's dark face.

Tristan Jr was hairless and, when he yawned, wrinkled. He stared fixedly at the unfamiliar man who was holding him. He looked surprised, and faintly alarmed, that it wasn't his mother or father. His little hands protruding from his clothing were deeply creased, ready to grasp anything.

What did Tristan Sr see? Not a future president of a company but the President of the United States. He saw a world-class athlete, a great musician or writer, a doctor, a church leader. He saw unlimited potential. Tristan Jr would learn a lot, forget a lot. He would be a force for good or for bad. He would shun the limelight or he would be up there, basking in it. He would earn a lot, or he would reject materialism. He would make lots of friends, some enemies. Whatever, Tristan Jr would always have Tristan Sr's love and support.

The boy was perfect. At least, he was perfect on the outside. Inside, he had one twisted gene that Tristan had hoped his company would be able to correct. This tiny, vulnerable creature of infinite possibilities wasn't even ill, but he carried an invisible flaw that would sleep inside him for ever. One day soon, though, it could be used to kill him.

40

March gave way to April. The daytime temperature had dropped to a merciful 25°C. The yard was dry but thankfully the rainstorms still came. With summer gone, though, they were much less frequent and thorough. Duma ducked under The Tap, turned it full on, and shook his head like a shaggy dog after it had been swimming. Water sprayed to each side of him and he laughed. It was kind of cooling. Really, the water was quite warm, the pipe having been heated by the sun, but the wetness did the trick. He poured some water into his cupped hands – still blotched but healed of the burns – and drank. Duma had never been able to muck around with water before. It had always been too valuable to waste. Now that The Tap had arrived, a whole new world had opened up. Duma had another source of fun. Already his dad's alcohol had become curiously dilute, Sister 1 had slept on a sodden mattress, and a bowl of water had mysteriously fallen on Sister 3 when she came through the door of their shack. Duma wondered how he had managed in the times before The Tap.

It was a special day. A member of the National Land Committee was visiting the labourers' quarters, checking for signs of the new South Africa emerging in Hartswater. He saw only The Tap.

The old man of the village, who had always fancied himself as a politician, was complaining, "The white farmers, they're a law unto themselves. We all know that. For them, a black life's worth less than one of their farm animals. That's the problem. You might've got rid of the No Blacks Allowed signs in the towns but you can't change the No Blacks Allowed thinking in the country." He tapped the side of his head with a wizened leathery forefinger.

"We've made great progress, passing equality laws."

"Laws! You can't change thinking with laws. You can't say, 'You're not going to think like that any more.' That's not how it works with people."

Standing there, still dripping, Duma overheard them and chipped in, "Our baas gave us water. And he tells us jokes about his favourite pig."

The committee member nodded. "Very good."

Good? It was much more than good to Duma. The Tap was a miracle, a godsend. OK, the baas was a hard man but, buried deep inside him, there was a heart after all.

The men who were masquerading as Knobel Industries were relaxing on the veranda again. Pieter gulped down a beer and Eugene sipped his iced water as if it were vintage wine. They were excited and expectant. Pieter talked and talked and talked. Eugene sat in silence, having learned how to wear an expression of interest in Pieter's constant chatter while turning off altogether so that he could concentrate on his own thoughts.

It was a special day. The e-mail that had arrived from England told them that delivery of something called SCP19 was imminent. The carefully worded, and laughable, message reminded them that the supply was for sickle-cell research purposes only. Soon, the investment of providing the blacks with clean water from the whites' irrigation system was going to pay dividends.

Pieter rose and said, "It's a good-news day. I'm getting another beer."

Eugene nodded distractedly. "Fill up my water, will you?"

41

After the maid had cleaned his hotel room on Monday, Paul examined every centimetre of it. He placed the tray containing the kettle and cups precisely where he wanted it, with a corner just touching the wall where he'd made a very faint pencil mark. Then he did the same with the small basket containing free biscuits and sachets of tea, coffee, sugar and powdered milk, aligning it with another barely visible pencil mark. He memorized the order and position of the various packets in the plastic basket. Carefully, he laid a hair on his bed where the duvet met the top of the pillow. In the bathroom, he checked the exact locations of his razor and toothbrush and the complimentary shampoo, soap, shower gel and toothpaste. He left the wardrobe door slightly open. He measured the gap by eye to be five millimetres. On the desk, he arranged his papers so that the tenth sheet up from the bottom poked out a couple of millimetres from the rest.

Anyone watching him would suspect that he was paranoid, a sufferer of some compulsive behaviour disorder. He wasn't. He just wanted to know, when he returned, if anyone had been in his room. He didn't want to be surprised by someone hiding in his wardrobe or by something placed in his bed. He didn't want to be pushed out of the window or electrocuted by a kettle with faulty wiring. He wanted to know if someone had been in and glanced through his paperwork or interfered with anything in the room.

Paul had thought it all through. If the bosses at YPI wanted to remove him, they wouldn't dare to fake another road accident, they wouldn't dare to repeat an arson. That would be too obvious. They would conjure up something else. Oh, he'd still take care every time he crossed a road, he would stay alert for the smell of petrol, but this time they'd have to be more creative. Paul anticipated that they'd consider the option of finding out where he was staying and arrange an accident for him at the hotel. That wasn't so bad. He could cope with it because it was predictable. He was worried more by the many other options that he wasn't anticipating.

Maybe they wouldn't opt for an accident at all this time. Maybe "suicide" would be the obvious way out. *Academic kills himself after death of his girlfriend*. Maybe they'd even spread rumours of a suicide pact between him and Helen to add a little weight to the deception. After all, according to Helen, YPI was practised at trickery. The company had already disguised some deaths as suicides.

Paul knew that he wouldn't get any joy from the police but he went to their headquarters anyway. The Brandon Fleetwood case was closed, he was told. The Helen Crear incident was one of a great many tragic road accidents, an ongoing investigation but unlikely to lead anywhere. Dwight Grant's health wasn't a police matter. The police saw no good reason to link the three episodes. And they had no grounds at all for quizzing the managers of a leading pharmaceutical company.

A low-ranking officer listened to Paul Turrell for half an hour. It was a token gesture, a community-relations exercise. The policeman was not really interested. He didn't believe Paul's accusations but at least he took down some notes. Paul persevered with the interview because the truth was important, even if some people wouldn't give it credence. Yet the policeman was, like the local MP, serving his purpose. If anything remotely suspicious happened to Paul, the law would know where to look for the culprit. Paul might not be around to say, "I told you so," but YPI would be where they deserved to be: under a police microscope.

After leaving the police station, Paul returned to Yttria to make himself even more of an annoyance. Yes, Drs Urling-Clark and Ingoe had got his e-mail message about a meeting. Yes, they might well be prepared to see him. No, they hadn't organized anything yet. Yes, they would be in touch. And no, they couldn't see him right now. That was final. When Paul left the gatehouse, two guards watched him keenly until he was completely out of sight.

Back in Paul's room, the tenth sheet up from the bottom of his pile of papers still stuck out slightly. The tray and basket were still touching his pencil marks and the sachets had not been disturbed. The strand of his hair was still lying across the pillow and duvet. In the bathroom, nothing seemed to have been touched and, next to it, the wardrobe door was still slightly open. He was satisfied that he was safe – at least for the moment.

According to the hotel barman, the new member of staff had already begun work in room service. That was very convenient if Yttria wanted a means of getting to Paul. The company had only to find a quality candidate in its own pay and get him to apply for the job. Or YPI could simply bribe whoever filled the vacancy. Either way, Yttria would have open access to Paul's hotel all of the time. Of course, the new worker might not be a YPI mole, his recruitment at this moment in time might be a total coincidence, but Paul decided to find out straight away. He gave the newcomer a golden opportunity. He rang for room service. "Can you have a fresh coffee brought up, please?"

"No problem, sir. You're Room 38, aren't you?"

"That's right."

Fifteen minutes later, the coffee arrived. It was delivered by a big brawny man with very short silvery hair. Paul had not seen him around the hotel before so he guessed that he was the latest recruit. Also, he was far too servile and he didn't wait for a tip. Definitely new to the game. Alone again, Paul held the coffee up to the daylight that streamed in through the window. The drink looked perfectly normal. It smelled entirely ordinary as well – quite tempting. Even so, Paul had no intention of drinking it. He poured it into a sample vial borrowed from the university, sealed it, and headed swiftly for the laboratories.

He spent the rest of the day at the university analysing the liquid. It turned out to be conventional Colombian coffee and it seemed to contain nothing worse than caffeine. As far as Paul could tell, it was perfectly harmless. Not a whiff of a poison. If the new member of the hotel's service staff was really on YPI's payroll, he had not taken the easy bait that Paul had dangled in front of him.

Paul's mind dwelled on the failure of his plan while he walked back towards his hotel. Waiting to cross Gonville Place, opposite the park, he felt a hand on his lower back. With a huge lumbering lorry bearing down on him, he was shoved from behind. For a moment, Paul envisaged himself falling in the road in front of the giant wheels, the massive unyielding cab. For a moment, he felt YPI's hand sealing his fate. For a moment, he was terrified. He threw himself backwards to resist the pressure, twisting round at the same time.

There was a surprised cry and Paul almost fell over a shocked child behind him.

Quickly, the boy's father said, "Oh, sorry, mate. It's just that he's, you know, eager. No harm done, though." The man was carrying a football and had obviously promised his son a kick-about in the park. He knelt down and admonished the boy. "You mustn't do that, see? It's very naughty – and dangerous. Someone might step in front of a car or something."

The lorry having gone past, Paul inhaled deeply and strode across the road. He had just learned how easy it would be for someone to cause his death. It didn't take cleverness or power, just a discreet push. It didn't take a man who looked the part of an assassin or a thug. It could be anyone, anywhere. It could happen when he least expected it. Paul would have to get used to living on the edge.

Suddenly, the whole business made Paul very depressed. His pace slowed to an aimless amble. He realized that he'd been holding back despair with anger and activity. Now, it all seemed just too much. Was he really going to beat a massive organization bent on his elimination? With Helen gone, he began to doubt his ability to fight on. He began to think that nothing really mattered any more. He began to think that if a weapon wiped out the whole human species, the planet would breathe a big sigh of relief and get on with nature. But. . . He shook his head sadly. It wasn't going to happen. The next generation of weapons would be specific. They'd eliminate just a carefully chosen selection of humankind. It wouldn't be the meek who inherited the Earth, it would be the ones with the resources to develop smart weapons.

Paul decided to spend yet more time in the hotel bar.

In a corner of one of Westminster's many bars, two prominent members of the Government talked quietly, privately, together.

The Defence Secretary had an ace up his sleeve. He'd just been briefed by one of his junior ministers, the Member of Parliament for Cambridge, who was anxious to make sure that her boss was fully armed with information and speculation that she'd learned in her surgery with a Dr Paul Turrell. The MP's willingness to share gossip about YPI had little to do with ethics and a lot to do with her career. The Defence Secretary knew that his understudy was eyeing jealously the next rung of the warped and greasy political ladder but he did not feel threatened by her. The only realistic way for the young woman to succeed him lay in his own promotion. He knew it and the MP, certainly no fool, knew it. She had a vested interest in her boss's political clout. So, the Defence Secretary learnt from her anything that would give him an advantage over his rivals in the party.

The DTI Secretary was saying, in her low but insistent voice, "What YPI's doing is *defensive* research and that's permitted under the terms of the Biological and Toxin Weapons Convention. I assure you there's no problem."

"You're speaking to a specialist in defence and yet I don't recognize what YPI's doing as defensive."

"You're not coming at it from the right angle, then. This SCP project you've somehow heard about, it seems it might – just might – harm certain races. They're not sure yet. It's still under test. Obviously they're still hoping it's a medicine for sickle-cell anaemia but, even if it *did* turn out to be a genetic weapon against black communities, work on it is totally justified. If a less ethical state than ours were to get their hands on it, or some similar technology, we'd have to have a defence against it for the sake of our own black population. That's just common sense. We've got to stay one jump ahead of unscrupulous states."

"But I hear YPI are *making* this potential biological weapon. To the press, that would sound like offensive work. I'm sure your average voter would think the same. It's like preparing for war – and that's forbidden by the Convention."

"No, no, no. Don't you see? It's quite simple," she said, a nasty tone to her voice. "Without making the weapon in the first place, scientists can't develop a vaccine against it and they certainly can't test any antidote, can they? On top of the health research, that's why they're making it."

"Think what you're saying," the Defence Secretary argued. "The steps to prepare a weapon for use and the steps to defend against it are identical."

"Well, that's true. Absolutely. But, believe me, YPI's working purely on pharmaceutical and defensive aspects, otherwise it'd be in breach of both the Biological Weapons Convention and British law. They're not going to do that, are they? For heaven's sake, YPI's a health care business, not a weapons research centre."

The Defence Secretary made a theatrical tutting noise with his tongue. "Even if I believe you, not everyone would. It's important these days not just to be clean but to be seen to be clean. To some this would look very dirty." He paused before adding, "There's something else. What if Yttria is . . . how shall I say . . . using underhand tactics to protect its product and its intentions?"

"What's that supposed to mean?"

"It means, if you keep your ear to the ground, you can hear all sorts of rumblings. Some very odd suicides, a former head of department downed in an aircraft failure, a doctor suffering a tragic accident, important samples going up in flames."

For a split-second, the DTI Secretary's face revealed surprise that her colleague had played a trump card that she did not realize he had. She thought she knew the game that he was playing, though. She believed that the Defence Secretary was keen to see her take a tumble – preferably in a nasty scandal – to halt her rapid rise through the ranks and demolish her chances

275

of rivalling him for the job of next party leader. Being on the same side, she would claim that they were friends first, colleagues second and competitors third but actually the order was the other way round. She would not admit that personal ambition came first, of course, because she was a politician. "I've no idea what you're talking about. None of these things has come to my attention and I doubt there's a shred of truth behind them."

When the Defence Secretary stood up, he looked pleased because he had unsettled her. "Let's hope not," he said before he walked away.

No one knew exactly what Uncle Akoda had done to get himself so much money. It was something on computers. He'd set something up and now he was into selling things. No one knew exactly what things. "Anything," Akoda answered. It wasn't that his business was raking in the dosh. It was all sorts of business-people wanting to throw money at him. They must have thought he was on to a good thing, somehow. But it wasn't real work. At the end of the day Akoda didn't have anything to show. No sweat on his brow, no product in his hand. "I put guys who want to sell in touch with guys who want to buy. I'm doing a valuable service. A ten-per-cent cut here, a fifteen-per-cent cut there, and lots of sponsors. It kinda adds up."

That's why Akoda's pockets were stuffed with money

when he sat with Dwight. That's why, if only Dwight would move his head, he would've heard a rustling from under his pillow. That's why nurses nudged each other and said, "Here he comes. Watch what he does." That's why the ward staff had a collection of tenners in a bottle, waiting for Dwight's recovery. That's why the nurses' beer fund was healthier than usual. Akoda gave them tips to look after his nephew really well. If only money could make Dwight better.

But Akoda knew no other way. He knew nothing about cures and drugs and doctoring and stuff. If he'd had a magic wand, he would've waved it over Dwight by now. But he hadn't. Not even his Internet site could locate someone selling a wand. Akoda had only sympathy and money so that's what he used at the hospital for four long months.

The usual doctor, the good-looker, had gone and left. Dwight's new doctor seemed to know quite a bit, but he wasn't getting anywhere. And he didn't care so much as the old one. He never seemed to have time. The old doctor, she was in a hurry, sure, but she always made time. Maybe she didn't get anywhere either, but she looked good and she really cared. It was written all over her face.

Arsenal's striker hadn't found the back of the net. The genuine Arsenal shirt hadn't got anyone to wear it. The drugs and the drips hadn't kick-started Dwight's brain. Another brain scan hadn't revealed anything. All the talking in the world didn't get a reply. And Akoda's money hadn't hit the jackpot. Even so, the tape still played, the football shirt still hung on the back of a chair, the doctors still pumped in this and that, still tried lots of tests, everyone still dropped by to talk. Uncle Akoda still left fivers and tenners under Dwight's pillow and still kept the nurses' collection box topped up.

If God Himself had been in the ward, Uncle Akoda would've bribed Him as well. But there was no sign of Him. Not anywhere.

42

In Memphis the number of casualties had escalated at first and then stabilized. Behind the mass of statistics, though, there were forty individual tragedies, sixteen dead and twenty-four in a coma. Forty distraught families were struggling to understand. To them, there was no comfort in numbers, no comfort in knowing that they were not the only ones. To each of them, their own loss was everything. The medics were struggling to cope with hundreds of lesser tragedies: people with depression, dizziness and fainting. Young or old, male or female, the disease had not made any distinction. But it had picked out black Americans unerringly. There was not a single white person among the casualties.

Media attention fell on Nathan McQueen, of course. He was never going to be the next Martin Luther King, the newspapers agreed, but he had become an effective and popular mouthpiece. Was he the target – and victim – of a far right group or was it just bad luck that the activist had eaten the same spoiled food as everyone else? One journalist speculated that the mystery outbreak was revenge for Shadow's fiery attacks directed at the white community. Perhaps Shadow was even one of the victims. No one knew, so everyone believed whatever they wanted to believe. In a way, the journalist suggested, it didn't matter. If Shadow had perished in a feud, another five Shadows would arise from its ashes. No one could ever totally wipe out their enemies by force because any act of violence would create a new generation eager for revenge.

There was no mention in the media of a cure for sickle-cell anaemia that had become a poison. Kyle was wondering if Tristan Lockhart would really do anything. Earlier in the day, Kyle had left that lofty Yttria office in a positive mood, as if he'd actually achieved something, as if he'd got the president on his side, but now disillusionment was creeping up on him. Maybe asking someone else to do something wasn't enough. Maybe he couldn't delegate his responsibilities to Tristan Lockhart in Atlanta and Paul Turrell in Cambridge.

Logging on to the Nathan McQueen website, Kyle read the expressions of regret and sorrow. Two abusive messages on the bulletin board were erased while Kyle browsed the site. Making up his mind, Kyle took a deep breath and began to write a message. It wasn't a personal reflection on the dead activist. As a white man who had never met McQueen, Kyle felt excluded from the emotion. No. Kyle's contribution was going to be different. He was going to explain Nathan's death, to stress the need to test all of the victims for the sickle-cell gene, to provide details of a chicken egg and a smart biological weapon that might lie behind the outbreak, and he was going to name Yttria. And, while he was on the Internet, he might as well book a flight to Heathrow because there was no doubt that he would lose his job. He did not intend to attach his name to the message but any computer buff would be able to trace his identity without breaking into a sweat.

No doubt a lot of visitors to Nathan McQueen's website would list Kyle among the cranks, but maybe someone would regard him as genuine. As far as Kyle was concerned, that chance made the sacrifice worthwhile. He clicked on the *Send* button.

Kyle's addition to the on-line book of condolence did not last long. The whole of the website was sabotaged within minutes of the arrival of the damning message. In those brief moments, hardly anyone saw it. But two people did read Kyle's theory. One was a friend and one was not.

At first, Kyle thought that it was the people upstairs. It took him a few seconds to realize that the thumping was at his own door.

"Police. Open up!"

Police? Surely not. What would the police want with him? He frowned, walked to the door and opened it warily.

The four people crammed into his doorway were not in uniform. Not police uniform anyway. They were wearing grotesque masks: plastic versions of George W

Bush, Arnold Schwarzenegger, Frank Sinatra and Jack Nicholson. Kyle did not react quickly enough. He tried to slam the door on the disguised men but Jack Nicholson already had a foot and a shoulder in the room.

"What. . .?"

The four men barged in and two of them grabbed Kyle.

A hand across Kyle's mouth stopped him calling out. He was bundled straight into a chair. Behind the back of the chair, his hands were tied tightly. The binding was soft, though, so at least it did not hurt by digging into his skin. Both of his ankles were bound to the chair legs with bandages.

From behind the hand that clamped the lower half of his face, he managed to mutter, "What do you want?" His garbled cry came out as series of grunts but it was obvious what he had said.

Quietly but very firmly, Jack Nicholson said, "We'll gag you as well if you try to shout out." He showed his prisoner a spare bandage.

Kyle nodded.

"No screaming?"

Kyle shook his head. He hated the thought of a bandage pulling back his cheeks, lying between his teeth, drying his mouth.

"Try anything – anything at all – and you're back to nodding and shaking, boy. OK?"

"Uh-huh."

"Good. Let's keep it that way." He nodded to Frank Sinatra on Kyle's left.

At once, a knife appeared at Kyle's throat. Kyle would have jumped if he had not been immobilized in the chair. He swallowed uncomfortably. "What's going. . .? I haven't got money. Honest!" But really he knew these people were not after cash. They would have grabbed his wallet and run out by now if they had been merely thieves. Kyle wished that they were ordinary muggers.

"You're all alone in Atlanta, aren't you? No one to come and help you."

"I've got. . ." Kyle stopped. He was going to claim Max Levine as a friend, but two things stopped him. He was no longer sure that Max *was* a friend. Also, he didn't want to sound even more desperate than he was already.

Someone behind him said, "We got ourselves a nigger-lover."

Kyle's eyes bulged with fright. Suddenly it was all clear. This was the group that had poisoned Memphis and murdered Nathan McQueen.

"We saw your Internet lies, didn't we?" said Frank Sinatra.

Fear took Kyle's words away. These men were totally ruthless and inhuman. Kyle's brain went numb and he could hardly focus on anything but the silvery blade that swayed menacingly in front of his face, like a cat about to pounce with its claws bared. Through a haze he saw Schwarzenegger drop his keypad and phone on the floor, stamp wildly on them, and then smash the computer itself.

The voice behind whispered, "No more surfing."

Kyle knew there was more to come. "What do you want?" he stammered.

"Mmm. Now there's a question," said Jack Nicholson. He paced up and down the width of the room, gazing at the carpet as if thinking. "This— what did you call it? – smart biological weapon. Who do you think took it from Yttria?"

"Urm. . ."

"Can you name him?"

Kyle still hesitated. He was not sure how to answer. Would it be best to deny any connection to Max Levine or simply to spit it out?

"You're not sure, eh? Well, that's good. What else aren't you sure about? Was the stuff from Yttria at all?"

"Yes."

"Wrong!"

The knife didn't move. It wasn't that. Something else – knuckles – caused the sharp pain in his side that winded him completely.

"Does it even exist?"

"Yes."

This time the pain was much worse. The punch to his side was delivered expertly.

Jack Nicholson halted in front of Kyle and turned face on. He was horribly close. "I think you'll find you're wrong there, boy. You certainly can't prove it. So, let's see if you can get it right this time. Does this smart thing really exist?"

This time, Kyle could only nod.

The blow came in from the other side, catching him out. He wasn't braced for it. His head lurched forward, his mouth opened involuntarily and he retched.

"You'd be the smart one if you agreed with us it's a figment of your fantastic English imagination. That'd be best all round, don't you think? Best for you, that's for sure. Best for your colleagues at Yttria as well."

Kyle felt a foot treading downwards on the bandage that tied his wrists. The back of the chair tore into the muscles of his upper arms and his shoulders yanked downwards until he thought that his arms were going to dislocate.

"You asked what we want. Simple. We want you to stop spreading lies about your work colleagues, don't we? That's all. Nothin' to it, boy. You see, it's a case of you realizing you were mistaken or, if you don't, it's up to us to find a way of stopping you telling lies. And trust me, you wouldn't like that."

"Please."

"Either way, we're gonna stay here with you till you see the light," George Bush chipped in. "We don't mind hard work but it's a waste of your time and energy. We don't really want to waste your time but if we have to. . ." He cracked his knuckles loudly. "You might as well make it sooner rather than later."

The counterfeit Nicholson walked over to the television, turned it on and hiked the volume. Homer Simpson bellowed even louder than usual. Cheerfully, Jack said, "That gives the neighbours something to listen to, don't it?"

Expecting the worst, Kyle cringed and slumped in his chair as much as the tethers would allow. The pressure on his shoulders lifted and he felt suddenly light, but a heavy boot crashed into his shin and he squealed, sitting upright again. He knew what the false stars were doing. They were working on different parts of his body so he didn't know what was coming next. And, once they'd run out of places to hurt, there was always that bright, sharp blade hovering in front of his face. Through the cloud of pain, Kyle also knew exactly what they wanted him to say. To put an end to the torture, they wanted a guarantee that he wouldn't name Max Levine to the authorities.

A fist slammed into his cheek and immediately he tasted blood in his mouth.

He was not quite sure what happened next. He thought that maybe he'd passed out for a while. Everything was fuzzy, but he definitely heard someone laughing. The torment had stopped and the four fake celebrities were looking at each other. Then Kyle heard it for himself. A thump and another voice.

Beyond Bart Simpson's laughter, someone called, "Anybody at home?"

Through unfocused eyes, Kyle saw the door to the apartment open and a figure appear. He screwed up his eyes, but he could not make out who it was – or if he was just hallucinating.

Without another word, Kyle's torturers all ran through the doorway, knocking the visitor over.

Then someone was kneeling down, untying Kyle's legs, saying, "Are you all right?"

Kyle's eyes opened again and, still disorientated, he recognized the man who was wiping blood from his damaged face.

"Yes," the visitor said. "It's me. I don't know what's going on here, but I held my grandson and knew I had to come and see you."

Kyle was lying down on the sofa and Tristan Lockhart was tending his wounds. It was quiet, so Tristan must have turned off the TV. "Your grandson?" Kyle uttered.

"You're going to be fine," Yttria's president said to him. "You should've seen me when I had time to go skiing. Skiing wasn't the problem. It was the accidents, the tumbles. Afterwards, I'd have bits gouged out and broken bones all over the place."

Kyle did not feel reassured. He ached all over. "Your grandson?" he repeated.

Tristan sat back and dropped some soiled tissues into the waste-paper bin. "He's got the sickle-cell gene."

"But you're... He's not..." Kyle was still groggy. The white man's words didn't make sense to him.

"My son-in-law's black."

"Son-in-law. Ah." Kyle began to nod but stopped straight away. He was dizzy and it felt as if his top-heavy head might roll off his body. "Got it. No wonder you came."

"Rest," Tristan ordered him. "You're not really with it yet. I'll get you a drink and painkillers. I'll have my doctor drop by and check you over. Don't worry, Yttria will pay. We'll talk later."

Kyle was able to sit up, but with every slight movement, he issued a groan. The inside of his mouth was swollen and uncomfortable, yet with an effort, he could speak softly. He had told the doctor only that he'd been beaten up but he explained why to Tristan.

Tristan sighed. "You called SCP19 a race weapon but, you know, it's not. It can't be, not really, because there's no such thing as race. Genetics has taught us that. The differences between blacks and whites are less than the differences within blacks or whites. See what I'm saying? A white man's DNA might be more like his black neighbour's than another white's."

Less nauseous now, Kyle nodded gently. "But there *are* races. There's no doubting that."

"People say there's whites, blacks, Asians and the rest, but there's no biological basis to it. Those labels stuck before we knew about genetics. They're superficial, based on appearance – and that's just an accident of geography, climate and culture." Tristan took a drink of the coffee he'd made. "Actually, when you think about it, it's crazy for sure. We all share the same African ancestors. And labelling people by skin colour doesn't make sense anyhow. No one's really white or black or anything else. There's just lots of different shades. There's no clear dividing line."

"You can still have a race weapon, though," Kyle claimed.

"SCP19's really a weapon against the sickle-cell gene, not against everyone with a particular skin colour. Again, it's a freak of geography."

"How do you mean?"

"Well, originally, sickle-shaped haemoglobin evolved in Africans around the equator as a defence against malaria. Did you know? Of course, you're a chemist, not a biologist. Anyway, when the malaria parasite gets into the red blood cells of someone with the sickle-cell trait, the cells curl up into the sickle shape and die, taking out the parasite with them. It's a neat piece of evolution, but you don't get something for nothing. It beats malaria, but it gave us sickle-cell anaemia. So you see, SCP19's not a race thing. It's turned out to be a poison for individuals evolved to avoid malaria."

"A lot of individuals," Kyle replied. "One in twelve blacks."

"I wouldn't say any of this at work, you realize. I won't repeat it outside this room."

"You haven't told the Memphis hospitals about SCP19, have you?"

Tristan looked hard at Kyle. "As head of Yttria, my hands are tied. I have obligations to the company."

Kyle exhaled and thought about it. "I've lost my job, haven't I? Time to catch a plane."

"Is it?"

"I should think so," said Kyle.

"I'm not going to sack you, not while you've still got some work to do."

"What sort of work?"

Tristan shrugged. "The sort of work you think you've got to do."

"But. . ."

"I'll give you as much protection as I can while you do it."

"What?" Kyle thought that he might still be groggy; he might be misunderstanding or mishearing.

"Come on. I can't do it for you. I told you my hands are tied. I can't do anything directly. I'm the president of the company! But you're a bright boy. Take a day off to get over this and think about it."

"Then?"

"Then, come into work and do what you've got

to do." From the doorway, Tristan said, "I don't know where Max Levine was on the day your Mitch got sick in Memphis, but he sure wasn't at YPI."

43

Paul told himself he could not afford to wallow in hopelessness when there was a job to do. OK, maybe as an individual he could only snap at the heels of the Yttria giant, yet he might just be able to trip it up. He was in no doubt that SCP19 was very smart and he was equally convinced that it was evil. He could give meaning to his life and, more importantly, to Helen's by doing everything he could to ruin its development. His next move, though, was anything but clear. The hair still lay across the gap between Paul's pillow and the duvet. Everything looked exactly as it had done after room service this morning. In a way, Paul was disappointed that no one had tried to harm him. His attempt to build a case of attempted murder against Yttria had ground to a frustrating halt. He had not even been granted a meeting at the pharmaceutical company yet.

He sighed and stripped off, ready for a shower. In the bathroom, though, something caught his eye. Yes, everything was exactly as it should have been but. . . He picked up the brand-new tube of complimentary toothpaste and his brow creased. The previous tube that must have been taken away this morning had not been empty. Why had it been replaced when it still had a few days of life left in it? It was an unlikely

292

extravagance on behalf of the hotel. Forgetting the shower, Paul got back into his clothes, put the small tube in his jacket pocket and raced to the university laboratories.

Paul held the tube in a fume cupboard and unscrewed the plastic lid to reveal a seal of aluminium foil. If someone was trying to poison him by spiking the toothpaste, they had made a professional job of it. It was not obvious how they had laced the paste with poison. Wearing gloves, Paul removed the seal and squeezed the entire contents of the tube into a sample vial. Carefully, he washed the small seal and empty tube to remove all traces of toothpaste and then took them out of the fume cupboard.

Using a magnifying glass and microscope, he looked for tiny openings into the tube. He found what he wanted in the aluminium seal. Near the edge, there was a hole, invisible to the naked eye. Of course, it could have been a manufacturing fault, but Paul believed it was a puncture created by a very fine hypodermic needle. And if it was, what had someone injected into the toothpaste?

He spent the rest of the afternoon examining the soft white mass and finding nothing at all. No arsenic, no dangerous drugs, no natural toxins, no cyanide, no weedkillers. Then he had an idea. He was performing familiar tests for toxic chemicals because he was a chemist, but Yttria had begun to move away from conventional chemistry and into biotechnology. They were working on viruses and bacteria. He needed to check for germs.

The biologist who agreed to help him took away a sample of the toothpaste and disappeared. While he waited for her, Paul drank coffee and paid his way by giving a lengthy tutorial to her research students. When she eventually returned, she looked fraught and demanded the rest of the toothpaste. She wanted it under lock and key in a secure laboratory.

"Why?" asked Paul, his heart suddenly racing.

"Because it's riddled with meningococcal B bacteria."

"Meningitis?"

She nodded. "It's a lethal strain, treatable by antibiotics but it's so rapid that patients often die before treatment kicks in. And there's no vaccine to this strain. It's the sort of thing we see every few years, usually in students arriving at the university or in babies."

Paul shook his head, speechless.

"How are you feeling?" the biologist enquired.

"How do you mean?"

"Have you had any headaches, rashes, vomiting, fever? Do your hands or feet feel cold? Is your neck stiff?"

"Isn't it just youngsters who get it?"

"Mostly, but adults catch it sometimes."

"Well, I'm fine," said Paul. "I didn't get round to

using the toothpaste and I handled it properly in the labs."

"I need to know where it came from."

At once, Paul replied, "So do I."

"It's a terrible threat. . ."

"Don't worry," Paul said. "No one's trying to pollute Cambridge as a whole. It's just me, not a whole lethal batch."

"It's clever as well. The bacteria live in the throat of lots of people and never do any harm because they don't get into the bloodstream. By putting it in toothpaste, someone's been very cunning. We all have little scratches and occasional bleeding from the gums: a sure way into the bloodstream. Then it can kill in hours."

"It's not a matter of 'we'. It's a one-off tube spiked for me."

"Even so. . ."

Paul touched her arm. "Thanks for your help. You've been great. I'm working on it, OK?"

"I've got to call the police and hospital authorities."

"Don't do that," Paul pleaded, "or you'll make it a lot harder for me."

"Look, this is *very* dangerous. You'd better have a bloody good reason."

Paul nodded. "I do. Create a fuss now and whoever's behind this thing goes underground. If it stays quiet, I can track them down in a couple of days. That's the way to eliminate the threat."

The biologist hesitated. Then, sighing and shaking her head, she said, "If our safety officer hadn't just left, I'd have had to consult him. Perhaps it's just as well he's gone. You take care."

"Thanks." Walking away backwards, Paul said, "I'll be in touch. Promise. I'll soon be telling everyone who did it – and why. I just need a bit of proof."

He went back to the hotel via a supermarket, where he bought a small tube of toothpaste identical to the one that had been placed in his room. As soon as he'd substituted the tube in his bathroom, he called YPI. It did not surprise Paul that Urling-Clark was now willing to see him tomorrow afternoon. Paul guessed that Yttria expected him to be confined to a hospital ward by then, so there would not be a meeting at all. What's more, Urling-Clark would deflect any suspicion from himself by claiming that he would never have arranged a visit if he'd had prior knowledge of Paul's infectious disease.

Yet again, Paul left his room.

From his parked car, Paul watched the hotel staff coming and going in the growing darkness. He glanced at his watch, working out the time difference with Atlanta, and then called Kyle on his work number. "It's Paul Turrell," he announced in a low voice.

"Oh? What's happening?"

"Are you all right? Your voice sounds . . . distorted."

"Just a sore mouth."

"Sorry to hear that. It's just a quick one. I'm making progress, slower than I hoped, but you can help."

"How?"

Paul hesitated as someone came out of the back entrance of the hotel, but it was a false alarm. When the worker was caught in the hotel lighting, Paul could see that the man wasn't the one he wanted to see. "Do you know if Yttria works with bacterial meningitis here in Cambridge?"

"Meningitis? Nasty. But, yes, I think Biology does. It wasn't my patch but I'm pretty sure I heard of someone trying out new antibiotics and vaccines for it."

"Thanks."

"Why do you want to know?"

"It's a long story. Sorry. I'd better not go into it now."

"OK."

"Thanks again. Must go."

Paul scrutinized every face while one shift of hotel workers handed over to the next. Smiling at last, he watched the new employee with short silver hair getting into a green Nissan and driving away. Waiting for just a few seconds, Paul took off in pursuit.

In Cambridge, it was never going to be a risky, high-speed chase. The only danger was in getting too close to the Nissan and being recognized by its driver. Still, nightfall would assist Paul's amateurish entry into the spying game. Paul kept at least three cars between himself and the hotel worker, but he also had to make sure that he did not get left behind at any of the crossings and crossroads. He wasn't familiar enough with the city to know where he was going, but he tailed the green Nissan, determined not to lose it.

It pulled into the car park of a pub and Paul drove straight past, coming to a halt by the kerb further down the road. He waited for a couple of minutes, then he walked back to the same pub and stepped gingerly into the smoky bar. Luckily, it was quite crowded so the room-service man would probably not pick out Paul immediately. Blending in but looking around constantly, Paul bought himself a pint. It took him a few minutes to locate that silvery head. The hotel worker was sitting in a corner of the pub, under a disused dart board, with another man. The two of them were leaning close and talking into each other's ears as if they were in a club filled with loud music. Paul thought that he recognized the second man but couldn't be sure. If he did know him, he could not recall his name or even work out where he had seen him before. Paul kept his distance, deciding it would be foolish to get closer in an attempt to identify the driver's contact.

When both men looked up vaguely in Paul's direction, Paul quickly lifted his glass in front of his face and drank. He noted with relief that neither of them took any particular notice of him. Instead, they resumed their talk. The man from the hotel was animated. His contact seemed to be much more weary and sober. The second man's expression suggested reservation. Perhaps he was sceptical about the news that the Nissan driver had brought.

After a few minutes, the hotel's new recruit got to his feet, furtively pocketed a brown envelope that the other man slipped into his palm, said a final few words, and made for the rear exit that led to the car park.

Paul threw back the rest of his lager – he needed it – and went out of the front door towards his own car. Walking along the road, he kept glancing back over his shoulder to see which way the Nissan would go when it emerged. Paul cursed when he saw it going back in the direction that it had come. The narrow road and a continuous stream of traffic stopped Paul making a U-turn. By the time he found a side-road in which he could turn round, he had lost the green Nissan. Instead, he pulled into the pub's car park and went back into the bar through the front entrance.

The second man was still there, sitting stiffly erect like a soldier, finishing the dregs of his drink. Discreetly, Paul watched him get up from his seat and head towards the back door. His purposeful walk also had something of the military about it. Realizing that this whole venture might be a total wild-goose chase, Paul followed him at a distance. This time, Paul would have to tail a white Mondeo.

And the car led him to a church. There, Paul could not follow the man inside because, in an almost empty church at night, Paul would be too easy to spot. He waited outside.

The man who had handed over the brown envelope stayed in the church for about fifteen minutes. Then he drove to a perfectly ordinary middle-class semi-detached house where a teenage girl greeted him in the well-lit hall before he closed the front door, shutting out prying eyes.

Paul got out of his car and, under the cover of darkness, took a good look at the house and its number. He wanted to be able to find it again later. He walked along the pavement, past a couple houses with *Sold* notices outside, until he found the name of the street. Then, having got what he wanted, he drove back to the city centre and his hotel.

He didn't go to bed, but he did clean his teeth because he wanted the tube to look used. He did not take that shower after all because it suited him to look rough. Before he went down to reception, he stood in front of the large mirror and ran his fingers through his hair so he looked even more dishevelled. When he was satisfied with his appearance, he left his room yet again. It was well past midnight and the corridors were dim and deserted.

The receptionist was surprised to see him so late.

"To tell you the truth," he muttered, "I don't feel so

good. I've got a bit of sickness and a headache – in fact, quite a lot of a headache – and a stiff neck."

"Oh dear. Do you want me to call a doctor, sir?"

"No, it's OK, thanks. But I'm a long way from my own GP so I'll just go over the way and get myself checked out at the hospital."

"Shall I call a taxi?"

"No. The fresh air might do me some good. Maybe that's all I need, I don't know. You can do me a favour, though."

"Yes?"

"If the worst comes to the worst," Paul replied, "and I don't show up later, can you tell room service? I don't want them clearing the room because it's not being used. I still want it."

"They wouldn't do that, sir, but I'll certainly tell them you're not feeling well."

"Thanks." Paul smiled weakly and walked away at a sickly pace.

At dawn, Paul was in his car parked opposite that semi-detached house, feeling semi-detached from normal life. He sat there and watched the world waking up: commuters making for the railway station and London, a paperboy on his rounds, a few joggers in tracksuits emerging from houses, early birds trying to beat the traffic to the city centre and business parks, the first lorries rumbling through, a milkman leaving pints on doorsteps.

That was what Paul was waiting for. The post or milk delivery. He didn't mind which.

He watched the milkman place three pints outside the house that he had targeted and then move on. Paul got out of his car and walked briskly towards the milk-float further down the street. "Sorry to bother you," Paul said, "but I'm just about to move into this area." He waved a hand towards one of the *Sold* signs. "And I want to sort out a milk delivery. I was speaking with. . . oh, I'm hopeless with names. . . number 25. . ." Paul left a gap for the milkman to fill.

"Mr Wooderson."

"That's it. Mr Wooderson," Paul replied. "He said I should speak to you. Have you got a phone number or something so I can contact you when I want to get going?"

Paul took out a notepad and jotted down the dairy's telephone number and thanked the milkman. Going back to his car, Paul allowed himself a grin. Now, he had a name as well. Unfortunately, though, it didn't mean anything to him.

An eternity seemed to pass before the white Mondeo crawled out of the neat garage beside the house. Paul's legs ached, his back ached, his head ached, and he had not slept at all. His chin was rough with stubble. Acting the part of someone with meningitis was not going to be very difficult. He felt awful. But he was also opti-mistic. Things seemed to be going his way.

44

Still sore, Kyle took a deep breath and approached the lab where Max worked, the transatlantic equivalent of Lab 47. Immediately, Kyle's spirits sank. The door had a security lock with a keypad and he did not have the combination. He looked around, hoping that someone who knew the entry code might come along the sixth-floor corridor, but there was no one. The door did not even have a window so he couldn't peer into the interior of the laboratory. He paced up and down for a while, wondering what to do, trying to keep hold of his resolve.

Within a couple of minutes, a guard built like an American football player on steroids marched up to him. "Yes?"

Kyle hadn't seen a closed-circuit TV camera but there must have been one trained on the door. "I need to get into the lab to see Max Levine," he replied, telling the officer his name.

"You got the code?"

"No."

"You don't have the code, you don't get in," the guard told him. "Doesn't matter if you're Prince Charles himself. No clearance, no go."

"I'll tell you what I do have. I think you'll find I've got Mr Lockhart's permission."

"Mr Lockhart?"

"Yes. The president. I think you'd better check."

While the guard was waiting for a response to his radio enquiry, he asked, "Hey, you *are* from England, aren't you?"

Kyle nodded. Trying to keep calm, he smiled clumsily.

"Do you know—?"

"No."

The officer listened to his radio for a moment and then replied, "Right. I hear you." Nodding at Kyle, he said, "You're right. You got clearance direct from Mr Lockhart's office." He punched some numbers into the keypad, keeping his big body between Kyle and the lock so that Kyle could not see the combination, and then he held the door open respectfully. He seemed to be impressed with a young Brit who had the confidence of the president of the company. "Have a good day."

Kyle thought it unlikely but he said, "Thanks."

Inside the large spotless lab, Max looked up. The surprise on his face soon gave way to a huge grin. He pointed towards Kyle and said, "It's your turn! That's a killer black eye and then some."

Walking up to Max, Kyle said brusquely, "Yeah." He was feeling edgy but he had made his mind up. There would have to be a confrontation. The barren biotechnology lab wasn't the best place for it but it had to be done. Kyle swallowed and said, "I figured it out."

"What?"

"That you were Arnold Schwarzenegger – the only one who didn't say anything, in case I recognized your voice."

Max looked blank. Then he glanced around him as if appealing to his colleagues to be saved from the ravings of a mad man who had broken into the laboratory. He put down the scalpel that he was holding and said, "What are you talking about, Kyle?"

"I'm talking about an egg, SCP19, you releasing it in Memphis, and the people who made a visit to my apartment on Monday."

Max was fast becoming irritable. "Have you got concussion or something? You sure are talking crazy."

Summoning the same courage that had got him into Tristan Lockhart's office, Kyle replied, "You took some SCP19 and grew it in an egg."

Max shook his head impatiently. "After all I've done for you—"

"You helped me settle in. I'm grateful. But I can't let you—"

"Can't let me what?"

Once, Kyle had regarded Max's amazing sideburns as a sign of masculine eccentricity but now they just looked silly. Kyle had regarded Max's worship of the great white Elvis as harmless; now he interpreted it as a sinister throwback to the bad old days of prejudice and supremacy. He swallowed and then uttered, "You're just a racist, simple as that. I can't let you go around poisoning—"

"Look, this isn't the time and place. I got a whole bunch of work to get through. Why don't you come to my apartment tonight? It's only a block away. We'll sort it out there – or fix you up with a shrink." He jotted down his address and handed it to Kyle. "Say eight o'clock? I'll be done here by then."

Kyle thought that it was probably the best deal he was going to get. "OK."

When Shadow had posted his memorial note on Nathan McQueen's website, another e-mail had arrived at the same time. Just before the whole site crashed, Shadow learnt from the anonymous message that some Atlanta drug company called Yttria was behind the Memphis outbreak. It wasn't a natural disease, it wasn't bad chicken. It was nothing but a deliberate attack on blacks, targeting anyone who carried the sickle-cell gene. Shadow didn't understand all of the technical biology stuff in the message but he recognized evil when he saw it.

He'd watched his brothers drop one by one like flies after a spray with insecticide, even those who'd been in Handy Park listening to him playing. He must have been exposed to the weapon as well. But he was feeling fine, physically, so he didn't need a blood test to know that he wasn't a sickle-cell carrier. Mentally, though, he

306

was seething. As soon as he read that e-mail message, he knew what he had to do. His brothers were relying on him. That's why he'd hitched a ride to Atlanta. Soon, Shadow would be as well known in Atlanta as he was in Memphis.

45

Things were going Paul's way until he lost the Mondeo in traffic. He pounded his steering wheel in annoyance and swore. Now what? His tenuous link to the people who might have assassinated Helen, who might be trying to assassinate him, had snapped. There was little to do but to try a long shot. Indicating right, Paul pulled out of the queue and headed towards YPI.

There were a lot of vehicles in the car park outside Yttria's security fence, but Paul walked among them, zigzagging his way along the rows, searching. He knew that his antics would probably be recorded on closed-circuit TV. He would not have long before the guards came out of the compound to check what he was doing. But he didn't care. Knowing that he would be on camera, though, he had to put on his performance. He wanted to stride along as quickly as possible, but he had to shuffle slowly, pause and take deep breaths like someone on his last legs.

Near the entrance, a young woman dressed entirely in faded blue denim was taking photographs. Paul hesitated and watched her for a moment. He took her to be an artist, maybe a student, snapping industrial buildings. He predicted that she wouldn't last long before she was ejected from the site, art project finished or not. When she took the camera from her face,

Paul recognized her. She was the person who had shown up at Helen's funeral. What was she doing at YPI? He was tempted to go and talk to her but he couldn't afford the distraction.

Paul carried on with his search, but his lame act did not leave him enough time to find what he was looking for. Three officers surrounded him, took his name, asked him what he was doing, and told him to accompany them to the security lodge. As they escorted him, though, they walked past a white Mondeo. *The* white Mondeo. Paul concealed a broad smile behind his pained expression. His long shot had paid off. At the entrance, the mysterious woman was being shooed away, but not before she'd taken a picture of Paul and his company minders.

Inside, when they directed Paul towards a seat, he almost fell into it, gasping realistically.

"Tell us again. What were you doing?"

"I'm here to see Dr Urling-Clark."

"Mmm. We're having that checked." The officer glanced at a colleague who was scrutinizing a computer screen.

The man called, "Yes, there's a meeting at two o'clock."

The guard looked at his watch and said cynically, "A little early, aren't we?"

"Two o'clock?" Paul repeated, feigning surprise. "I thought it was supposed to be nine o'clock."

The security officer sneered. "What were you up to in the car park?"

Rather than answer the question, Paul decided to make things more interesting. He said, "I want to see Mr Wooderson."

"Mr Wooderson?"

"That's right."

"Why?"

"Because he might be able to throw some light on why I was in the car park."

"Have you got an appointment?"

"I do now," Paul retorted. He put his hand on his neck and let out a low moan.

The guard was not going to offer any sympathy for Paul's obvious illness. "Do you know our security chief?"

"Oh, yes," Paul answered. "I know a lot about him. You can tell him that."

The officer looked puzzled but said, "All right. I'll see if he's in."

"I think you'll find he is. Just tell him I'm here to see him."

Paul kept his eye on the guard while he telephoned from an adjacent room. Through the open door, Paul could not hear what the man said but his expressions were quite lucid. He nodded, turned to look at Paul, frowned, and his lips formed the words, "Yes. He looks sick." There was a pause as the guard listened to his

310

boss, then he put down the phone and returned to the unwelcome visitor.

"Mr Wooderson can't see you now and he suggests you leave the premises."

"Why?"

"Because there's nothing for you here."

"I might as well hang around for this meeting with Dr Urling-Clark. Or you could ask him to bring it forward."

"It's a waste of time. Mr Wooderson tells me this afternoon's meeting will be cancelled."

"Why's that?"

"He didn't say and I didn't question it. The meeting's off."

"Why is everyone avoiding me all of a sudden?"

The security officer shrugged. His innocent expression told Paul that Wooderson had probably left him in the dark. The chief of security had not told him that he was speaking to someone who was infected with meningitis. That made sense to Paul. Wooderson would not want to let on that he knew that his visitor was diseased. How could he have known – unless he'd had something to do with the infection?

To make sure, Paul remarked, "It's almost as if you think I'll spread some sickness around."

"I don't know about that." The guard was embarrassed and wanted to change the subject. "It's probably just an unavoidable change of schedules. Now, if you'd

311

just. . ." He waved both arms towards the door as if ushering a lamb out of a pen and into a field.

Paul got to his feet, sighed and stumbled out. He had learnt a little more – not as much as he'd hoped for – but enough. His next step was clear.

Paul did not return to the hotel. He wanted its staff to think that he was suffering – possibly dying – in hospital.

At the end of the working day, shortly after Mr Wooderson had returned home, Paul was staggering about on his doorstep. When the security chief answered Paul's ringing, his face was a treat. It was a mixture of real shock and absolute fear.

Paul's foot was in the door straight away and he lurched drunkenly into the hallway, a hand supporting his neck.

"What. . .?" Mr Wooderson leapt back.

"I just had to see you," Paul muttered, "before I go to hospit . . . a . . . a . . . a . . ." He hesitated, pretending that he was about to sneeze.

If YPI's chief of security had planned the attempted murder by meningitis, he might well know that the disease was spread through nasal discharges. While Paul faked an imminent sneeze, Mr Wooderson flinched, plainly alarmed. His rapid retreat meant nothing in a court of law but it told Paul everything.

Wooderson's daughter appeared at the end of the

hallway and her father cried, "Get back!" He waved her away in a panic.

So, Paul thought, Wooderson knows all about it. He knows that the meningitis bacteria's favourite hosts are teenagers.

Paul sniffed and smiled. "Sorry. Just a sneeze. I think it's gone for the moment. It'll come back when I least expect it, no doubt." He looked at Mr Wooderson and added, "I seem to have frightened you. Why's that?"

Squirming, Wooderson replied, "Sorry, I was... taken aback, that's all. Look, I don't think you should be here—"

"You know who I am?"

"Dr Turrell. I saw you once at Yttria – in a bit of a state. You were shouting, accusing everyone of ... all sorts. And I've seen you on video, making a nuisance of yourself. I really think ... I insist you leave right now."

Paul took his right hand from his neck and applied it instead to his nose. Still, the feigned sneeze did not come. "Why are you so keen to get rid of me?"

"We're ... er ... eating."

In a croaky voice, Paul asked, "What did you give to the room-service guy last night? Money in a plain brown envelope, like a sleazy politician? Why?"

Mr Wooderson became even more stiff and alert and scared. "I ... er ..."

"While I'm still capable of standing up, tell me Urling-Clark's address and I'll leave you alone."

"Yes," Mr Wooderson replied, suddenly more cheerful. "It's him you want to speak to, not me." He rattled off the manager's address.

It was easy for Paul to memorize the details. Ironically, Urling-Clark lived just along the lane from Helen's house. Paul said, "Thanks. I'll let you get on with that meal now. You don't want it going cold."

The church bells were in full cry. Their unimaginative and monotonous clangs fell on the entire village. Beyond the church, it was painful for Paul to drive past that half-wrecked house where he had spent so few days and nights, blissful days and nights. One side of the property was supported by scaffolding, like bones holding up weak flesh.

Of course, it was possible that Wooderson had telephoned Stuart Urling-Clark, but Paul doubted it. He had got the impression that the security chief was keen to pass the blame to his work colleague so he was unlikely to provide Stuart with advance warning. He'd want Urling-Clark to face Paul's wrath. As well as Paul's imaginary disease.

There was no response at the Urling-Clarks' house but their next-door neighbour, washing one of the cars on his ample drive, kept a suspicious eye on Paul.

Going over to the low fence, Paul asked him, "Do you know where Stuart is? I'm from YPI and I'm supposed to be having an out-of-hours meeting with him."

The man nodded, apparently convinced that Paul was genuine because he had dropped YPI and Stuart's first name into the conversation. "If you listen carefully, you can hear him."

Paul paused. It took a couple of seconds to figure it out. "The church bells?"

"Stuart'll be there with his wife. They're into the church and campanology," he said, clearly showing off his vocabulary.

"Thanks." Paul didn't feel like exchanging witticisms about bell-ringing. He walked away, got into his car and cruised back down the lane, once more passing Helen's disfigured house. He was occupied with a thought. How could a religious man plot against Brendan Fleetwood, Helen and himself? How could he cover up deaths among volunteers at Westland Young Offender Institution? How could he work on an offensive weapon? It was a peculiar Christianity, a peculiar way to love thy neighbour.

Thankfully, the bells were stilled by the time that Paul wandered into the dimly lit church. He had never seen the Urling-Clarks but somehow Paul was able to pick them out straight away. It was an educated guess. Stuart was dressed in trousers, middle-aged cardigan and garish tie. His wife was dressed sensibly, nothing daring, nothing interesting.

The small group of bell-ringers looked at Paul briefly and then carried on whispering among themselves.

Head bent, Paul waited on the back row of pews.

Luckily, the Urling-Clarks were the last ones to walk down the aisle. When they were opposite Paul, he got to his feet, clutching the back of the pew as if he needed the support to remain upright. "I'd like to have a word with you," he said.

Stuart's face creased with disapproval. "Pardon?"

To make sure, Paul asked, "You're Stuart Urling-Clark?"

"Yes."

"I want to have a chat," said Paul.

"Who are you?"

"Paul Turrell."

"But you—"

"What?"

Recovering quickly but taking his wife's hand and edging away, Stuart said, "You were supposed to see me this afternoon."

"Your security people – Mr Wooderson – cancelled it. I'm sure he told you and I'm sure you agreed."

Mrs Urling-Clark put in, "I don't know what's going on here, but are you feeling all right?"

Paul shrugged it off. "It's nothing. Just a headache, stiff neck and a bit of a temperature." Quoting every symptom he could recall, he added, "I'd shake hands but they feel very cold. Must be poor circulation."

Ignoring Paul's remarks, Stuart snapped, "Make another appointment with me – when you're feeling better. I can't see you now. We're busy. Full stop." He did not see the irony of snubbing a sick man in a church.

"You *will* see me now," said Paul. Then he let out an enormous cough, making no attempt to cover his mouth politely.

Immediately, Stuart put his hand over his mouth and nose. He staggered back, leaving his puzzled wife, and mumbled, "If you pester us, I'll call the police."

"Be my guest." Paul extracted his mobile phone and held it out towards Stuart. "I'd like to hear you explain my illness to the police, especially after what your Mr Wooderson told me earlier tonight. I'd like to hear you explain why you're so afraid to be near me."

"You've got a fever, young man, it's rather obvious," Mrs Urling-Clark said. "We don't want you around us if you're going to spread germs."

"You're into pharmaceuticals," Paul said to Stuart, "so what do you think I've got? A cold? Flu? Something that aspirin will shift?"

"I don't know. How could I?"

"So why are you backing away as if I've got leprosy?"

"Look—"

"It's too late for pretending you don't know anything," said Paul. "I put some pressure on Wooderson and he told me all about it, told me exactly what *you'd* got him to do, all your murky dealings."

"Told you everything? What are you talking about?"

317

Stuart retorted, now in the vestibule, dragging his wife, hoping to escape from Paul Turrell. He probably thought that he had to ride out only the next few hours and this sick lunatic would be out of the equation.

Following the couple, Paul asked, "You didn't expect Wooderson to talk, did you? Do you want a list of YPI's crimes?"

"I don't know what you're on about." Stuart tugged on his wife's forearm.

As a parting shot, Mrs Urling-Clark said, "I think you're delirious. You ought to be in hospital."

Yet Paul would not leave them alone. Pursuing them into the fresh air, where the daylight had begun to fade, he continued to harangue them and he continued the bluff. "I've got fingerprints on the tube of toothpaste, I saw Wooderson paying his fixer off and I've got Wooderson's word on where his orders come from. A clear trail from a poison to you."

"None of this makes any sense to me," Urling-Clark claimed as he made for home, eyes fixed ahead, not looking at Paul. "It's rubbish. Just what are you after?"

"Charges of murder and attempted murder for starters. But I might be persuaded not to talk to the police and the press in exchange for closing down the SCP19 project." After all, that's what Helen wanted most of all.

"You're mad," Stuart muttered. "Completely. Utterly."

Yes. Perhaps a little mad. Paul had every reason for being mad about YPI. But, despite his bravado in front of Urling-Clark, he didn't have any concrete evidence. All he had was the bogus disease and the fact that Urling-Clark and Wooderson had recoiled from it. To Paul, their reaction illustrated their guilt but it hardly amounted to proof. He had failed to get either of them to mention meningitis. If they had, they would have incriminated themselves immediately because only those who had plotted against him would have known the nature of the sickness.

Paul had pushed it as far as he could for the moment. Yet the evening was a long way from ending and he still had something to do.

46

Kyle was not daft. He knew that he could be walking into a trap. Even so, he had no choice. It was almost eight o'clock and he was standing in the corridor outside Max's sky-high apartment, close to Yttria on the west side of downtown Atlanta.

Inside the spacious and uncluttered room, some rock-and-roll singer was describing in detail and repetitively how he was going to dance his blues away. It could have been Elvis but Kyle wasn't sure. At least Kyle was relieved to see that he had not walked into a den of lions. Max was on his own. Behind him, out of the large window, there was a dramatic view of the Centennial Olympic Park and CNN TV Center.

Max turned the music down but not off and then went to get Kyle a bottle of beer straight from the fridge. Sitting again, Max took a drink of his own beer and then said, "I trusted you. You've lost a brother. You know what it's like."

Kyle was bewildered. "What's that got to do with it?"

"Everything."

"I'm not with you," Kyle admitted.

"You seemed pretty sure I'd polluted Beale Street with SCP19. I was going to deny it but why should I? I did it for Shannon. I did it for the nigger who killed Shannon. I'm not ashamed. In fact, I'm proud."

"Shannon? Is that your sister?"

Max nodded.

"She died on the street, you said. What are you saying now? She was murdered by a black American?"

"As good as. She was just a kid – sixteen – and he hooked her on drugs. He got her on the streets where she died."

"That's. . ." Kyle could not find the words to express his horror. "That's terrible, but. . ." He shook his head. "I can't wage war on all cars because of one accident. You can't persecute an entire race for one man's crimes."

Max was on a short fuse. "You think he's the only one? Christ, you've got some learning to do. Who d'ya think's behind the crime here? Who are the muggers and murderers, the pushers and the pimps? I did it to get back at Shadow as well, and a whole bunch like him. I'm taking a stand against the black tide of crime and violence and drugs. Simple as that."

The cold beer forgotten, Kyle said, "Don't you feel . . . guilty?"

"No. This is the Land of the Free and what I've done, it's justice. It feels good to exercise my rights." Max was genuinely amazed at Kyle's inability to see the virtue of his cause. "What are *you* saying? That I'm not supposed to do anything about it?"

"I think you've got to let the law—"

"Are you some sort of champion for the blacks?"

"No, I'm no one's champion. Not even close," Kyle

replied. "I'm no activist and I'm no campaigner either. I'm . . . ordinary. I just want to see a bit of humanity, that's all."

"People got to earn humanity. Some don't deserve it. They're holed up in prison, some are on death row, some are still out there on the streets."

Kyle could not believe that he was sitting comfortably in the home of a racist, a multiple murderer, discussing the merits of genetic cleansing. He should be running, screaming, calling the police. Before he decided what to do, though, he had a terrible thought. He asked, "Have you got any more SCP19 eggs?"

"Sure do."

Kyle swallowed. "How many?"

Max shrugged as if the exact number didn't matter. "Four." He glanced towards the kitchen.

They'll be in the fridge, Kyle realized. Like the beer. He glanced down at the bottle, frozen in his hand.

Max laughed. "No. There's nothing in the beer. Even if there was, it wouldn't affect you."

The CD finished and a welcome silence replaced the ancient rock and roll.

"You've got to let me take the eggs back to work," Kyle said. "That's where they belong. They can be handled safely at Yttria."

"What planet are you on? No one gives up his best weapon."

"It's wrong, Max."

"You're new here. You don't understand."

Kyle leapt out of his chair and dived towards the kitchen. Quickly locating the fridge, he knelt down and grabbed the only egg box that he could see. Getting back to his feet, he expected Max to be there, right in front of him, ready for a fight or an argument. Having taken the American by surprise, though, Kyle was hoping to persuade him to back off by threatening to break his precious eggs. At least here, in a closed apartment occupied by two white men, SCP19 would not do much damage, as long as no one opened the door or a window. But there was no contest. Max was still seated in the living room, not making a move. He wore a wry expression as if amused and puzzled by the weird antics of his British guest.

Cradling the egg box in his right arm, Kyle headed for the door and flung it open with his left. Then, stunned, he came to an immediate standstill.

Jack Nicholson, Frank Sinatra, George W Bush and Bill Clinton stood in the doorway, blocking his escape route.

A firm hand from behind whisked the egg box away from him. "You appear to have forgotten my friends," Max said. "Welcome to a Storm Force Brigade meeting." Calmly, he opened the cardboard carton and took out one of the deadly clutch. He held the light brown oval between thumb and forefinger. "Beautiful

323

container, isn't it? Kinda strong but fragile as well." He walked over to the window.

"No!" Kyle cried.

Kyle was dragged back to the centre of the room by the rest of gang and behind him the door slammed shut. It sounded final.

Max opened one of the windows and looked down at the distant ground.

"You won't drop it here," Kyle said. "They'll know it was you."

Max laughed again. "You haven't got inside the American mindset at all, have you? Work out how many people live on one side of a high-rise building like this. Hundreds. It could have been any of them. Anyway, who's going to think of a smashed egg on the sidewalk when blacks start falling ill?"

"Everyone I tell."

"Aw, you're not going to do that. You see, it's easy to have an accident up here. It's not just eggs that fall out of windows." He poked his hand outside, still holding the smart weapon in its protective shell.

It was no use struggling. Not against five of them. Kyle didn't stand a chance. He had to use his brain, not muscle. Kyle's main strength had always been in his head anyway. He took a deep breath. "No," he said. "I mean, everyone'll know because I'll have told them already – whether you push me out or not."

"What are you talking about, boy?" Jack Nicholson snapped.

Kyle felt the sweat running down his back and cheeks. "I'm not daft, you know. I guessed you might try it on tonight so—"

"What?"

"I did something about it."

George W Bush muttered, "He's bluffing."

Max withdrew his hand but did not put the egg back in its box. "I'm really disappointed in you, Kyle. What have you done?"

"It wasn't hard. It's at work. I put all the details about you and SCP19 in an e-mail message. It's protected with a password and self-timed. Tonight, it'll send itself to every computer in Yttria. It'll go to the police departments and regional medical centres in Memphis and Atlanta, whatever happens to me. Need I go on? You get the picture."

Kyle thought of himself as a chemist. He didn't know a lot about computers. He certainly didn't know how to send out e-mails automatically at a prearranged time. But, ever since his accident, he had been employed in computer chemistry. Perhaps Max would believe that he had acquired enough expertise to set such a trap. In reality, Kyle had left a note with Tristan Lockhart's secretary so that, in the morning, the president would know where Kyle had gone. That was all. From his own apartment, he had not been able to

325

inform anyone about his activities because Max had destroyed his computer and phone.

There was a searing pain in his right arm, twisted up behind his back. A voice in Kyle's ear whispered, "It's a bluff, isn't it?"

"No," Kyle squealed through the torment.

The stabbing intensified. "You've really set an automatic e-mail?"

"Yes," he cried. "I can stop it if I get to work – with the eggs."

"That's the trade-off, is it?" Max asked, coming close. "SCP19 for deleting the message?"

"Yes."

Deliberately, Max put the egg back into its cardboard cushion and picked up a table lamp. He waved the bright light in front of Kyle's contorted face.

Kyle felt his right arm go limp and it no longer seemed to hang in its natural position. No bones were broken but something felt out of place. The throbbing was almost unbearable but he tried to ignore it. Instead, he screwed up his eyes as he watched the menacing movement of the bulb.

Suddenly, the light went out as Max yanked the electric flex out of the base of the lamp. He was holding the defunct table lamp in one hand and the mains cable in the other. The two wires poked out of their insulation.

Kyle turned his head away. "No!"

The collection of men held him firmly, refusing to

allow him to recoil. Behind him, someone held his head full on to the bare metal wires.

"You're not bluffing?"

Kyle didn't know who had spoken. He focused only on the live cable.

"Well?"

"It's the truth," he spluttered.

The wires inched towards his face. They wouldn't need to touch his skin or even the salty sweat that would conduct electricity. Soon, any moment now, when the gap was narrow enough, a spark would leap, sending a crushing jolt through his body. Maybe even a fatal shock.

"Mr Lockhart's not going to burst in and save you this time," Max said. "Now, are you really sure?"

It was difficult not to blurt out that he was making it all up. It was difficult to concentrate. Yet, in his mind, something was telling him to hang on, telling him that *they* were bluffing. Yes! Of course. Max wasn't actually going to give him an electric shock. If he really meant it, Max's friends wouldn't be holding him because they'd take the current as well. Even so, the bare wires were so close, like the flickering tongues of poisonous snakes. Trying to keep his nerve, Kyle uttered, "I'm not joking!"

"All right," Max said, withdrawing the cable and turning it off at the mains. "He's telling the truth."

"Is he?" George Bush queried.

Kyle's heart sank as he heard someone say, "Let's get

serious. Get his pants, shoes and socks off, strap him to the seat and stand well back."

No time seemed to pass. The next thing Kyle knew, he was taped to a chair and there was only Jack Nicholson kneeling in front of him. Everyone else was hidden behind him. That snaking electric cable slithered closer and closer to his bare feet, ready to strike.

"No more games. Have you set up an e-mail?"

"Yes."

He was not sure if the tingling around his foot was the start of a shock or his own anticipation.

"Sure?"

"Yes," he muttered.

Then it happened. His head jerked agonizingly back and the pressure pushed all of the wind from his body. His heart and lungs seemed to be on the point of bursting. He was shocked rigid, falling back in the chair and collapsing on to the carpet. His head thudded against the floor. He was empty, finished.

"Just think. That was only the sole of a foot." The manic actor came alongside Kyle as he lay crookedly on the floor, still attached to the upturned chair, still conscious. The wires followed the contours of his bare legs, a few centimetres away from the skin. "Just think what it's going to be like. . . higher up."

Breathless and afraid, Kyle stared, unable to speak. He imagined a sadistic smirk behind the mask. His eyes darted back to those dreadful mesmerizing wires.

"So, is this automatic e-mail really real?"

A sound, a groan, escaped his throat. "Uh." Kyle didn't recognize it as his voice.

"This is your last chance, boy."

The cable was nearly touching his thigh yet, from his drained body, Kyle somehow summoned the spirit to nod his head. Then he braced himself, ready for the agony.

"I told you so," said Max's voice. "He's not lying. We've got to negotiate."

Abandoning the flex, Jack Nicholson stood up and joined the others.

Kyle was barely aware of the conversation among the members of the gang but he understood the outcome. They had decided that Max would take Kyle into work and witness him destroying the imaginary e-mail in exchange for the rest of the SCP19. After all, with Max still in his job, they could get more of the smart weapon once this annoying Brit had been disposed of or sent back to England.

When Max pushed the chair upright with Kyle still attached to it, Kyle nearly blacked out. He was dizzy, still unable to speak or feel much of his body. The rest was purely an ache. His phantom fingertips were screaming at him as if the nerves had just been severed. Some cold water was splashed in his face and the tape stripped from his legs and arms. Normally it would have hurt, but Kyle was numbed. He felt nothing but a slight tug. Released, he fell sideways off the seat and someone laughed at him.

There weren't many vehicles left in the company car park. Not enough to provide good cover, but plenty to provide a distraction. Shadow smiled. He had spotted a plush white Lexus. His favourite. In the dark, he knelt by the car's fuel tank, the perspiration glistening on his brow and arms. Like rain on dark glass, a drop of sweat ran down his left cheek, over his short muscular neck and into the cotton of his shirt. The night was not hot but he perspired with excitement. And with the anticipation of releasing his anger, of course. At his side were the tools of his trade: a rag, a can of gasoline, a box of matches.

Shadowtime. His fingers gripped that little box, slowly extracted a match. A simple strike, a twist of the wrist, and the cleansing began with a graceful yellow plume. Shadow's spine tingled, his heartbeat raced. He dropped the lighted match and the eager trail of fuel reached up and embraced the gift of life. The flame danced silently towards the white car. The yellow fingers clawed up the side of the Lexus, loitered for a few seconds on the soaked rag, blistering the paintwork, and then wormed their way into the interior.

Time stood still. It was the moment that Shadow craved. Flames flashed out into the darkness, sucked the oxygen from the night air, and fanned the Lexus.

330

After a delicious delay, the windows blew out and the car leapt off the tarmac in an exquisite explosion. The flame shot upwards into the night, pushing aside the darkness, illuminating the sky. The shock wave rushed past Shadow where he knelt, hidden from view behind another car. A split-second later, he felt a ripple of heat wafting over him. This was why he was alive. To exact revenge for Nathan and all the others, using the cherished weapon of fire. But the Lexus was only the start, only a means to an end.

He left a holdall under the car, between its rear wheels. Then, when he heard the guards, it was time to move towards the building emblazoned with *Yttria Pharmaceuticals Inc*. Once Security was occupied with the flaming car, Shadow could mount the fence and make a dash towards the premises. Against the background of shouting, roaring flames and, soon, approaching sirens, no one would hear Shadow smashing a window. No one would notice him clambering into the building.

There was a commotion in the car park when Kyle and Max arrived at Yttria. A vandal had set fire to a night-shift worker's car. Perhaps it was just as well that there was a diversion. The sole guard left at the gate did not notice that Kyle seemed to be staggering, a little stunned. "Are you cleared for night work, Mr Proctor?" he asked.

"Er. . ."

Max looked a little alarmed and began to say, "I think you'll find—"

"Oh, it's OK," the security officer said, glancing up from his computer screen. "I see your clearance has been upgraded. You can go almost anywhere, any time."

All three of them glanced outside where the darkness had been dispelled by the bonfire. Now, the quiet was being dispelled by a wailing siren.

"Huh. Local trash," the guard muttered. Opening the gate for the two workers, he added, "Have a good night." Distracted by the disturbance in the car park, he forgot to search Max Levine's bag.

47

It was night-time and Paul felt a great wave of fatigue flood over him. It wasn't just the lack of sleep, it was the constant tension. To stop himself drifting unintentionally into sleep, he had left the relative comfort and warmth of his car. He had crept around to the back of the house where a cold wind kept him alert. Besides, if there was to be action tonight, it wouldn't be at the front under the yellow streetlights, in full view of any late-night neighbours.

At the far end of the Woodersons' garden there was a shrubbery, and Paul sat in it on the cold, damp ground. He was still, quiet, vigilant and, blending with the bushes, invisible to any other intruder. He was also bored. It was two-thirty in the morning and nothing had happened – apart from an unconcerned hedgehog that had trundled across the lawn. Perhaps Urling-Clark had not taken the bait. Perhaps he didn't believe that Wooderson had turned against him. But Paul was following his instinct. By saying at the church that Wooderson had opened up, Paul intended to make Urling-Clark feel threatened by his own senior security officer. Paul was sitting in the garden, getting chillier and wetter by the minute, because he thought that it was in Urling-Clark's nature to strike back hard when he felt intimidated. Paul didn't know what he was looking

333

for but he thought that he would recognize it when he saw it. Whatever it was, it would be designed to put an end to the threat posed by Wooderson.

Paul yawned and looked skywards as something flew overhead: a bird or a bat perhaps.

Then he heard something. Not footsteps. It was a quiet click at the back gate. It could have been a cat or the wind or anything, but Paul thought that it was a human being. He held his breath.

A figure – almost certainly the man who had taken the job in room service – appeared in silhouette at the corner of the house. He was carrying a bag of some sort and he moved without a sound. He knelt by the back door, put the bag down silently, removed something from his pocket and began to fiddle with the lock.

Paul strained his eyes, watching and waiting, shrinking into the shrubbery but safe from detection. He told himself that only he could hear the exaggerated thumping of his heart and his uneven breathing.

The man with short silvery hair put something back into his trouser pocket, pulled out a different device, then carried on his patient work on the back-door lock.

Three, maybe four minutes had passed, but to Paul, it seemed like for ever. Then there was another faint click and the intruder stood up. Gently, he pushed open the door and stepped inside the kitchen, taking his bag with him.

No, not a bag. As the man turned to enter the house,

Paul got a good look at what he was carrying. It was a can, almost certainly a petrol can, perhaps five litres in volume. Of course. It made sense. Suddenly, Paul was sure that he was watching the arsonist who had demolished the research wing of the hospital, who probably fixed Helen's central heating system to explode. Paul took a long breath, trying to keep calm, and edged towards the back of the house.

Inside, by weak torchlight, the hotel worker was dousing the hallway, front door and kitchen with petrol. A perverse kind of room service. Plainly, he was hoping to trap the Woodersons inside a cage of fire. At one moment, this cold-blooded fixer was accepting a pay-off from Mr Wooderson in a homely pub and, at the next, he was plotting to kill the same man in his own home.

Paul knew that he did not have long to decide what to do. This hired assassin might strike a light and burst out of the kitchen at any moment. By then, it would be too late to alert the family sleeping upstairs. But, if Paul chose to rush in straight away, he could be playing into the arsonist's hands. Paul guessed that the hitman would welcome the opportunity to knock him senseless and abandon him to the inferno along with the Woodersons. If the meningitis hadn't done the job, maybe fire would. This professional might even set it up to look as if Paul had burnt down the house to exact revenge on the security chief and inadvertently ensnared himself.

Paul swore silently. He felt responsible for getting the Wooderson family into this mess so he had to do something. But what? He was not really cut out for espionage. He knew all about the fierce chemical reactions that were about to obliterate the Woodersons' home but he didn't know what to do to stop them.

In the hallway, the man was squatting by the mains socket, attaching something to it. Then he shifted to a lamp. He had something in his hand, a screwdriver, and he was doctoring the electric flex.

Of course! At last, Paul saw a lucky break. Surely, the man inside had added a timer to the electric socket and was now fiddling with the lamp's wiring. That made sense. Nothing as crude as a match. The silver-haired assassin would be away from the site of his crime when the mains timer turned on the lamp, the lamp's defective wiring caused a spark and the spark initiated a fire in the petrol-drenched atmosphere. It was the same tactic that he'd used in Helen's house: the central heating system's automatic timer had initiated the explosion.

Quickly, Paul retreated to his hiding-place in the bushes. He could afford to wait. He could afford to let the assassin go. He did not need to risk a confrontation because Wooderson could identify him later. Besides, Paul was angling for bigger fish. Yet how long would there be between the killer leaving and the spark flying? How long would Paul have? Was the delay measured in seconds, minutes or hours? Not hours. In hours, the petrol vapour would have dispersed. The longer the delay, the more likely one of the Woodersons might wake up, smell the fumes and alert the family. No. Paul would have minutes or seconds to get to that timer and turn it off.

When the dark figure slipped sideways out of the house, Paul was frustrated to see him bend down by the back door and fiddle again with the lock. He was making sure that the Woodersons were entombed in their home.

As soon as the man tiptoed away through the alley by the side of the property, Paul came out of his hiding-place and tried the back door. As expected, he found that it was locked. There was no time for thinking. He had to get in quickly and disable the incendiary device. Paul looked around for a brick or heavy stone. Nothing. Instead, he braced himself and then kicked the back door near the handle. His foot juddered to a halt. He had made no impression on it but the boom thundered throughout the quiet house. Paul didn't worry about the noise any more. He had to wake the Woodersons anyway. He tried again, slamming the sole of his shoe against the wooden door. There was a wrenching sound but the door refused to budge. Then, grunting aloud with the effort, he let loose as much strength as he could muster in a third kick and this time the back door flew back and crashed against a wall. He dived into the kitchen. Paul knew that he was now at his most vulnerable. If the timer activated, there would be an almighty flash and he would be consumed in the blaze.

He was dimly aware of someone on the stairs shouting, "What's going on?"

Paul ignored everything. He dashed into the hall, clattered into the small table and lunged for the mains switch, turning it off. To make sure, he yanked the plug and timer from the socket.

"What?!"

Paul looked up to see Mr Wooderson in a dressing gown at the bottom of the stairs. He was reaching for the main light switch.

"No!" Paul cried in panic. "Don't turn anything on. Can't you smell it?"

Mr Wooderson murmured, "Petrol."

"Yes," Paul replied, getting to his feet. "Petrol. Leave the lights off. It's ready to blow."

Still dozy, Wooderson was perplexed. "What's happening?"

"YPI's getting its own back for you talking to me."

Wooderson said nothing for a few seconds. He was still coming to his senses, thinking it through, working it out, trying to combat the heaviness of sleep. Then he stammered, "Someone's tried to kill us in our sleep!"

"Urling-Clark."

Shock displaced drowsiness and Wooderson growled, "Maybe it was you."

"Why would I break in and stop it, then?"

In the darkness, Mr Wooderson shook his head in exasperation.

"Call the police," Paul told him. "All right?"

There was a female shout from upstairs and Wooderson said, "Hang on." He mounted the stairs again. After a minute, he was back.

Clearly, he had told his wife and daughter to get up and leave the house without turning on anything electrical in case of sparks. He wanted them to go to a neighbour's house, out of the way of the fire risk and out of the way of meningitis bacteria.

Hurriedly, the two men opened both doors and all of the windows in the house to allow the petrol fumes to escape on the through-draught, then they waited outside on the hollow street. Adrenalin was now pumping through both of them, making them alert.

"I told Urling-Clark you'd shopped him," Paul confessed.

"Oh?" Wooderson was still suspicious of Paul, not yet convinced.

"Yes. He sent your mate with the short hair and plain brown envelope. And a can of petrol. That's what he thinks of you – you *and* your family."

Wooderson still kept his distance. "I ought to give you a good thumping or thank you. I don't know which." He paused before adding, "But no one threatens my family. No one."

To the sound of sirens in the distance, Paul replied, "Tell the police what you know, then."

The senior security officer nodded slowly. He was distracted. Paul's words had not won him over but something was certainly gnawing at him. "I've been looking at myself a lot recently. I've even been to church." He let out a long weary breath. "I'm tired of doing YPI's dirty work. It's wrong. I'm tired of Urling-Clark trampling all over me."

"Here's your chance to put the record straight," Paul replied as the police car's headlights carved up the night.

Later, at the police station, the low-ranking officer who had once listened impatiently to Paul Turrell's allegations reappeared. He approached Paul warily. "Mr Wooderson's just told us you've got meningitis. I've called an ambulance."

Paul smiled wryly and scratched at his stubble. "No, I haven't got meningitis or anything else. But you've got to ask why he thinks I have."

The policeman nodded. "He's already told us. He's told us a lot."

"About Helen Crear?"

The officer nodded again.

"Brandon Fleetwood?"

"That wasn't an accident either, it seems."

Paul sighed with relief.

"We've got a call out for some people at the top of Yttria Pharmaceuticals. And we've got the name of a hired fixer. He's the one who drove the car into Dr Crear, according to Wooderson. In fact," the policeman admitted with a sidelong glance at Paul, "it's pretty much as you told me on Monday."

Once again, Paul felt an immense wave of tiredness. This time he could afford to succumb to it. Shortly, he would be able to take a long, long bath, wash his hair, shave, tuck into a huge beef curry, sleep. At last, he would allow himself to relax, but he could not be happy. He could not be satisfied. He had not brought Helen back. He could not bring her back. And, whilst he had plucked the rotten apples from YPI, he could not be sure that he had consigned SCP19 to history. Despite the coming scandal, Yttria could still pursue the smart biological weapon.

He was too tired to think about it now, though. Sleep was inevitable and irresistible.

Tipped off by an unusually well informed contact at the Ministry of Defence, the journalist with cropped dark hair and denim clothes went over the DTI's list of export licences once again. For a moment, Victoria Scates wiped her tired eyes. When she put her glasses back on, she found herself peering yet again at the only conspicuous entry. She'd smiled when she'd seen it for the first time. The second time, she'd frowned. The third time made her think. Now, she was deeply suspicious. Yttria was exporting genetically-modified ostrich eggs to an ostrich farm called Knobel Industries in Hartswater, South Africa. Why? Why send eggs to a farm? Shouldn't it be the other way round? The consignment was marked for research purposes only. Strange. Very strange.

The whole thing was odd. Victoria had received a whole catalogue of allegations against Yttria to investigate. They had been leaked to her from the MoD by an anonymous source that might well have been the MP for Cambridge. After all, the MP was a junior minister in Defence. But why would the MP release the rumours when her own Government would be tainted if any of them were true? And why would the MP now leak information on the fate of Yttria volunteers? The Government had gagged Victoria when, a while back, she had got much the same story from the Black and Asian Defenders. Perhaps an internal cleansing was under way. Perhaps the MoD was locked in a dispute with the Department of Trade and Industry. Whatever game the politicians were playing, it was bread and butter for a journalist.

Government intrigue wasn't top of Victoria's priorities right now. First, she had to dig deep into the export of an illegal racial weapon, the cover-up of those disastrous drug trials, the removal of opponents. She had to reassess Helen Crear's death: not a suicide after the baby organ scandal but a possible murder after the drug trial fiasco. If someone in the MoD or DTI was toppled by the publication of Victoria's investigations, great. But politicians didn't really matter. It was people who mattered, and modified ostrich eggs for research were on their way to a farm in a country that was still coming to terms with issues of race and land ownership.

With her newspaper's faithful Visa card by her side, Victoria logged on to a travel site to book herself a last-minute flight from London to South Africa.

48

The building wasn't totally empty but it felt as if it were. Max and Kyle took the elevator to the sixth floor where the dimmed corridor was eerily deserted, the labs dormant. Inside some of the rooms, automatic equipment churned and buzzed. Liquids were being stirred in flasks, air was bubbling through fermentation jars, a robotic arm was transferring solutions from one set of sample tubes to another, analytical equipment was generating and storing data. Neither Max nor Kyle had ever fully got used to the fact that robots, unlike human workers, performed perfectly well in the dark and never wanted to go home at night. It always seemed odd that the machines' ominous humming emanated from unlit labs.

Max sniffed the air and said, "Someone's left the top off the ether bottle again." The two men stood for a moment outside Max's laboratory. It was not clear who was the captive and who was the captor but it was Max who tapped in the code, opened the door and turned on the strip lights.

Kyle closed his eyes and then blinked before he could open them fully. Under the harsh laboratory lights, he was pale and weak. He looked more like the sheep than the wolf but, in a way, he was in charge. At least for the moment. He was in control until it became obvious that he didn't have a bargaining chip at all.

"What now?" asked Max, his tone loaded with open hostility.

"You put the eggs in a secure unit, crack them open one by one and pour the contents into concentrated sulphuric acid."

"You're sure not leaving anything to chance."

"No."

"I want to see this e-mail first," said Max.

Quickly, Kyle glanced around the laboratory benches. "OK. But there's no computers in here."

"They're in the office at the end."

Kyle tried not to sound disappointed. "No problem, but. . ."

"What?"

"Why don't you put the eggs somewhere safe first? They make me nervous."

"Squeamish, eh?"

"Yes," Kyle replied bluntly. He didn't feel talkative. He just wanted to get it over with and then rest. Hopefully, sleep would repair his various injuries.

To Kyle, the reek of solvent seemed to be getting more powerful. And he thought that he heard someone outside in the passageway.

Max walked to a sealed cabinet, put his briefcase on the floor and carefully lifted out the box of eggs. At the side of the unit, there was an airlock. He slid the opened cardboard carton into it and shut the small but weighty door. A pump sprang into automatic action, sucking the air out of the cavity. Then came the hiss of a chemical sterilization spray followed by clean air. The eggs were now in limbo. They were sealed from the outside world but not yet drawn into the sterile cabinet itself. The giant latex gloves lay limp and unused against the glass side of the unit.

"You show me the e-mail," Max said, "and I'll come back with some acid so I can destroy the SCP19."

In the next fume cupboard, some microbes were growing in a broth while a mechanical stirrer whisked the grimy fluid round and round. Beyond that, there was a large reservoir of purified and sterilized water.

"How do I know you'll really kill it off?"

"Because I say so. I only want to see this clever message you've set up. You can delete it after I've done the eggs. That's fair," Max claimed. "I isolate the eggs, you show me the e-mail. I kill the SCP19, you kill the e-mail. I'm not doing my side of the bargain for nothin'."

"All right."

A robotic arm in the middle of the lab lifted a syringe, stabbed it through the rubbery seal of a sample vial, drew up some of the liquid, swung round with an unusually loud squeal and injected it into a chromatograph with a whirr and a click.

Both Kyle and Max glanced towards it and sniffed again. Perhaps the equipment was about to develop a fault because there was a smell of burning now. But they both ignored it because they had other things on their minds.

Kyle followed Max towards the computer room, desperately trying to come up with an idea to get him out of a hole but his brain was dull with pain and anxiety.

Max flung the door open. "There. You can use any of them. It sounds like you've got high-level clearance now so you can access everything you want from here, including your e-mail."

Kyle hesitated. Still nothing had occurred to him. He had no choice but to relinquish control. "There is no e-mail."

Max was clearly shocked. "You what?"

"There's no e-mail. I was lying."

"No. You're lying now," Max replied angrily. "You're trying it on."

Kyle shook his head. "Sorry."

"If you were bluffing. . . No, it's not possible."

"I was."

"No chance, not under that punishment."

"It's true," Kyle said. "I *was* bluffing."

The burning smell was much stronger now.

Max turned away and, with his open palm, scattered everything within reach on the bench. Flasks and dishes clattered to the floor. Then he inhaled deeply and swung back to Kyle. "You've sure got guts. I'll give you that. But. . ." His hands were clenched tightly into fists now and there was hate in his face. It was the hate of someone who didn't like to be duped. "My friends won't like that. I don't either," Max said menacingly.

Kyle shrugged. Both physically and mentally, he was exhausted. Just before Max's furious fist knocked him unconscious, he heard something. Something loud. It was the building's fire alarm.

The place was huge. Shadow didn't know where to start. It wasn't like torching a car or a house. This was an immense job. But he wasn't going to be put off. Yttria did not deserve the space that it occupied on the planet. Shadow was determined to reduce it to ashes. This time, he was so annoyed, so outraged, that he didn't care if a few people were still in the building. If they worked in a dirty multinational company like this, they deserved everything they got.

On the fifth-floor maze he stumbled across something interesting. There was a locked room labelled *Solvent Store*. He didn't need to be a scientist to understand the hazard symbol painted on the door. It showed wild yellow flames and underneath was written in black capitals, FLAMMABLE LIQUIDS. Shadow smiled.

He picked up the heavy fire extinguisher that stood in the corridor and, using his power, slammed it into the door. The metal buckled under the force. One more strike and the solvent store lay open before him.

There were shelves and shelves of large dark bottles, each one containing two and a half litres of highly flammable liquid. Shadow unscrewed the plastic cap of the nearest jar and breathed in the fragrant smell. It reminded him of gasoline. Perfect. In the storeroom there was even a trolley meant for wheeling the heavy bottles to different laboratories. At once, Shadow got to work. He removed the screw-caps from every bottle that carried a warning of extreme flammability and dangerous flash point. Then he loaded the trolley with as many opened bottles as it would take.

No one encroached on the corridor while Shadow perspired over his arduous work. There were few sounds from inside the building apart from his own clanking of the heavy bottles. The guards would still be outside, dealing with the fire and the other little presents he had left in the car park. He was pleased that he'd had the foresight to leave some suspicious-looking bundles under a few of the cars. It would keep the authorities distracted for a long time – until they found that the shoebox contained stones, the McDonald's package was full of cold chips, the two-bit holdall held a homeless man's mangy sleeping-bag, and the plastic bag held waste paper topped by suggestive batteries and wires. Shadow hadn't planted an incendiary device but the guards didn't know that. They would have sent almost their entire staff out to deal with the emergency in the car park. He could imagine the sniffer dogs, the robots poking around in the packages, the empty surveillance room, the unwatched security screens.

Shadow smiled as he lugged the trolley down the passageway, pouring the solvents behind him as he went. Each time he came to a side-room or laboratory, he drenched it with solvent and ditched the empty bottle inside. When he had exhausted his supply of liquids, he went back to the store to get more.

Shadow had taken other precautions. He had already been down to the basement, found the main water supply and turned it off. Then, to make sure the sprinkler system did not spoil the fun, he flicked its master switch to the off position.

He thought that he had probably soaked the entire fifth floor with flammable liquids. Finally, he scattered solvent liberally around the stairs and elevator shafts so that the fire would spread more quickly to other storeys. The whole place stank. At first the smell had been sweet, then it became sickly. Now it was nauseous and Shadow had a gnawing headache and choked lungs. But the building was ready to become a bonfire. It was waiting. Just to make sure, Shadow tipped over more bottles in the storeroom itself and carried two jars up the stairs to the sixth storey.

There, he hesitated. Did he hear voices? No, there was nothing. It was just his nerves, his bursting head, his imagination. He scattered the contents of the bottles down the passageway and fled. He needed fresh air.

If he didn't get away from the fumes soon, he would pass out and fall victim to his own trap. Yes, he needed clean air but he also needed to see flame. It was shadowtime.

Using the stairs, he went back down to the ground floor and found the window that he had broken to gain entry. It was also his escape route and it was still clear. Everything was in place. Shadow would light the trail of fuel on the stairs, retreat quickly, climb out of the window, and find a safe haven where he could watch the coming spectacular. And it was going to be very spectacular. Box of matches in hand, heart pounding, he went back to the dripping stairwell. He was feeling very sick and dizzy now but he was also on a high. It wasn't just the effect of the solvents, it was the risk and the thrill of his biggest job yet.

He would have to be careful to keep the lighted match away from his own shoes and the bottom of his pants, which were wet with liquor. He couldn't afford to linger over the ignition this time. The place was a ticking fire-bomb. He was about to strike the match and flick it towards the eager pool of liquid that had gathered at the bottom of the stairs when he heard a voice behind him.

"What's this?"

It was a cry of surprise and outrage from a white guard gripping a thick baton in his hand.

Shadow did not fancy his chances against a trained

security guard with a weapon. Truth be told, Shadow had never been any good at fighting, despite his strength. He didn't have the stomach for it. Now, though, his escape route was cut off. The only way was forward and upward towards that heady mixture of solvents. Unable to complete his job, Shadow pounded up the stairs at speed, taking the shiny wet steps three at a time.

Shadow's legs were already tired but he forgot about his fatigue, forgot about his headache, as he flew upwards. He was faster than the security officer, who was carrying his baton in one hand and shouting something into the radio in his other.

Shadow was breathing heavily, clogging his lungs with yet more vapour. He decided he'd have to play a trick. It was the only way. He could not keep climbing when the exit was five storeys below him. He needed to double back. As soon as he could get one flight ahead of the guard – out of his sight – Shadow dived down the corridor. It was the sixth floor and he turned into a darkened laboratory, flattening himself against the internal wall. He was gasping the polluted air for breath, trying to keep quiet. Most of the fumes were concentrated on the storey below but they were slowly permeating the whole building. Shadow could not get away from the sickly vapour. He waited in the blackness, trying to ignore the ghostly buzzing of some machine in the room with him. It sounded as if it were alive. Once the guard had gone past, he would race out of the lab and back to the stairs or the elevators.

The officer was about to mount the next flight of stairs when he realized that he could no longer hear the boy's footsteps above him. The young intruder had slipped into the sixth floor. Damn him. The guard tiptoed into the long gloomy corridor. Where the hell was the lad? He turned up his nose. And just what had the scientists got up to? The place reeked of chemicals and he couldn't stand the stink. Still, he was paid to look after security, not to worry about the stench created by the company's scientists. He was never going to find the boy in this light. He cursed the shadow and hit the light switch.

Immediately, his hand went to his face for protection. There was an immense whoosh, almost a dull explosion, and a mass of flame filled the corridor. The guard cried out as the dancing yellow curtain enveloped him and headed for the stairwell. There, it flashed downwards, eager to seek out more fuel on the storey below. It left behind a smoky corridor, small pockets of flame, and a writhing guard whose screams were lost in the howling alarm.

Max reopened the exterior door of the airlock and hurriedly grabbed the small cardboard carton. He was not going to lose the opportunity to reclaim the eggs. In fact, it was all turning out very well. The alarm and the smell told him that there was a fire somewhere in the building. He would escape with his smart weapon and let the flames take care of Kyle, still unconscious in the lab.

Out in the corridor, Max came to an abrupt halt, taken aback by the sight that met his eyes. He grimaced and recoiled from a scorched body lying inert on the floor. Yellow flames licked triumphantly around the figure. The fire had taken hold of its victim so fiercely that Max could only imagine that someone had doused him in gasoline or something. Open-mouthed, Max surveyed the hazy passageway. It was obvious that flame had flashed along it, engulfing the security officer. Here and there, parts of the carpet and walls smouldered or burned like oversized candles but, for now, the brutal blaze had retreated. Max could do nothing for the tortured man and, besides, the eggs were more important to him. In an emergency, though, he should not use the elevators. They could lose power and he'd be trapped inside. Clutching the egg box, he made for the stairwell. After all, he was only six storeys up. He'd be down and away in no time.

Trying not to look at the smoking remains, trying to avoid breathing the appalling smell, Max sidled past the body and headed for the stairs. He was worried that, behind the clamour of the siren, there might be a roar, but he wasn't sure. The alarm pounded his ears and played tricks with his hearing. He turned the corner and halted abruptly. Instead of a stairwell there was an inferno of flame and heat. Immediately, Max felt his hair shrivelling, his skin twitching, his sideburns sizzling. There was no doubt now. A howling fire raged. There was a massive explosion – the solvent store down below detonated – and windows crashed and blew out. The fresh air added more oxygen to the blaze, feeding a huge fireball that came up the stairs towards Max.

For a moment it was like looking down into fiery hell. Max staggered back, the eggs toppling out of his grasp. The box hit the floor and the eggs cracked, oozing their innards. The fluid turned white on the floor as if instantly fried and then burnt to black. Every last molecule was utterly destroyed.

Max turned to flee but he wasn't fast enough. The clothing on his back burst spontaneously into flame and, shrieking with pain, he tripped over the guard's body. The inferno rolled mercilessly over him.

Shadow stood in the dark. Above the piercing fire alarm, he heard at least one explosion, probably more, and two human screams – inhuman screams, really. He'd never heard anything like that before, he'd never hurt anyone before. He was crying softly. The wall against his back had suddenly got hot and he leapt away from it. Now what was he going to do?

There was no way out of the building. He'd made sure of that. The stairs and elevators would be seething with unruly flame. He was six storeys up. Even if he could find an external window, there was no way he could jump to safety and live. There was only one course: up and as far away from the conflagration as possible. But, even if he found a way of accessing the upper floors, how would he escape? He would just have to hide in one of the top storeys and hope that his plan to reduce the whole place to a pile of charred rubble would not succeed.

Cautiously, he put his head out into the corridor and a warm blast engulfed him. When he saw the two bodies lying close to each other between him and the stairs, he let out an involuntary groan. He could see no sign of life in either of them. He swallowed with discomfort. Now, that combination of yellow and black – flame scavenging on charred remains – had lost its magnificence. He hadn't expected to be so close to death; he'd anticipated being able to watch from a safe distance. Then, any victims would have been anonymous and out of sight. These blackened shapes, fixed like grotesque statues in a horror film, brought him too close to his own crime. He turned and vomited. Wiping his mouth, he tried to steel himself. Later, he could afford to regret what he had done. Now, he had to save himself, if he could.

It was definitely useless to go back to the elevators or stairs. That end of the passage was aglow. The snarling fire prised a whole panel from the wall and it toppled to the floor in flames. Shadow stepped out of the doorway, into the deathly tunnel and headed the other way. Black smoke stained the ceiling, converting the corridor into a cave. Overhead, the light bulbs that had come on had since blown. It was so hot, it felt as if he were moving inside a volcano, looking back constantly in case a stream of lava threatened to flood over him. He had taken only a few steps when there was another explosion and the unearthly whoosh of a fireball behind him. Luckily, Shadow was next to a different laboratory and its door had been left slightly open. He lunged nervously inside, slamming the door shut behind him.

He found himself inside a well lit lab, blowing on his right hand. The door had been surprisingly hot. The room had no windows at all. Shadow had felt heat before, smelled toxic fumes before, watched flames many times, but he had never put himself in any real danger. He was scared and breathless. Yet he had no intention of becoming a victim of his own arson. He wondered if it would be safe to go back out again. Seeing a cloth lying on a bench, he took it and tied it round his hand for protection before he opened the door gingerly. He could no longer see the two men. That part of the corridor had succumbed to the blaze. If he had stayed inside the last room a moment longer, he would have been trapped, consumed. This lab would be the next to fall prey to the pyre as it crept down the passageway. Already smoke was billowing in from cracks along the wall.

Panicking, Shadow looked around the laboratory for anything that would help him to get away. It was then that he saw someone lying on the ground, stirring slightly. Really, Shadow didn't have the time to worry about anyone else, especially not a worker at Yttria Pharmaceuticals. He should leave the white and get out, but he couldn't. He had already seen too much cruelty for one night. He went over to the young scientist and squatted down. "Are you OK?" he panted.

The man muttered something incomprehensible.

Seeing a large tank of water, Shadow grabbed a beaker, held it under the tap and filled it. Then he flung the water over the man's head.

"Ugh!"

Shadow did it again. "Come on! If you want to get out alive, you'd better wake up."

Kyle sat up and winced. "What's. . .?"

"The place is on fire and we're in deep, man," he shouted above the din of the alarm.

"Fire?" Kyle groaned and accepted the boy's muscular arm to drag himself upright.

"Is there a way up on this side?" Shadow pointed away from the stairs.

"Up?"

"We can't go down. That's where the fire is. Can we go up?"

"I don't know. No. The lifts are. . ." The wounded white waved in the other direction.

He was English, Shadow realized. "Think. There must be something."

"No. There's. . ." Kyle hesitated. "Yes, there's a big goods lift."

"Right. Let's go."

"No!" Kyle cried, shaking his head, trying to shift his fuzzy vision and clouded judgement.

"What's wrong? Quick!"

"There's something. . . Just a. . . You don't use a lift in an emergency."

"You got a better idea?"

Kyle shrugged helplessly.

Shadow said, "Look. I'll soak you with this water. You chuck it all over me. Right?"

"Yes, that'll . . . you know."

They stood there, throwing water over each other until they were both saturated. Water ran down their flattened hair, their faces, into their clothing, which stuck to their skin. The soaking reminded Shadow of what he had just done on the fifth floor but this time the liquid wasn't flammable. The water flushed the solvent from his clothing. After the impromptu shower, at least the Brit looked a little more alive, his face a little less pasty.

The wet rag around his right hand, Shadow opened the laboratory door. It was like a glowing furnace outside. He shrugged. "Look, it's coming down the passage. It's gonna be on our tails. The only thing we can do is run. You go first. You know where the elevator is."

Kyle stared at the boy, trying to understand, and then nodded. "Yes."

"If you don't want to fry, run like you've got the cops behind you."

They charged down the smoky cavern, the intense heat on their backs. Steam flew from them. "Faster," Shadow called.

Near the end, Kyle stopped and looked around. "There!"

Just around the corner, there were the large zigzag doors of a goods elevator. In the semi-darkness, Shadow grabbed the door handle and yanked. Nothing. The elevator was parked on a different storey. He fumbled for the call button, pushing it over and over again as if he could speed the elevator's arrival. He could not hear if the mechanism had sprung into action because of the alarm that swelled like feedback. He banged frantically on the door.

"Just a minute," Kyle cried. "There's a fire escape."

"Where?"

"Over here. Out the window, I think."

They both looked out. Sure enough, spiralling metallic steps were fixed to the side of the building.

"Great!"

But, from out of the broken window on the floor

below, a giant flame leapt up in front of them on the other side of the glass. Anyone on the frail exit would not have stood a chance.

"No!"

Hopes shattered, they both turned away from the escape route.

A wall of flame was coming along the corridor towards them, incinerating everything in its path. They dashed back to the goods elevator. Water was evaporating rapidly from their skin and clothing, drying them, stripping away their only protection. They were coughing and choking on the thickening smoke that descended lower and lower till it was just above their heads. They ducked down and tried to squash themselves against the warm, inset door.

"The lift's not coming!" Kyle yelled against the uproar of the fire and the alarm.

But Shadow had felt the vibration against his back. "It is. Hang on in there."

A wave of scorching heat swept past them and a large section of the burning ceiling crashed down at their feet.

"It'd better be now or—"

A flaming panel dropped off the wall and on to Kyle's trousers. The last remaining dampness in the fabric stopped it from catching alight. Kyle crushed himself against the door and cried out from the pain in his knees.

Shadow pushed Kyle aside unceremoniously and tugged on the door again. This time, it folded back. Shadow grasped the handle of the metal inner door and the wet rag sizzled in his palm. The elevator cage was blisteringly hot. Through the tiny gap between the solid floor and the elevator, Shadow could see flame. Below them, even the shaft was on fire. He grabbed Kyle and yanked him inside. He pushed with all of his might on the outer door, shutting out a surge of flame that singed his hair and parched the skin of his face and hands. For a moment, the billowing fire scorched his unprotected hand. Not paying attention to his injuries, he slammed the inner door shut and hit the top button on the keypad.

The heavy-duty elevator rumbled and lumbered into life, climbing upwards unwillingly.

"It's going up!" Kyle cried.

"You wanna go down? It's hell down there. Just don't touch anything," Shadow warned.

"I can feel it through my shoes," Kyle muttered.

Shadow nodded. "We're in a frying-pan." He coughed violently. "If we went down at this speed we'd be well-done steaks before we got past Floor 5. We got to go up, away from the fire." Then, impatiently, he yelled, "Doesn't this thing go any faster?"

Kyle shrugged. "Never been in it before."

"How many storeys has this place got, man?"

"Er. . ." Kyle paused to think. "Nineteen, I think."

Shadow looked at the keypad. "This only goes up to fifteen."

"It's for lab equipment. The labs stop at fifteen."

The button showing the figure 9 lit up as the elevator crawled higher at its sedate pace, refusing to acknowledge their urgency.

The air inside was still hot, dry and smoky. They were high above the seat of the blaze but the heat and smoke followed them relentlessly. They shuffled from foot to foot to ease the scorching on their soles.

"Come on!" Shadow urged.

Kyle was too exhausted, too hurt, to say anything. It was all he could do to stay on his feet. If he sat or lay down in the precarious cage, he would be burnt and blistered.

Gradually, far too gradually, the metal cage hauled them perilously higher.

"At least we're still moving," Kyle muttered.

Then, sauntering past the door to the twelfth floor, the tired contraption shuddered to a complete halt.

49

So, this was it. Kyle thought that his life was over. Everything that he loved had been taken from him. In turn, his family, music and career had been wrenched from his grip. First it was his brother's death, then his own silly accident, and now a fire was going to complete the job.

The boy in the elevator with Kyle had the body of an adult weightlifter but he was obviously a teenager. It was bizarre to see him taking charge yet Kyle had little option. He was mentally drained and he had been hurt more than he would ever admit. He felt like an overused punch-bag, its stuffing hanging out limply like his useless right arm.

"Give me a hand, man." By sheer force, Shadow had managed to prise open the inner cage door just a crack. His eyebrows and black curly hair were burnt away. What was left was a pale brown colour. He'd taken off his sweatshirt and wrapped it around his hands as he forced the door back. His black body bore signs of blistering but he didn't complain. Rivers of sweat poured down into his trousers. "Shove your foot in the gap and push," he said.

Kyle tried to shake off his morbid thoughts. He still believed that their situation was hopeless but he owed it to the boy to help. After all, he'd already saved Kyle's life once.

Together they heaved on the metal door until it creaked open a few more centimetres.

Then Shadow kicked the iron gate until he was satisfied with the gap. "That's enough," he yelled. "We can get through." Then he started to work on the massive outer door on Floor 12, reaching down to yank on the handle and pull it back. His knees contacted the bottom of the cage and he groaned with pain.

This time, Kyle didn't need to be asked. Because the door folded back like a concertina, Kyle could get a good purchase on it with his foot. He aimed a kick over Shadow's head as the boy ducked down to grasp the handle. Kyle's foot crashed into the fold and opened a chink. He did it again and saw a slot of light from the twelfth floor. He was relieved to note that it was an electric light, not a flickering flame.

"Let me," Shadow said. Freed from having to hold the handle in the open position, he stood upright and let fly at the outer door with his powerful legs, first the right and then the left.

It was easier than they'd dared to hope. The lame door limped open.

Abruptly, the fire alarm stopped. The emergency wasn't over. The fire had probably disabled the alarm, just like it had disabled the goods elevator. The electricity supply had died a fiery death. The end of the discordant screech came as a huge relief to Kyle and Shadow but, in their tormented ears, the ringing seemed to continue. Below them, there was an ominous crackling noise that reminded them both of the sound of bonfires.

Shadow squeezed through the gap first, burning his bared chest on the metal, and jumped down on to the dimmed floor, a metre below. He coughed and spluttered then called, "Phew. It's OK. Come on."

Shuffling sideways, Kyle joined him, landing much more awkwardly on shaky legs.

Shadow grabbed him to stop him toppling over.

"Now what?" asked Kyle.

"We climb."

"More?"

"They won't get that fire under control for ages. It'll come up. The higher we go the longer we've got. First," Shadow said, "let's find the toilet."

"What?"

Remembering that he'd been down to the basement and turned off the main water supply, Shadow answered, "The cold taps won't work but maybe we can use the hot. There's got to be water tanks somewhere with plenty left in. Or we can use the flushes."

By the glimmer of emergency lighting, Shadow dunked his sweatshirt in a bowl of warm water and then pulled it over his scarred chest. He flushed each toilet while Kyle reached down and caught some of the gushing cold water in a jug that he'd found in an office. Kyle drenched himself and Shadow with the life-preserving liquid.

There was a hot draught blowing up the stairs, but because Shadow and Kyle were saturated with water it was bearable. The air carried an acrid stench, though. Both of them could feel it stinging their throats and lungs.

The two of them were pushing themselves to the limit, demanding yet more effort from their aching limbs. The sound of their footfalls was lost in the thunderous noise from the fire. Each flight of stairs seemed taller and longer than the previous one. The darkened storeys went by slowly, exhaustingly, the only light coming from battery-powered safety lamps.

"What's up on the nineteenth?" Shadow shouted over his shoulder.

Kyle's answer was delivered between short breaths. "The boss's office and other stuff, I suppose."

"There's a phone, then."

"Yeah. We can call. Tell someone we're stuck up here."

They resumed the climb in silence, saving their breath.

At last, they tumbled into Tristan Lockhart's office, lit only by one backup light, and slumped into seats. Straight away, Kyle picked up the phone but the receiver did not make a sound. The inferno was doing its best to cut them off completely. Mr Lockhart's computer was driven by the mains so Kyle could not e-mail the authorities either. He could not see a mobile phone or any other way of making their presence known. "Damn!"

Ironically, on the president's desk by the phone, there was a sealed envelope that bore Kyle's handwriting. *Mr T Lockhart. Confidential.* Kyle picked it up, shook his head ruefully and dropped the note into the waste bin. Even if his written accusations against Max Levine survived the fire, they were redundant now.

It was the middle of the night. Outside the window, four huge blocks were lit up like Christmas trees towering over Yttria. One of them was Max's apartment block. The CNN Center housed a 24-hour news service. Its cameras were probably pointed at Yttria right now. Most of its windows were shining. In the few unlit windows, Kyle could see the reflection of the still ferocious fire. Limping to the window and looking down, Kyle gasped.

"What?" Shadow asked.

"See for yourself."

Halfway up the block there was a skirt of fire and a long trail of smoke drifting into the night sky. Flames were bursting out of smashed windows and stroking the side of the building. The blaze was now centred on the tenth floor and it was rising rapidly. Beyond the prancing yellow ring, ineffective appliances like toys had their hoses aimed at the seat of the pyre. Compared with the ferocity of the firestorm, the hoses provided a mere dribble. Behind two panes of glass, Kyle could hear the shrieks of sirens.

"Very spectacular," Shadow mumbled to himself.

Kyle felt the window with his hand. It was already unnaturally warm but not yet hot. They had a little time but how did they attract attention? If they waved in the barely lit window no one would notice them. They would be gesticulating still when the flames overtook them.

Kyle coughed loudly and gripped his aching chest. "You know what's happening, don't you?"

"What?"

"The fire's using all the oxygen. Soon, there won't be much left in here for us. If the flames don't get us. . ."

"We'll suffocate."

Kyle nodded.

Somewhere below them, there was yet another explosion and the sound of glass splintering above the noise of the conflagration.

Shadow slumped back into a chair. He reckoned he'd earned a bit of luxury as his life came to an end. In a broken voice, he asked, "What's your name?"

"Kyle. Yours?"

The boy hesitated.

"If you don't want to say. . ."

Shadow changed the subject. "Why do you work in a place like this?"

"That's what I ask myself sometimes." Kyle sat down as well.

"If you knew what they did here, you wouldn't."

Kyle looked into the boy's roughened face and replied, "I know everything they do here."

"Really?"

"Well, not everything but . . . enough." He coughed through a raw throat.

"You know, something horrible happened in Memphis. This company's behind it."

Kyle was amazed. "How do you. . .?" He stopped himself. "Who are you?"

"I saw it on the Web."

Kyle nodded slowly. "It was you! That's why you're not saying who you are. You started the fire to get your own back."

Shadow didn't deny it. Why should he? Neither of them would be around much longer. "This company's got it in for blacks with something called the sickle-cell gene. That's an awful lot of us."

"I know."

"Why do you work here, then?" Shadow uttered incredulously.

"After today, I won't," Kyle said. "I'm out of here." Then he looked down at the soft carpet, realizing that he didn't expect to have a tomorrow.

"You weren't surprised when I said about the Web."

Kyle shook his head. "No."

"You saw it as well."

Kyle smiled wryly. "Yeah, I saw it. I wrote it."

"You?" Shadow sat upright, the emergency light picking out the startling white of his eyes. "Then you're. . . You're OK, man. I'm glad I found you." He reached over and slapped Kyle's hand. Then he grimaced with pain, wishing that he hadn't. The impact set his palm on fire again.

Above them, there was a deafening crash and they both jumped up. "What's. . .?" Suddenly, water cascaded down the outside of the windows. They both dashed to the dampened glass to see a helicopter with a huge tank dangling and swinging underneath. The double glazing reduced the racket from the rotors and engine to a muted vibration.

"They're dropping water on us from a chopper!" Shadow said.

Uselessly, Kyle waved his left arm and Shadow jumped up and down in the darkened office. The helicopter vanished into the night sky, becoming two distant flashing specks.

When Kyle looked down again, he saw that the fire had progressed. It was only three or four storeys below them. Last time Kyle had been caught in a laboratory fire, a trivial one in comparison, he'd lost the tips of his fingers. He was going to lose a lot more in this awesome blaze.

Shadow was still gazing up into the night sky, dotted with lights. "That's the answer!"

"What is?"

"Choppers. We need access to the roof. Come on!"

The atmosphere in the corridor was stifling. Smoke had begun to penetrate even the top floor. They didn't have long before black fumes obscured what they were looking for. "It could be anywhere," Shadow called out, amid a fit of coughing. "A hatch or something."

They went down the passageway, peering at the ceiling in every dusky room as they went. Nothing.

Then came another thunderous crash followed by a gush of water.

Afterwards, Shadow muttered, "Hush. Listen."

Kyle nodded. He heard it as well. A dripping sound.

They made for the noise as quickly as they could. Water was seeping from a panel set in the ceiling near the end of the corridor. The trapdoor had not been built to withstand the impact of water-bombs that a succession of helicopters were dropping on it.

"That's it," Shadow uttered.

"But how do we get up to it?"

Shadow dashed into an office. "Help me drag this out." He nodded at the desk and brushed everything from its surface with his forearm. Flowers, papers, disks, pens and telephone scattered across the office. He blew on his burnt hand, and then gripped one edge of the desk.

Kyle took the opposite edge with both hands but only his left arm was capable of lifting.

Between them, they lugged it out into the passage and positioned it directly under the hatch, ignoring the drops of water that plopped periodically on to it. Shadow vaulted on to the surface of the desk and reached up. He could touch the metal plate and the lever that held it in place but he wasn't close enough to apply much force to either. "Get me a chair."

Once Kyle had lifted up a secretary's seat, Shadow clambered on that as well. He pushed, shoved and pulled on the lever but it would not budge. Friction and possibly rust had locked it in the closed position. He decided on brute force. It was a tactic that had worked already tonight to get him through doors. He pointed at another fire extinguisher. "That should do it."

"Be careful," Kyle warned him.

The ugly sound of the fire hungrily consuming the building amplified. As the flames approached them, the crackling was becoming a roar.

Shadow shuffled to get balanced in the right position, paused to wipe the sweat and splashes of water from his face, and then rammed the heavy cylinder against the jammed handle. It turned with an unaccustomed screech. He hit it twice more before he felt something yield. "Yes!" The lever opened, Shadow threw the extinguisher to one side and shoved the access plate aside, revealing the open sky . . . and a hovering helicopter. This time its reverberation was full-throated. The gate in the suspended tank was opening and a wall of water was about to hurtle towards him. There was no time to lock the plate back in place. "Get back!" he shouted, jumping down.

He grabbed Kyle and pushed him into the office. Following him, Shadow banged the door shut and leaned all of his weight against it. A second later, a downpour came pounding through the cavity in the ceiling. It crashed down onto the chair and swept it away on the torrent. The desk slid further down the passageway and slammed against a wall. The powerful cascade shook the office door and water leaked in around the bottom, but it could not budge a determined Shadow. After twenty seconds, the flood ceased. It had drenched everything, flowed into every crevice and the bulk of it had surged down the stairs like a boisterous waterfall.

"Right. We've got a little while before the next one."

"And the water down the stairs will have knocked the fire back a bit."

Under their feet, the carpet squelched like a bog. They shifted the sodden desk back to its position under the dribbling hatch and found another sturdy chair. Shadow got his head, shoulders and arms out into the air and heaved himself up on to the flat tarred roof, then waved at Kyle. "Your turn."

But Kyle was lopsided. His left arm provided the leverage he needed, but his right was still useless. When he tried to put pressure on it, agony enveloped his shoulder and he fell back. Coming to his aid, Shadow put his hands under Kyle's right armpit and heaved. Clumsily and painfully, Kyle clambered out on to the roof. In the squally wind, he staggered around until he found his balance. There was a low barrier around the edge of the rooftop, a couple of receiver dishes, and various vents letting off steam into the night air. Everything was dripping wet and shiny. The pools reflected the lights of the surrounding tower blocks. Kyle felt very dizzy.

Shadow disappeared down through the hatch again, saying, "I'm going to get something."

He was gone for only a minute but in that time Kyle felt dreadfully alone and frail. He was a tiny creature standing precariously on top of one enormous concrete block, buffeted by the howling wind and surrounded by fire.

Shadow's head poked up through the hole. "Any more choppers yet?"

Kyle knelt down where he felt more firmly attached to a solid surface and glanced upwards, scanning the sky. "No."

"Good. Grab these then." Shadow shoved up through the hatch a bundle of vertical blinds that he'd torn from an office window and two white tablecloths from a meeting room.

Tucking the stuff under his left arm, Kyle said, "OK, we wave the cloths but what're the blinds for?"

"You'll see."

Shadow came through the hole athletically and immediately laid out two of the blinds on the rooftop, two strides apart. The standing water acted like glue preventing the wind from whisking the heavy material away. He joined the two parallel strips with a third blind across the middle, forming a giant H. Next, he started on a capital E. Kyle joined in as best he could to spell out a giant HELP on the flat roof.

"If we don't get the next chopper's attention. . ." Shadow gasped as he went about his task.

"I know," Kyle replied. "The tide washes us over the side."

"I guess you call this all or nothing."

At one corner of the building, a bright flame reared up suddenly and then fell back. To Kyle, it felt as if an enemy scout had just spotted them and their pathetic attempt to escape. He imagined a wrathful fire with a mind of its own, determined to reach them while they were at their most vulnerable.

Shadow had no idea if an incoming pilot would be able to see his simple message but he had to try. He hadn't finished the P when the air shuddered menacingly with the blades of the next helicopter, weaving its perilous way between the towers, giant bucket swinging heavily underneath.

Kyle and Shadow abandoned the P and began to wave the tablecloths with all their remaining strength. They swayed and tottered in the wind, the cloths acting like huge sails, making them unstable and unsteady. Angry flames sprang up on opposite sides of the building at the same time, closing in on them.

The wild drumming of the rotors was painfully loud now and reaching an ear-splitting crescendo. The helicopter showed no sign of noticing the small agitated figures. Closer and closer it came until the tank loomed immediately above their heads. The pilot was making last-second adjustments to her position before releasing the next deluge.

"No!" Kyle cried in anguish.

Camera 2 tracked the next helicopter as it approached the flaming Yttria building. "That's nice," the CNN producer shouted. "Steady." To her Personal Assistant, she added, "The fire chief must be getting desperate. Pouring water down the outside's not going to put the fire out."

"He's trying to cool the whole show, I guess," the PA replied. "And get a fine spray at the broke windows. That'd help."

The producer turned her eyes to a different screen. "Keep it there, Camera 4. Let's see the water hit the roof and follow it down. Hey, what's that? Give me more zoom on the roof." She squinted at the scene.

"Is that really what I think it is? That's right. Move in closer. It is! There's someone on the roof. A couple of people. If they don't shift, they're going to go overboard in the wash." She watched the figures waving at the incoming helicopter, desperately trying to attract the pilot's attention.

The producer yelled at her PA. "Get on the phone to the fire crew! Tell them to stop that 'copter. They need an airlift, not water."

Her finger lingered over the *Release* button and she frowned. Her headphone was telling her to halt the operation. Asking for clarification to make sure she'd heard correctly, she said, "Repeat that, Control."

"Abandon drop, Five Seven. People on the roof."

"Abandon drop?"

"Affirm, Five Seven. Two men on the roof. Drop your load in the park. Copy?"

"Roger, Control."

"The park's cleared. Ditch the tank there."

"What? Water *and* tank?" the pilot asked. "Say again."

"Roger. Water and tank. After you uncouple, can you land on the roof?"

"That's risky, Control."

"Can you do it, Five Seven?"

She looked down at the flat roof with its aerials and vents. There wasn't enough space. "Negative, Control. Negative. But I can get in close and drop a harness."

"Roger, Five Seven. But that's just as risky if you get a snag. It's your call."

Now she could make out two young men waving blankets or something. They'd even tried to spell out HELP on the flat surface. The chopper's down-draught had disintegrated the makeshift E. The previous water drops had slowed the fire but still it crept up through the storeys. It was nearing the top floors now. The men on the roof would soon be consumed. "You sure the park's clear, Control? I don't have time to do this gently."

"You'll smash a statue at worst."

She banked the chopper, hung over Centennial Olympic Park, released a shower of water and then uncoupled the whole contraption which plunged heavily to earth. A few seconds later, she was hovering over the Yttria building, balancing the pedals, joystick and lever delicately at the same time, getting in dangerously close. One landing skid touched the housing of a ventilation shaft and, momentarily, the craft tilted. She had just brought it back under control when she felt the other skid snag on something. No. It couldn't be. There was nothing on that side, she was sure. Glancing back, she saw that a boy hadn't waited for her to stabilize the chopper. He had jumped up and grabbed that skid. He was now scrambling aboard. She lifted the craft to safety with the lever, positioning it a few metres above the highest aerial. A huge solitary flare came up the side of the building, uncomfortably close, illuminating the rooftop for a moment. She ignored the danger. There was still one person to be plucked from his uncertain sanctuary.

She pointed at the harness and the boy behind her got the idea. He fed it out of the open side of the helicopter. She put up her thumb and lowered the harness with the electrically operated winch.

Sensibly, the boy was lying across the floor, peering out and down. He held on to a fixture with one hand and the movements of his other arm told the pilot to move left and keep lowering the harness. Then he looked up and waved her to stop. She steadied the chopper, counteracting the wind, waiting.

There was another bright flare and then the boy excitedly lifted his arm, palm upward, again and again. She gathered that, down below, the man had figured out the gear and strapped himself into it. She wound in the winch and at the same time lifted the helicopter clear of the blazing building, hoping that the man dangling under her had a good head for heights. Still, better a bit of vertigo than an excruciating death. She hovered as smoothly as possible while the winch reeled in the battered victim like a fish that had given up the struggle.

Looking back, she saw the teenager grappling amateurishly but effectively with a slightly older and very pale man strapped awkwardly into the harness, gathering him into the refuge of the cabin.

She put up her thumb again, pushed the joystick forward and headed for home base.

50

Water was the most important commodity in Hartswater. Not weapons, not crops, not property, money, gold or diamonds, not even a white skin. It was good, clean Vaalharts drinking water.

Inside the farmhouse, Eugene and Pieter were hunched over an ostrich egg. Eugene's bright boyish smile reflected the delicious piece of mischief that was taking perfect shape. "It's a beautiful container, isn't it? Strong and delicate at the same time."

Pieter wasn't really interested in aesthetics. He just wanted to get on with it. "We break it into the kaffirs' tank."

Eugene nodded. "Yes. That's where the research project begins," he said with a grin. Tapping the report sent with the five eggs, he said, "Apparently, the virus carries well in air if it's warm and windy, but it dries out and dies pretty quickly if it doesn't find a host to infect. In water, it's a different thing. Diluted, it's active for quite a long time. And, of course, it gets delivered exactly where it's wanted. It's not reliant on a co-operative wind."

Pieter stood up. "Let's get on with it."

"You don't like to savour the moment – appreciate the fine technical achievement – first."

"No."

"You're missing something in life, my friend."

Victoria Scates had followed the consignment of ostrich eggs all the way to Knobel Industries, a remote farmstead in Hartswater. She'd left the hired Land Rover in the labourer's village and paid a boy called Duma a ridiculous bribe to look after it for her. Then she'd walked furtively across the maize fields towards the lavish farmhouse. It was the only way of getting close without being seen from five kilometres away. Just in case she was spotted, she had disguised herself as a hiker by wearing a huge rucksack on her back. Crouching down close to the bush road but remaining hidden in the crop, she saw two men emerge from the front door and head for the large sheltered tanks at the side of the property. Both of them were dressed from head to foot in khaki, a pseudo-army uniform. They were too preoccupied to scout the land for intruders.

Victoria grasped her trusty digital camera – the best that her newspaper's money could buy – and focused on the men. The larger of them, the one with enough hair to stuff a mattress, picked up a ladder and propped it against the water tank. What was going on? He didn't look like the type to scamper up ladders but up he went, clumsily, clutching something in his big hand. At one point, he hesitated and the object fell from his grasp. The second man caught it neatly and shouted.

He spoke in English with a deep Afrikaans accent but Victoria could not distinguish his words.

What had he caught? Yes, it could have been an ostrich egg. Victoria wasn't close enough to be sure but she continued to snap away.

The big man carried on to the top of the tank, shifted a large plate to one side, then sat on the edge and looked down at his friend. The man on the ground slipped the egg, if that's what it was, into a pocket, mounted the ladder and soon joined his companion at the top. He stayed on the ladder, holding out the treasured prize. While he retreated, the big man cracked it on the edge of the tank, like a haughty chef cracking an egg on the lip of a frying-pan. He let the fluid ooze out from the splintered shell down into the water supply.

Victoria shook her head sadly. Whatever they were up to, it was going to be bad news for someone. Ducking down into the maize, Victoria plugged the baas's name – the one Duma had told her – into the Internet search facility on her phone and waited. It didn't take long. Articles in *The Mail and Guardian* weekly told her that Pieter Fourie was a leading member of the Afrikaner Freedom Front who had been convicted of shooting a black teenager. Pieter's brother was serving a prison sentence for killing a black worker who'd had the cheek to call him Wouter. Victoria guessed that she was spying on Pieter Fourie and someone else. She also guessed what they were doing. These buffoons – dangerous buffoons – were consumed with fear of change and race hatred.

She abandoned the idea of revealing herself and getting an interview. There was something much more important here than a story. Stuffing the phone and camera into her bag and strapping it across her back, keeping her head down, she began to skirt around the house, looking for evidence of a pipe. If she found one, she could simply follow it to find out what was attached to that tank. Then she would know who was about to be supplied with contaminated water.

There was a sharp hollow bang and, to her left, the soil erupted and a maize plant keeled over. She dived to the ground in panic as another small explosion kicked up dirt behind her. Someone was taking potshots at her! She felt like curling up into a ball, not daring to move but the person on the other end of the rifle – she assumed that it was the landowner – knew exactly where she was. She adjusted the glasses on her nose, flattened herself against the ground and started to crawl towards the track. The next bullet thudded into the soil to her right and Victoria squirmed. But when the fourth shot landed some way behind her, she realized that Fourie was not trying to kill her. He was using her for sport, scaring her off. If she had been black, his sights would probably have been very different.

Then she heard another Afrikaner voice. "This is private land! No backpackers allowed."

It could have been a lot worse. He might have recognized her as a prying journalist, but her crude camouflage was working.

As she got to her feet by the dirt track, her hand contacted metal. It was the top of a poorly buried pipe and it had been laid by the side of the track. Now she could trace the water to its destination. She got to her feet unsteadily and took off down the road at speed. She counted three more bullets hitting the road at her heels, encouraging her on her way, and then the rifle ceased to fire. She was out of range but she still ran. If she dallied at all, she had little doubt that Pieter Fourie would be after her in a jeep. While she scurried away, she kept an eye on the half-heartedly buried pipe.

Out of sight of the farmhouse, the pipe took an unexpected turn to the left and followed a rough path made by tractors. Really, the track was little more than two ruts carved out by giant tyres. Victoria soon found herself heading back towards the workers' quarters. She halted, drawing breath heavily, as the truth hit her. Pieter Fourie was poisoning his own labourers! He was deranged and destructive. In his warped mind, no doubt he regarded workers as cheap and easily replaced. He had probably volunteered them for some deadly experiment before he tried it on all of the nation's blacks. Sweat poured down Victoria's back and soaked into her denim shirt where the bag dug into her back. She broke into a sprint which soon deteriorated into a painful, breathless jog.

Once again, Duma had his head under The Tap and water dribbled pleasantly over his hair and head. He filled his mouth with water and then, cheeks bulging, squirted it from his lips over Sister 3. He laughed.

"Duma!" the little sister shouted in a temper, before she ran off to tell someone how horrid he was.

Behind her, there was the woman from the next hut. Her husband had died and she was wanting water to clean out their shack. Perhaps she thought that she could wash away his disease and her own memory of it. She was joined by one of the young women of the village who needed water for her chickens, children and pumpkins.

Duma filled a bucket with water, walked past the parked Land Rover and, when no one was watching, headed towards the school room. He had already plugged all of the holes in the teacher's desk so it should be leak-proof. Now Duma could turn it into a small pool. He wished that he had some fish. It would be great to see his teacher open her desk and find some fish swimming in it. Still, a pool was good enough. After carefully tipping the water in, he peeped under the converted desk. Hardly a drip. Great. Outside, he returned to his guard duty by the white woman's Land Rover. Sitting behind the wheel, he pretended to drive the car, but the only revving noises were formed in his own throat. He would've put the four-wheel drive through its paces but the woman had taken the ignition key.

The old man of the village had wheeled a large basin on a home-made wooden trolley to The Tap and was filling it so that he could take it home and do his washing. On the other side of the street a labourer was taking a shower. Wearing just his shorts, he stood there while his son mounted a box and tipped water over him from a big jug. By the look on his face, he thought he was in paradise. "Again," he said, and the boy ran back to The Tap with the thirsty jug.

Duma began to feel a bit dizzy and he had a headache like he sometimes got when he'd been driving a tractor all day through the heat of mid-summer. But summer had gone and he was only pretending to drive. He went back to The Tap and, mouth underneath it, drank freely. Water trickled pleasantly over his cheek and down his neck. Some spilled on to his bare legs, rinsing away the dried dirt. When he looked up again, the weird white woman was charging down the track like an agitated ostrich, waving her arms, shouting something at the top of her voice.

The men decided to let the British journalist speak. They listened carefully to her and each of them formed their own conclusions. Many of the labourers distrusted her, fearing that she was endangering their jobs, but some accepted her words.

"That's the baas all right."

"Why should we listen to her?"

"A poison we can't see or taste?"

"I'm not drinking no more."

They turned to the old man of the village for guidance and waited for his verdict.

The elder looked at The Tap, at the sky, the fields, and then back at his fellow workers. He nodded. "She's right," he uttered. "You could never trust the baas – any baas. Nothing's really changed around here, apart from The Tap. Maybe we know why now. He gave us it so he could poison us. We mustn't use it. At least, not until we see if anyone gets sick."

"I got back quick," Victoria added. "If the water's poisoned, I don't think much can have got through yet – not unless you've been using it a lot."

The old man eyed her closely and said, "It's our only one. Of course we use it a lot."

Duma sat beside Victoria in her hired car and watched, almost speechless, fascinated by her English technology. She fed the digital photographs of the farmstead into her laptop. She zoomed in on the hairy one, the buffoon, and asked Duma, "Is that Pieter Fourie?"

Duma nodded. "The baas."

Focusing on Fourie's friend with the childlike grin, she said, "Who's that?"

Duma shrugged.

Victoria gazed at the screen. For some reason, maybe it was that cheeky smile, her instinct told her that he was the really evil one. Her brow creased and she shook her head. Then she had a crazy idea. Maybe, just maybe... Using PhotoSuite, she drew a crude beard on the mystery man. Then she painted out his glasses and examined the altered image. She was not satisfied but she knew what she had to do next. She removed most of the man's hair, guessing the shape of his bald head underneath. Then she sat back and gazed at the face that she had created – or re-created.

She smiled to herself and then immediately inhaled sharply with the shock of her discovery. OK, he'd lost weight and his nose was smaller than she remembered, but she was looking at Dr Adriaan Bresson. Dr Death himself. P W Botha's prized physician, international criminal and hated racist. Victoria could not remember all of Bresson's crimes against humanity but she knew that he was a mass murderer and drug trafficker and that he'd once plotted to poison Nelson Mandela. Of course, he was also a known expert in chemical and biological warfare, aimed at the black races.

And Yttria saw fit to deal with this type of man.

"Do you know him?" she asked Duma.

The boy shook his head again. He didn't understand the white woman's reaction. Normally, he would've ached to get his hands on such a toy – he would've loved to paint Sister 3's head on an ostrich's body – but he felt faint and queasy.

"Can you get the elder, or whatever you call him? I think he should see this."

Duma got down from the jeep gingerly and went for the old man. He didn't make it, though. Fifteen paces away from the white woman's vehicle, he collapsed.

The old man and the rest of the workers agreed. They'd seen his dreadful face on posters. It *was* Dr Death. And his presence at the farm explained it all. But there was nothing that they could do. If they went to the baas's farmhouse, a few sticks would not be a match for white guns and rifles.

Victoria offered a different way forward. She sped back to Kimberley in the Land Rover with an unconscious Duma and his mother. Her first stop was the hospital and the second was the police station.

Seeing a white policeman on desk duty, Victoria hesitated, for once unsure of herself.

"Yes?" he prompted.

It was too late to turn back now. Victoria said, "I need to see a black officer."

"Why?"

To the left, Dr Adriaan W Bresson peered at her from a faded poster that no longer captured the cruel twinkle in his eyes. "Because it's a matter of race, an ANC matter."

391

He snorted but he was too intrigued to deny her wishes. "You'll see both, then." He called for a black colleague.

"Are you ex-ANC army?" she asked the second policeman as he strolled towards the desk.

He nodded suspiciously at the Englishwoman. "So?"

Victoria pointed at the poster of Bresson. "I know where he is."

Simultaneously, both policemen cried, "What?"

Victoria produced her laptop and showed them the original photograph of the man at the Fourie farmhouse and then her doctored version.

"No chance," the white officer muttered. "I could make my son look like Mandela with a box of tricks."

But the policeman who had come out of the ANC's army was thinking and nodding. His trustworthy face was totally transparent. If there was even a remote chance that he could get his hands on Dr Death, he'd take it. "If this is Bresson, what's he doing up at the Fourie place?"

Victoria explained everything she'd learned from a leaky British Government and everything she'd seen at the farm. The black officer listened carefully and patiently. Behind him, the other policeman paid just as much attention but he was smouldering, occasionally grunting with derision.

Afterwards, while Victoria prepared her big story on

the laptop and an armed unit headed for Pieter Fourie's farmstead, the white duty officer was on the phone. By the time that the police got to the mansion, there would be no sign of Eugene Knobel, Adriaan Bresson or Dr Death. There would be no hint of the man he would become next and the name he would adopt. And, no matter how thoroughly the police searched, there would be no trace of the remaining four ostrich eggs.

51

Lying exhausted in the helicopter, Shadow made up his mind. He had lost his appetite for arson but not his appetite for freedom. He needed to make one final effort. Above the din of the engine and thrashing blades, he could not make himself heard to his new and shattered friend but, when the craft descended towards the helipad, he clasped Kyle briefly in a hug. Directly into his ear, he yelled, "Good luck, man."

Shadow didn't wait. As soon as the skids settled on the ground, he jumped on to the brightly lit tarmac and, blown by the down-draught of the rotors, took off unsteadily into the night. Almost immediately he dissolved in the darkness outside the ring of landing lights.

Kyle frowned at first and then smiled. He didn't know the boy's name but he understood his sudden departure.

Sitting beside the sergeant's desk, Kyle was eyeing cynically the vast array of weaponry at the policeman's disposal. Kyle's right arm ached in its sling and his face bore the purple imprint of Max Levine's knuckles. Under Kyle's trousers, both of his knees were bandaged.

The first cop was saying, "We're pretty sure it was an arsonist called Shadow."

"The one from Memphis?"

"That's 'im," a second sergeant replied. He was white and he'd been imported from Tennessee. "So, anything you can tell us. . ."

"I can't. I was. . ." Kyle shrugged. "Out of it."

"What was his name?"

"He didn't say."

"Even so, you must know what he looked like. You were with him for ages. How old was he? How tall? How fat or thin? Describe him."

Kyle shook his head. "He was . . . black."

"You don't say. Is that all?"

Kyle thought about it and then said, "Sorry. They all look the same to me."

Both cops stared hard at him. "Where are you coming from? You don't believe that. You're protecting him."

"He saved my life."

"He didn't care nothing for you. He set the place on fire."

Kyle shook his head again. He wasn't denying the act of arson. He was thinking about the irrelevance of it all. "What's the point? After that, he's not going to set anything else on fire, is he?"

"He killed two, injured seven."

"He was provoked," Kyle replied in a weak defence of his own tight-lipped stand.

"You're the best lead we've ever had on this Shadow.

What did he look like?" the Memphis cop repeated firmly.

"I'll tell you what," Kyle replied, determined not to be side-tracked. "I'm more interested in talking about something much nastier: Yttria and something called SCP19."

52

Victoria's series of newspaper scoops caused earthquakes in British politics and the pharmaceutical business. After the first article, Victoria had been contacted by an academic called Paul Turrell. She already had a picture of him being manhandled by Yttria's security staff and, after hearing his full story, her newspaper reports became ever more spicy. Then, after interviewing a young chemist called Kyle Proctor who had just been deported from America for failing to co-operate with the police, the stain on the world spread even wider.

The Secretary for Trade and Industry had not been able to answer Parliamentary questions satisfactorily and, after less than a year in the job, she retired to the obscurity of the back benches. The Defence Secretary's smile was never caught on camera. He was far too careful, far too experienced a politician, to be seen gloating over a scandal involving one of his own kind. But he had done more than defeat a rival. He had averted a disaster and kept his party's ethical policy intact. At Westminster, a whisper was going round that the MP for Cambridge was about to take over at the Department for Trade and Industry.

The gates of YPI in Cambridge were besieged by a very vocal group of protestors who could not be shifted as easily as a homeless beggar. Victoria's revelations, the scandal in Atlanta, and Wooderson's confessions shocked three honest managers within Yttria. Astounded by the extent of their colleagues' scheming, they came clean. They revealed that the company was trying to find a way forward for the smart medicine at the same time as it recouped its losses by selling a money-spinning smart weapon. In an interview, they told Victoria that they had always had their doubts about YPI's policy but that they'd kept their dilemmas to themselves. Their misgivings had been eclipsed by economic necessities. Yttria Pharmaceuticals was a broken and discredited company. Urling-Clark, Ingoe and a host of top brass were arrested.

Ironically, Lab 47 really had been trying to improve the formula of a drug against sickle-cell anaemia. Dwight Grant was a casualty not of a racial weapon but of another failed medicine. The "suicides" at Westland Young Offender Institution were the unfortunate result of trials with SCP19 before the company knew that it was toxic. The deaths were covered up with a little help from the on-site medic and a Dr Padley. Both doctors were taken into custody for questioning.

The silver-haired assassin, the man with the green Nissan and the last person to see Helen alive, slipped the net and was never seen in Britain again. The YPI scientists who had worked knowingly on the advanced biological weapon would not be out of a job for long.

Their expertise would soon be snapped up by other organizations, other countries, same agenda.

The Arsenal striker was still going on about the thrill of scoring goals. Eyes still hidden behind shades, Uncle Akoda was saying quietly to Dwight, "I just can't stand it no more, man. There's your mam and dad. . . There's a whole world out here." He pulled a bundle of notes from his pocket and slipped a tenner secretively under Dwight's bulging pillow. "There's plenty more of that if you wake up," he muttered. But Dwight was as unresponsive as ever. Akoda shook his head, got up and left his nephew. He was a few steps away when he heard an unfamiliar noise behind him. It was a sort of groan, a half-hearted attempt at communication. It could have come from any of the patients nearby but Akoda knew. He spun round to see Dwight's eyelids flicker. Akoda dived towards the bed and shouted at the top of his voice for a nurse.

The patient in the next bed sat bolt upright in shock and nearly had a heart attack.

"He moved. I saw him move!"

A dry tongue appeared between Dwight's lips and, almost inaudibly, he whispered, "Did I score?"

"Score?" Akoda repeated through his tears. "You've scored all right, man."

The doctor did not attempt to claim any credit. "No,

we didn't do anything. We just kept him ticking over, that's all. No, Dwight did it all. He did it for himself – and a good few others."

"Others? How do you mean?" asked Dwight's mam.

"Well, it took a while but his body's worked out how to produce antibodies for this drug. His defence has finally figured it out. Now, we can produce an antidote for anyone from his blood."

"I don't care about—"

The doctor interrupted. "If you've been reading the news, you'll know there's victims like Dwight in Memphis and South Africa. They need Dwight's help and I need your permission to take a blood sample."

"Will it hurt him?"

"No."

Mr and Mrs Grant shrugged.

"Good," the doctor said. "Because I'm sure it's what Dwight himself would want."

53

Duma did not really understand how some boy in England had made him better. He didn't understand why either, but he *was* getting better. Already, the nurses' missing thermometers were appearing in the most unlikely places. Already, the chart at the end of Duma's bed showed some impossible swings in his blood pressure – and his hands showed give-away ink stains. Already, the bottles for collecting urine samples contained the most improbable looking liquids. Duma's favourite was cherryade. The drink was good but it was worth sacrificing half of it to his urine bottle for the joy of seeing the horror and alarm on his nurse's face.

"Duma," a doctor pronounced with considerable relief, "I think you're ready to go home."

"Oh." It would be good to go home but he'd miss the hospital's cherryade and food. Still, he wanted to see how things were back on the farm. It might even be good to see his sisters again, if only to play more tricks on them. He knew that the tank and pipe had been flushed of the poison and The Tap delivered good clean water again. He knew that the baas had been arrested and sent to jail. And his mum had told him that, because both Pieter and Wouter Fourie had been prosecuted, the National Land Committee was thinking about redistributing the Hartswater prairie. Maybe, in a few years' time, Duma's dream would come true. Maybe he would have his very own field after all. That was worth going home for.

54

Johan knew that a smart weapon can't be unmade any more than the nuclear bomb can be erased from history. Once produced, the knowledge is always out there. Oh, the law could ban the weapon but, because knowledge cannot be destroyed, it can always rise again. Dr Johan Uys, as he now styled himself, arrived in the Middle East with four ostrich eggs, offering a smart biological weapon that could be used to strike at any nation with a black community. It was an enticing prospect for a state with a grudge against America or Britain. In return, all that Dr Uys wanted was a laboratory where he could begin his own work again. There were bound to be governments that would accept the deal. There were bound to be chemical companies that would be intrigued. There were bound to be scientists who would welcome the curious, red-headed man with the charming smile and the eyes that shone with patient anticipation.

Author's note

The crimes described in Chapter 7 are not a product of my imagination. They have all been reported in South Africa. Ony the names of the culprits have been changed. The fictional Internet site described first in Chapter 9 has been modelled closely on existing web-sites, of which there are over 1,000, based mainly in the USA. Several real institutions appear in this book but the events attributed to them are entirely fictional.